PRASE FOR '

'IF YOU LIKED JACK REACHER,
YOU'LL LOVE HARLAN'

'SMART, SEXY, AND HARD AS NAILS'

'SUSPENSEFUL, SEEDY, AND HARD-NOSED

'THE U.S. HAS JAX TELLER. NOW THE U.K. HAS HARLAN'

cheers!

I NEED YOU

HARLAN ACTION THRILLER SERIES

HARRY HUDSON

MICHIE LONDON LTD
71-75 Shelton Street
Covent Garden, London
WC2H 9JQ
www.michielondon.com
First published in the United Kingdom in 2023

*What matters most is how well you
walk through the fire.
-Charles Bukowski*

MC TERMINOLOGY

1% - Referring to a statement that said '99% of motorcyclists were law-abiding citizens', implying the last 1% were outlaws

Brother – A member of an MC

Charter – A local division of an MC where they have more than one physical presence

Clubhouse – Where MC members meet to discuss club business and to party

Cut – The leather vest worn by a member of the MC

Full Patch – A title given to a member who has passed their probationary period

MC – Motorcycle club

Old Lady – The wife of an MC member

Patch – The clubs livery as worn on the back of their vest/cut

Patch Over – When a motorcycle club becomes part of a different, often bigger, MC

Prospect – Someone serving their minimum 12-month probationary period before they become a full member

President – The elected leader of the MC at international, national or individual club/charter level

Sgt at Arms – An elected position and responsible for the discipline of MC members and the protection of the club

Vice President – The under-study to the President

STREET TERMINOLOGY

Bag or Bag of Sand – £1,000

Blow – Cocaine

Burner – A cheap mobile phone for anonymous use

Charlie – Cocaine

Kettle – Watch, derived from the phrase 'kettle and hob' to rhyme
with fob (an old pocket watch)

Monkey – £500

Readies – Money

Sky or Sky Rocket – Pocket

Ton – £100

Trap phone - An untraceable, prepaid mobile phone used for
making narcotics deals

Weed – Cannabis

Wifebeater - A sleeveless vest or t-shirt

1

The end.

That's what Harlan knew, the second his right fist connected with bone. His assailant's brain would shake so hard inside his skull that his eyes would be closed before the body had a chance to brace itself for the fall that was to follow.

It was always the same. Harlan would stand over them, waiting to see if they wanted to get up and go again but he knew that they wouldn't, they never do.

The math was simple; when Harlan hits you, you hit the floor. Harlan wasn't a bully, he was a bouncer, and contrary to popular belief, the two aren't the same. But he was also more than that. Much more.

She took to the stage, wearing not much more than she was born with. Men of all ages and sizes were salivating at the spectacle. Barmaids were working in between the tables. Black short skirts and tight, red t-shirts, doing their best to avoid being pawed by drunken hands as they served.

It wasn't always like this. This was, first and foremost, a

wine bar; plush with leatherette sofas and mood lighting. The back wall behind the bar was stocked with reds, whites, and rose-coloured wines. It attracted those with healthy credit cards who wanted a classy evening to socialise or do business. Guy had opened it in the summer of the previous year, ploughing every pound he had into it, even selling his beloved Porsche. And it had been a success. Had been.

Carla gripped the pole and started to climb; her legs outstretched. Five minutes of high-octane sexual cavorting followed as she rode, slid and simulated, the stainless-steel tube between her thighs. At the end of her dance, she knelt down and collected her winnings, as she called it. Money had been thrown at her like confetti at a bride. Carla collected the tens and twenties.

Fifties were the holy grail but tonight's dance hadn't produced one. And then, as quickly as she had arrived, she was gone, behind the curtain and into her robe. She hated what she did. But it was better than the alternative.

Guy hated these nights, too. This was an upper-class establishment, not a seedy strip club. Five nights a week he was proud of his business. Customers would be welcomed by suited door staff with shiny shoes, the door held open and an 'Enjoy your evening' as you entered. The bar staff wore waistcoats over crisp white shirts rolled up at the sleeve and a short tie. Extensive training was undertaken before you could work behind the bar and high-end cock-tails were sold, expertly shaken and stirred.

Once a week or, if he was lucky, once a fortnight, that would change. The plush seats and mood lighting remained but the knowledgeable, smartly-dressed staff of both sexes were replaced with young girls in short skirts and tight tops. The well-mannered door staff were replaced with gym junkies dressed in battle black. The resident saxophonist who played on the oval stage in the middle of the room was replaced with a pole and women wearing thongs and heels. Guy paid for all of it. The profit though, that went to a different guy altogether.

'Get off me,' the waitress said, as a hand crept onto her thigh and teased the hem of her short skirt. She had brought over a tray of beers to yet another table full of drunken, raucous men. 'I mean it, stop.' The hand in question didn't stop and continued to wander. She tried to pull away but the hand grabbed a handful of fabric and held her there. He looked up at her as she struggled to free herself. In a split second of outrage, she emptied a bottle of beer over his head. How dare he maul her like she was a piece of meat?

'You stupid bitch,' he roared, standing up in temper and with the contents of a beer bottle running down over him. He slapped her hard in the face with the back of his hand, sending her stumbling back. Then, a split second later, came the sound of bottles smashing against the white-washed wooden floor. The waitress held her cheek, burning from where he'd hit her.

'Fucking feminists,' he said with a sneer, his face just inches from hers. She looked over at the bouncer. Their eyes met and she hoped he would be her hero. He broke the stare first, looking away and back to the stage, uninterested in her plight. She turned and raced through the bar into the back room where, safely out of sight, she cried tears of embarrassment and anger.

It was close to 4am when the last of the stragglers finally left. The floor was wet and sticky and beer mats had been shredded and scattered. The whole bar was a mess. It was like his business had been burgled. The first few times this had happened, Guy was close to tears; now, he was close to quitting. Two things stopped him; the lease, and his pride. He knew he had to stop it, to fight back, somehow. He took the mop and bucket from the storeroom and started to clean but was soon interrupted when he saw them walk in. Thugs in cheap suits.

'Busy night by the looks of it,' said the shorter of the two. He was barrel-chested and had a buzzcut.

'Yeah. The usual bunch of animals. Still, I suppose it is a zoo,' replied Guy. The resentment was clear, so too, the anger.

'A profitable zoo, though,' Buzzcut snapped back.

'Yes. For you two.'

'Correct. And let's just see how profitable, shall we?'

Guy hated this bit. Cash was king but sadly for Guy, the cash wasn't his to keep. It would be counted up and taken by the two thugs in suits. On these nights the bar staff were told to only take cash and a portable ATM was brought in specially. But this wasn't a machine hired out by a company that had all the legalities in place. The ATM was a colossus of a man, Schwarzenegger crossed with the Hulk. He would sit there, a card machine in his hand, acting as a human cash dispenser. Customers without cash were sent over to the booth to see him.

The rule was simple. You paid the machine in fifty-pound denominations, no less, and for that, you got forty pounds back in cash. If you complained at the deal or fancied your chances at trying to take the fat stacks of cash that sat on the table, the sheer sight of him would make you think twice. On top of that were the stories; if you did get abusive or brave on these nights, it was well-known that the beatings were swift and severe. You paid, you tipped, and you left. On these nights, Guy paid the bills and they took the takings; zero outlay meaning maximum return. It was simple, fool-proof, and based on fear.

. . .

The night had been uneventful for Harlan. Just how he liked it. The DJ had been good and the club had been busy. The bar itself was L-shaped, so drinks could be served on two sides of the building. Each side had six pumps, four base fridges, and a stocked wall full of spirits. It was well-run, popular, and profitable.

It hadn't always been that way. It was a place known for trouble. Fights were common. Dealers had moved in and women had stayed away. Police and ambulances were often called. Until one day, when Jay knew it couldn't carry on like this, it wasn't the emergency services he called, it was Harlan.

Harlan waited for Jay to balance the tills. Jay was the manager, fair-haired, freckled, and funny. He enjoyed his job and enjoyed happy customers. He took out the excess notes and coins, leaving each till with the float required to start a shift. Harlan stood outside the office as Jay opened the safe. Yesterday's cash takings were already in there, with Sunday's still to go in. Today's customers mostly paid with their cards so there would only ever be a few grand in there before it could be banked on the following Monday. Even so, Harlan was diligent in his shutdown procedures once the last person had left. He would check, and double-check, the exit doors. He'd added steel bars through the push handles for added security. Toilets were checked and the cubicle doors opened.

Harlan wasn't the owner or the boss. He didn't even appear on the payroll. But Jay never cashed up until Harlan was happy. Jay put the cash inside the red velvet bag and pushed it to the back of the safe. He added the diary and the credit card receipts. Jay closed up the safe and set the code. It was time to go home.

They walked down the stairs and stepped out into the night; their eyes taking a couple of seconds to adjust. Jay set the alarm and they stood and waited for the beeping to stop, meaning the building was secure.

'Another day done. Don't know about you, but I'm bushed,' said Jay, adding a yawn.

'I'm not too bad, but then, it was an easy night.'

'I can't believe the difference in just a few months.' Jay was referring to the trouble or lack of it. 'Can I ask you something?' Jay added.

'What is it?'

'What made you get into this line of work? I mean, you're more than just a bouncer.'

Harlan gave him a wry smile. Jay knew he wouldn't get an answer. Harlan was an enigma to everyone who worked there. He had appeared from nowhere. There was no back-story. He was, well, Harlan.

Harlan cut through the side street and walked over to his van. He opened the door and got in. It was a German-made panel van. It was nothing fancy to look at. It hadn't been modified or pimped up. It was a means to an end. Mechanically it was sound. Harlan made sure of that. Every week checks were done; liquid levels and tyres. Belts were replaced in advance and it was serviced when scheduled, all by him. Harlan was a gifted mechanic with the dirty finger-nails to match. He turned the key bringing the engine into life, and more importantly, the heater. The van wasn't equipped with any aircon, meaning the engine needed to heat up, before he did. Harlan rubbed his hands together, trying to elicit some warmth whilst waiting.

He reached inside the glovebox, feeling peckish. He pulled out a Mars bar first, decided against it, and reached back into his sugary treasure trove for an alternative. This time his hand came out holding a Snickers, that would do.

He tore open the wrapper and took a large bite as he felt around the glove box for his two mobile phones. A smartphone and a street phone. One would ring frequently. The other, never. One was full of contacts, the other one just had two. He touched the screen on the smartphone. Nothing there. As always. He dabbed his thumb on the other, much smaller phone. A pay-as-you-go Nokia. There was a message. It said: **I need you.**

The street out front was quiet except for a few taxis taking their fares back to their homes. He was at the end of his candy bar when he heard voices outside. It sounded like a group. Three voices, or more. His senses heightened. He knew in his line of work that bouncers were most likely to suffer retribution at the end of the night when the odds were heavily stacked against them. The group came into sight. Harlan sized them up, running a checklist in his mind: Five men. Two carrying bottles. Two with tattoos running the full length of their arms. Laughing. Lively. Drunk. But dangerous? He wasn't sure. Not yet. But he would be, and soon. He felt his body tense. He knew that feeling; it was his subconscious talking to him: *Flight or fight?* But flight, for him, was never an option. Ever. In his line of work, if the fight's on, the fight's happening

The group walked straight past him. They were about twenty metres from him. They didn't even acknowledge the van, or Harlan sitting inside it. A minute later they were out of view, then out of earshot. He gave a sigh of relief and then wound down the window and threw his empty wrapper to the floor. He depressed the clutch and put it into gear.

There were two parking bays outside the Bed & Breakfast. One was reserved for Carol, the owner, and the other for whenever her daughter visited. Carol's customers would park around the back of the property, on the main road, where parking was at a premium. Harlan reversed his van into the daughter's parking space. Carol had said it was his to use.

Harlan had rented a room for just five days at first but that was nearly four months ago. He had become her longest-staying guest, ever. He killed the engine and then the lights, went through the gate, and up the path to the front door. It was the middle of the night and the black sky was just starting to turn a dark blue. In a few hours, it would be another new day and he wanted to be fast asleep before that happened. He turned the key in the lock and walked through the paisley-carpeted hallway and out into the kitchen to grab a glass of milk. He stood up against the worktop with the message still on his mind. **I need you.** A message he had received many times before. The message meant he'd be moving on. Again.

Harlan walked up the stairs to his room. By now he knew which steps to avoid, so as not to make the creaking noise that might awaken other guests. His room was at the far end of the hallway. He had started out with one of the three smaller rooms, sharing the communal bathroom, but as his stay lengthened, he had been given the only double room that had its own shower. He sat on his bed and kicked off his boots, which were weathered and scuffed. A bit like him. He put his arms behind his back and stretched. The years of standing in pubs and clubs played havoc with his posture and he was slightly stooped at the shoulders because of it. He took off his t-shirt and tossed it onto the reading chair in the far corner of the room. He was a man of few words but many tattoos; some tattoos were there to cover scars; some scars cut through the tattoos. His body had become a canvas of combat. He put the two phones on charge, checking both. The message was still visible on the

Nokia, the one he'd purchased in a back-street shop, and would top up using only used notes. The second, the smartphone, showed nothing more than his chosen screensaver. He brushed his teeth and splashed some cold water over his face. He would shower in the morning, before breakfast, before replying.

The dark Mercedes sedan pulled into the driveway, shingle crushing under the tyres. It was a large Georgian house, with grand proportions and an air of authority. The car stopped short of the large, front door and the passenger got out. He was taller than his counterpart and had a more fashionable haircut. He walked over to the mailbox that was mounted on the wall and dropped in the envelope. It was all there, to the pound. Nothing taken. That would have been classed as a cardinal sin. *You don't touch the cash. Ever.* The occupants of the car, both wearing suits, were merely employees, The money wasn't theirs to keep, only to collect. It belonged to the owner of the Georgian mansion. They would be paid tomorrow, in a layby and in the dark. The passenger got back in and the driver gently turned the car around inside the sweeping driveway, being careful not to hit any of the large terracotta plant pots that were dotted around and spaced equidistantly for grand aesthetic effect. The sedan made its way quietly out of the grounds and onto the main road. Once the property was no longer in the rear-view mirror, the driver pressed down hard on the throttle, twisting and turning through the country lanes.

2

The traffic lights were red. Enough time to send a quick text. **5 mins. Wait outside.**

She placed the mobile phone back on the seat, between her legs and out of sight. She was careful not to have the phone in view of her windows in case she needed to text and drive. She knew never to stay exactly at the speed limits, as that would be too suspicious. The trick was to act, and drive, normally. If she was ever stopped, her ruse was at the ready, 'I'm picking up my mate from a party.' The mate was in on it. If needed, he could be called to corroborate the lie. So far, she hadn't needed to play that hand.

The lights turned green and she pulled away, humming along to an RnB track. It had been a good night. Saturdays always were. The cash was shoved down inside her bra as she had been told that male officers never frisked a female unless a female cop was present. There still more punters to see, still more cash to collect. She knew her bra would be bulging later, which made her smile and sing just a little bit louder. *Nothing to it*, she had once been told. And up until now, there hadn't been.

She pulled up to the roundabout, looked to her right and then pulled out. From nowhere, the bland car behind her switched on the blue lights that were concealed behind the lower plastic grill, and the driver started flashing his headlamps for her to pull over. The shock to her system from the glaring lights was instant. Rihanna knew she had two choices. To pull over or to try and get way. She gripped the steering wheel, her knuckles turning white. Adrenaline and fear. It was decision time.

Common sense prevailed. Rihanna wasn't a hardened criminal; she couldn't just flee and sofa surf at friends' houses trying to stay one step ahead of the law. Rihanna was a well-raised young woman. She was a middle child, with an older brother and younger sister. This was just a way of earning some extra cash. Easy cash, her friend had told her. But right now, as she indicated to pull over, it didn't seem so easy after all.

The undercover police car pulled up behind her, the headlights now on full beam. Rihanna was dazzled by the light shining in through the rear window. She didn't know that this was a common tactic, used to startle and disorientate, but it was working. Rihanna felt the waves of panic start to swell in her stomach. The bravado she felt when driving around, the lie prepared and ready to deliver, the attitude of being 'a someone', was nothing more than façade. Right now, she was a frightened little girl who needed her daddy.

The knock at the window made it real. 'Miss, step out of the car.' The request was formal, not threatening but not pleasant. She undid her seatbelt and felt the sweat on her back. Would she be strip-searched? Cuffed?

'Miss. Now, please.'

Rihanna gripped the door handle. She was momentarily frozen. Her world was crashing around her. She was not yet twenty and had her whole life ahead of her, but here she was, about to be found out.

He banged the palm of his hand hard against her window. It had the desired effect as Rihanna opened the door and like a rabbit caught in the headlights, turned to face him, guilt written across her face. She was a novice, not a gangster.

'Get out of the car, hands where I can see them,' he barked.

She did as she was told.

He flashed his badge. It was too fast for Rihanna to read, not that she tried. Her thoughts were only on her parents. What would they think when they found out what their daughter was doing most weekends? They were good people. Law-abiding people. They deserved better.

'Empty your pockets.'

The first tear fell. Slowly. Like a small trickle of water running down a warming window.

'I won't ask again. Empty them or I'll get some constables and we will strip you right here.'

If Rihanna was as streetwise as she pretended to be, she would know her rights. She would know this couldn't happen until at the station. But she didn't. She fumbled her hands into her pockets. She knew what was in there but she prayed to whatever god may be listening to make all this go away. But it wasn't going away.

'Want me to do it?' he asked. The hint was clear. *Empty them yourself or I will.*

Her hands emerged. She opened up the fist of her left hand. In it was a screwed-up tissue, a hair band, and a packet of gum, half eaten with the foil wrapper folded down. It wasn't that hand that was the problem. It was the right one.

'Now the other one. Slowly.'

The second tear fell. Then the third. She was facing prison. Years. Her imagination was running wild. 'Miss, open your right hand. NOW.'; his patience thinning by the second.

And then, slowly, as if aiming for suspense, she opened her right fist.

'Well, well. What do we have here?'

Edward made sure the car had gone; the CCTV system, high spec and bespoke. There were as many covert cameras as those in plain sight. There were even two outside the property on the main road, high up in the trees. One catching cars from right to left, the other, left to right. Controlled wirelessly and fed directly to his phone. If you were coming or going, he knew about it. He walked down the staircase. Dressed in black trousers, black designer turtleneck, and shiny black brogues. It was 5 am and he had been up all night at a private members club. His profession allowed him access to such establishments, and his reputation ensured it.

He stepped outside, looking out across the lawn as he did so. He understood jealousy and envy, and what jealous and envious people were capable of. He felt sure nobody was outside, and felt safe with the 10st Rottweiler he had beside him. He opened the mailbox with the small key he had in his trouser pocket and pulled out the envelope. It felt fat, a good night. He scanned around one last time and then went back inside and shut the door. He walked back upstairs with the envelope in his hand and a smile on his face. Business was booming.

They sat in silence until finally, he spoke. 'Have you been in trouble before?'

Rihanna was sitting in the back. Cuffed and scared. 'No. Never. I'm, I'm –'

'Save it. My job is to catch you. It's the court who will decide how long you'll get. First offence, generally they tend not to go to town. But not with you, no, no you've got far too much here to be classed as an amateur.

He was messing with her head. Rihanna had no idea if what she had been found with was a lot, or just loose change.

'I reckon 4. Maybe 5. You'll do two and a half, easily. Driving about selling little wraps of coke, not proving to be such a good idea, after all, eh?'

Rihanna looked away from the policeman's glare in the rear-view and out into the night from the window she was leaning against. He was right; why did she do it? To fit in? To be cool? The money? It didn't matter now; she was going to prison for two and a half years. He had just told her that, and he knew. He was a policeman. The tears started again and this time they didn't stop.

The sound of a horn beeping in anger woke him. Harlan checked his watch; it was nearly ten. He sensed the smell of egg and bacon coming from the kitchen. His stomach told him he needed food more than he needed sleep and he listened to it. He got out of bed, naked, and walked over to the reading chair where last night's clothes were. He stepped into his jeans and fastened the belt. He picked up the t-shirt and smelt under the armpits. Stale sweat and beer. He tossed it to the floor, went to the wardrobe, and took a fresh top from a hanger. Black. Cheap. Comfortable. Harlan wasn't a designer dresser. He needed a shower but wanted breakfast. He put on a pair of clean socks and then his boots. He ran his hand through his hair and then stroked his cheeks through to his chin to smooth down his beard.

By the time Harlan got to the dining room, he was the only one there. The other guests had either eaten or checked out. Harlan didn't mind. He preferred eating in silence. He was paid to protect people, not to like them.

'Good morning, Harlan. Did you sleep OK?' asked Carol, who had come out of the kitchen to greet him.

'Yes, thank you. You?'

'Yes. Eventually. Once my headache passed.'

Harlan had gotten used to the many ailments Carol had. Or said she had. Harlan put it down to being busy, and lonely. Carol ran her bed and breakfast single-handed, no cleaners, cooks, not even a window cleaner but she was closing in on sixty and she needed to slow down. She had told Harlan that her partner had died after suffering a stroke at the age of forty. They weren't married but he proposed to her the year before and Carol had told him her biggest regret was that she was widowed without a wedding. Not for selfish reasons, rather for Kevin, as he wanted to marry her sooner but Carol had said there was no rush to wed.

'Full English?' she asked, already knowing the answer.

'You read my mind. Need a hand?'

'No, dear, you sit there and rest. Tea?'

Harlan nodded. He liked Carol. She was mumsy but not overbearing. Nor was she a stickler for house rules. Over the years he had stayed in more B&Bs and cheap hotels than he cared to remember and had argued with many an owner and guest, but Carol was one of the better ones. Definitely in the top ten at least. Reminiscing is so often interrupted by reality, and the reality was last night's text: **I need you.**

The message wasn't as random or as vague as it appeared. If you needed him, then that was what you messaged. Nothing more. It was code-like. Harlan couldn't be found online, on websites, or via social media. There wasn't an ad for his services in shop windows or in the back pages of the free papers. The service he offered relied on secrecy. Over the years his number had become a sort of SOS. Harlan was your antihero. Nobody wanted him in their clubs until they needed him. He pulled the phone from his pocket and typed his reply:

Will call shortly. Make sure you answer as if you don't, I won't be calling again.

The message set the scene. Harlan was in charge. From the very get-go.

Carol came back in with a mug of tea and placed it on the table. 'Breakfast won't be long, toast or bread and butter today?'

Harlan smiled at her.

'Both? I knew that's what you would say.'

Harlan could see she was troubled. It seemed more than just a headache.

'Carol, what's wrong?'

'It's nothing. It will be alright,' she replied, but the uncertainty in her voice was clear.

'Carol, tell me. Take a seat.' Harlan stood up and pulled out the chair opposite his.

Carol looked like she wasn't sure whether to sit and share. She was a private person at the best of times.

'Please,' he said, his outstretched arm and open palm gesturing towards the empty chair. Carol sat down, gingerly, looking embarrassed.

'So, tell me. What's stressing you?'

Carol took a hankie from her pinny, as if it were some sort of comfort blanket.

'Go on.' Harlan was direct.

Carol went to speak, stuttered and then dabbed her mouth with the hankie.

Harlan took a sip of his tea to allow her time to compose herself. She began.

'You know that, um, that large gentleman in the side room?'

Harlan had to think. The guests would come and go regularly, it was a stop-over business. People would be here for a night, a weekend maybe. No more than a week. It was only him that was four months in. 'No, not really' he said, with a slight shake of the head.

'He moved in a couple of weeks ago. He works on the roads, I think. He is, what's the word, a subtractor?'

'You mean sub-contractor,' Harlan said, a little smile appearing on his face.

'Yes. That's it. Silly me.'

'So, what's the problem?'

'He hasn't paid. I mean, he did. He paid the first night but then said he was going to be here a week and could he pay at the end. Normally I don't do that but he said he was really stuck for cash and had to pay his child support but he would pay me on the Friday.'

'And he didn't?'

'No. And when I asked him, he said to stop hassling him and I would get it at the weekend.'

'And I take it you didn't?'

'No. But he sure had enough money at the weekend. He was out both nights and was rolling drunk.'

'And now we are what, three weeks in and he still hasn't paid?'

'Nothing. I left him a polite note on Monday asking if he could clear his bill and asking him how much longer he wanted the room but when I went in to change the sheets, I found the note screwed up in the bin. I don't know what to do.'

'I do.'

'No, please don't get involved, it's not your problem. I'm sure it will be fine.'

Harlan went to speak but as he did the smoke alarm screeched into life.

'Damn it, I've burnt your breakfast.'

Ten minutes later and he had cleared his plate, mopping up the last of the bean juice with the bread and butter that she had cut into triangles. He shouted his thanks to Carol but she was busy tidying the kitchen. She had the radio on and didn't reply.

He was in need of a shower and to make the phone call. He got to the top of the stairs and heard snoring from the side bedroom. The room of the non-payer. How could he not get involved? She was a lovely woman and she prided herself on her little business. She kept a clean home and kept Harlan fed and watered. It was time to wake up sleeping beauty. Harlan got to the door and knocked.

Nothing.

He knocked again, a little harder.

Still nothing.

He clenched his fist and instead of knocking, he thumped.

He heard stirring and then movement. Carol had said the guy was big so it would take a moment for him to get his sorry ass up and across to the door. Harlan heard the latch release and as the handle started to turn, he shoulder-barged into it and sent the big fella reeling backwards. Harlan stepped through and shut the door behind him.

'What the –'

Before he had time to finish, Harlan had the guy by the throat and slammed him hard up against the wardrobe.

'You're taking the piss. It stops. Now.' Harlan relaxed his

grip just a little, enough for the guy to speak. Enough to see if he'd got the message.

'Get your fucking hands off –'

He hadn't. But he also didn't get a chance to finish his sentence. Harlan threw a half-left and followed it up with a bone-crunching right. It was fast, precise, and got the desired result. He was out cold and ready to fall but Harlan stopped him, holding him by the throat before lowering him down to the floor, leaving him sitting upright and unconscious. He closed the door and went for his shower.

Five minutes later Harlan was back knocking at the door, this time barefoot. He heard the big fella get up, which Harlan took as a good thing. Sometimes they needed medical assistance to wake up. Harlan had really wanted him to get the hint *before* he had sparked him out, but, oh well. He was here again to see if the fella had come round, and more importantly, come to his senses. The door opened slowly, the big fella standing there, naked except for a pair of shorts. There was a red swelling across his left eye and jaw. Harlan spoke softly, to keep it out of Carol's earshot.

'You owe three weeks' lodge. Pay it and bung an extra week on top. And you'll be checking out today. Do we understand each other?'

Harlan waited for an answer. He had moved to a 45° stance, ready to spring from his foot, twist through his hip and destroy this guy's jaw for good. There was no need. The big guy in the shorts nodded. He looked like his ego had left him and was in no rush to return. 'Yeah. Understood.'

'Good, don't make me knock again.' Another nod and then the door closed.

Harlan walked back into his room, sat down in the reading chair and pulled out the cheap burner phone. He then hit the call button. Guy answered on the second ring.

'Is this who I think it is?' asked Guy, nervously.

'Depends who you think it is.' replied Harlan, no emotion in his voice.

'Erm, I. I am, I'm –'

'Yes, I can help you. Now convince me on why I should...'

Harlan listened intently for the next ten minutes, barely interjecting. Guy told him the full story, from the struggles in setting up his business, to being the prominent wine bar in town, to it now being slowly, but surely, taken from him. By the end, Harlan could hear the distress in Guy's voice. Distress, like sincerity, was hard to fake.

'Let me get this straight. A couple of fellas take over your bar once a week or so, set up a strip club, fill it with geezers and take all the cash?'

'Pretty much.'

'Pretty much?'

'They also put some steroid junkie in the corner with a card machine who hands out cash after you pay him.'

'Clever.'

'Yeah. I guess. They supply all the staff, which I pay for. I have to pay for the promotion for these nights, too, and if the numbers are below what they want, they expect me to make up the shortfall.'

'Expect?'

'Yes.'

'And I take it this expectation is *painfully* enforced?'

Guy went silent. Harlan knew what Guy was doing, replaying whatever they had done to him in his own head. The fear of repeat meeting the fear of remembering. Not a nice combination.

Harlan didn't push for specifics. 'Give me an hour.'

'Will you help me? Us? As there are a few owners that this happens too, it's like a round robin.'

'I said, give me an hour.'

'OK,' said Guy, not wanting to push his luck any further. 'Can I ask your name?'

The line went dead before Guy got his answer. All he could do now was wait.

Harlan had made his mind up. He would help. If the price was right. Harlan had morals, he didn't like bullies, but he wasn't a saint. He was a criminal himself, although he preferred the word outlaw. He would help those in need but he also understood the complexities of war, money, and greed.

Harlan mixed with what the straights would call 'the wrong crowd'. He knew most of the major players in most of the major cities, one way or another. But those he knew, didn't target the straights. Only bullies and scumbags targeted them. It was time to move on. Time to live somewhere else for a while.

He took the holdall from the bottom of the wardrobe and cleared out the row of clothes on hangers, which wasn't a lot. A handful of cheap shirts and tees. But what was in there, like a shining beacon, was his cut. Like his boots, and himself, it was weathered, worn, and scuffed. Harlan removed it from the hanger, savouring the touch of soft yet hardened leather. It gave him a soothing, calming feeling when his fingertips caressed it, a feeling that said he was home. Like the Paul Young song about his hat.

He turned the vest around and held it aloft to see the emblem on the patch that adorned the back. It was more than a cut, it was a statement to the world, a statement that had only two words; **SATAN'S SECURITY**.

That was the name of the club; the police, well they called it a gang. But it wasn't, not really, it was a group of men that paid their dues when due and partied hard when it was party time. It was a club. A gentleman's club. Of sorts.

The emblem showed the devil at the doorway of hell with two burly bikers standing outside, depicted as doormen with skulls for faces. It was crass, colourful, and chilling. To members, it was a badge of honour, of cama-raderie in numbers. To the public, it meant a mixture of bad men. To rival clubs, it meant just that, rivalry. Bitter, bloody, rivalry.

Harlan had seen, and been in, a lot of battles with his club. He had once held the prestigious title of Sgt at Arms but had left the charter for reasons only known to his Presi-dent, a secret that remains between them to this day. His loyalty and his bravery had allowed him to stay on as a nomad; he kept his patch and they kept a trusted ally.

Harlan stared at the vest; it told a thousand stories. Even after ten years, he still felt privileged to wear his patch, though he had earned it the same thousand times over.

Rihanna's phone was showing a slew of notifications. Messages. Missed calls. Tweets. Snaps. She didn't care. She wanted the world to open up and swallow her whole but knew that it wouldn't. She had been caught with class A's and the copper had been honest with her. Blunt, but honest; two and half years. Minimum. Rihanna was out of tears, her eyes puffy and her nose, sore. She looked around her bedroom, knowing the creature comforts of home would soon be replaced with a prison cell. Her mum had shouted up the stairs a few times, once for breakfast, then for lunch. Each time Rihanna had shouted back that she wasn't hungry. She knew if she ate, she would be sick. He had told her she needed a solicitor. And a good one. But he'd also told her they cost. A lot.

The money she had hidden down her bra was now in her bedside cabinet drawer, plus her earnings from the night before. She wasn't a saver. What she earned with her side hustle, she spent. New trainers, gilets, underwear. The money she earned from her day job paid her car finance, her keep, her ISA and what she called her pocket money, used for food and fuel. It was her hustle that got her the luxuries. She had counted it up, a little over two-hundred quid. She didn't know how much a good solicitor cost. A lot, he'd said, and two hundred quid didn't seem a lot. She suddenly regretted buying the handbag. It was nice, one-hundred pound nice, but right now she wished she had the cash instead.

She felt lucky she hadn't been taken to the police station. Instead, he had driven her around, probing on who it was that supplied her. He had scolded her on her stupidity before finally dropping her back to her car, telling her to expect his call for the next steps in the proceedings regarding her bust. He had seemed a little menacing, but then again, she hadn't been arrested before so had no-one to compare him to. It had been an awful ordeal, and she knew it wasn't over.

She looked around her lovely bedroom with its cream walls and walnut coloured furniture. The carpet was soft and she had a make-up desk where all her designer perfumes were lined up. There was an ornate, oval mirror that could pivot slightly and dress jewellery hung from it. She kept her trainers in their boxes inside one of the wardrobes. The other was stacked full with clothes and coats.

Rihanna's parents worked hard and were proud of their children. Her dad was a self-employed accountant and her mum was an admin clerk for the local hospital. She knew she had let them down. The shame she was about to bring on her parents was palpable, even if they didn't know it yet. They would, though, when she went to court and got sent down.

She buried her head into her pillow and started to silently sob again.

Harlan was all packed. All in one large black holdall. He took out his watch from the top dresser drawer. A Rolex, silver and with a green dial. He liked to turn his income into assets, distrusting banks. He opened the curtains and made the bed, leaving the room just as he had found it. He walked out and closed the door behind him, crossed the landing and descended the stairs. Carol was hoovering the hallway and didn't hear him when he called her. He tapped her on her shoulder which made her jump.

'Oh, I'm so sorry, I didn't see you,' she said, after catching her breath. She noticed the bag in his hand. 'Not leaving me, are you?' she asked, hoping it wasn't the case.

'I'm afraid so, Carol. I have work in another part of the country.'

'What a pity. I got used to having you around. A big, strong man around the place. Made me feel safe, if I'm being honest,' Carol said, blushing.

'I'm sorry. Needs must. You know how it is.'

'If you're checking out now then I owe you some money as you have paid until the middle of next week,' said Carol, running her finger through her diary to be sure.

'It's fine. Keep it. It's only a few quid.'

'No, no, I insist.'

'Keep it, please. Treat yourself.'

Carol smiled. She liked him; he would have made her a proud mum. He was a man's man; she knew that, but he was polite and treated her with respect.

'Can I give you a hug?' she asked.

'Course you can. Come here.'

Carol needed to stand on tiptoes to reach her arms around him. She hadn't hugged one of her guests before, but he was different. She liked how he felt, solid. Hard muscles and a broad back but he came with a gentle touch, she could hardly feel his hands on her.

The hug ended and Harlan made for the door when she called out to him.

'That little problem I had. Well, it's gone away. He checked out earlier and paid what he owed, and a little more?'

'Oh, really? Harlan put his hand on the door handle, about to push it open and leave.

'Harlan?'

'Yes?'

'Thank you.'

He nodded his head and left.

3

_____

Rihanna's phone rang. The screen told her it was an unknown number. The call she didn't want. She thought about letting it ring through to her voicemail but that would only prolong the nausea she had felt since her arrest. She pressed on the green button.

'Hello?' The trepidation in her voice couldn't be hidden.

'Rihanna, this is DS Sharman, the officer from last night.'

'Hi. Yes,' unsure of what she was supposed to say.

'I need you to come into the station for your formal interview.'

'Oh, um, OK?'

There was a pause. Rihanna wasn't sure whether to speak or not. Then DS Sharman spoke again.

'Have you managed to get a solicitor yet? Like I said, it needs to be a good one.'

He reiterated the seriousness to her and she felt her bottom lip begin to quiver.

'Rihanna?' he added, pushing her for an answer.

'No. No I haven't.' She tried to hide the panic in her voice.

'OK, listen, this is what I am going to do. You seem a nice girl, naive but nice, so I will throw you a lifeline. Put this number in your phone.'

Rihanna listened as he read out eleven numbers. She stored it in her notes.

'Call this number, when it answers I want you to say DS Sharman said you could help, OK?'

'OK? But –'

'No buts, you say that. He is a solicitor friend of mine and he will help you.'

'Really? Thank you. Thank you so much.'

'He will want paying, though.'

'Do you know how much?'

'How much have you got? As in, on you now? Including what you can get from a cash machine?'

Rihanna totalled up what she had now and what she could withdraw.

'Just over £500.'

'Um, not sure. He isn't cheap. Tell you what, I'll call him now and ask him to do it for that.'

'Really? Thank you.'

'He may even set up some sort of payment plan, but I'll leave that to him to discuss."

'That would really help. Thank you, again.'

'I'll call him now then call you back.' He ended the call.

Harlan drove a couple of miles across town to the garages that sat behind a row of council houses. Ten houses, each with painted brickwork and each with a blue front door. Behind were ten garages with black up-and-over doors. Each one the same size, just wide enough to fit a car in. The doors were a mixture of chipped paint and explicit graffiti. Harlan had seen the advert in the local paper, Garage to rent - £10 p/w, and had called up and negotiated it down to a score a month.

He pulled up and parked parallel to the first four garages, making sure not to have the bonnet of the van over-hanging his. He got out and took a set of keys from his pocket, kneeling down to undo the padlock before getting up and taking the handle of the garage with him, pushing it up and over until it slid back on its runners. The garage smelt musty and there were no lights. It didn't matter, though. What he had come for was right there, dead-centre and pride of place.

He took off the dust sheet and folded it up, as far as his patience would allow. He pressed the ignition button and the bike fired into life. Hate and fury leaving the exhaust pipes; that was how he had once described it. He stood back and listened to her idle, he found the sound soothing. The bike met the club's criteria. The rule was that no bike could be under 500cc in engine size and had to be a Harley, keeping with the American counterparts. If you were an outlaw, you had a Harley, it was just that simple.

His bike was powder coated in matt black that contrasted with the shiny chrome. The fuel tank had been airbrushed with the club's emblem on both sides. It was a real head-turner and befitted the position he had held at the club. The bike, the boots, and the beard gave him the stereo-typical look of a biker, the profession, nightclub bouncer, gave him the title of 'thug'. He would agree wholeheartedly that he was a biker, but venomously deny that he was a thug.

He threw his leg over the bike and then kicked away the stand. After a few quick, hard bursts of the throttle, he rode the bike outside leaving himself enough of a turning circle to drive his van into the garage ready for its hibernation. He removed the key from the ignition and then went around to the side door of the van and opened it. He took a few clothes from the holdall and transferred them into a rucksack. The rear of the van had been fitted out with plywood panels. Harlan peeled one of the side panels back to reveal a dirty and dusty plastic bag. Inside the bag were two brass objects, each with four holes. Four holes for four fingers to go through. Brass knuckles. These were only used if the odds were stacked heavily against him. One-on-one, child's play. Two-on-one, a walk in the park. Three-on-one, he may break a sweat but still doable, same for four. But five against one, then the knuckle duster would come out. Fair's fair, after all. He removed the plastic bag and then shoved it down to the bottom of the rucksack. He locked the van and then placed the key on top of the rear passenger wheel. He pulled the garage door back down and snapped the padlock shut.

Harlan walked over to the bike and looked around for prying eyes but there weren't any. He took the burner phone from his pocket and hit redial. Guy answered on the second ring.

'I'm in.' It was the two words Guy had been hoping to hear.

'Great, um, thank you, I, I don't know what. I mean, um, what happens now?'

'Send me the address of the club. I'll meet you there tonight.'

'Yes. Of course. What time? 7, 8?'

'I'll call you. And you're buying dinner.'

'Good. Great. I'll see –'

The line had already gone dead. Harlan opened the rucksack, took out his cut, and put his arms through. He could faintly feel the stitching on his back. He liked it. It let him know the club was behind him, literally. And to those who were literally behind him, it let them know that the club was between him and them. It was more than a badge; it was a badge of honour. He put on his sunglasses, kicked back the stand once again, and roared out of the estate.

Her phone rang again. Unknown number. She knew it was him. She answered.

'Rihanna, DS Sharman.' Formal. Direct. Minus any pleasantries.

'Yes.'

'So, I have spoken to him, and he will work out an arrangement with you.'

Rihanna went to speak but he carried on before she had a chance.

'You need to meet him before you come to the station, he is funny like that. Do you know the coffee shop on Beckett Street?

Rihanna had to think. 'No?'

'It's just past the Cat and Mouse pub.'

'Oh, yes. I know where you mean.'

'OK. Good. He will meet you there in an hour. Don't be late, as from there you'll need to come to the station for your formal interview.'

Rihanna thanked him and said she would be there. She was still nervous about her interview, just not as much now. She checked the time on her phone. She had enough time to shower. She was meeting a solicitor, she needed to look good. She went to the bathroom.

DS Sharman rang off and rang another number. 'Yes, she will be there, in one hour.'

'Good work. So, what do you think, serving or stripping?'

'Difficult to tell. She doesn't seem that confident, stripping may be a stretch for her. Carla would have her work cut out to get where she needs to be. Doable though, at a push.

'Nice body?'

'Yes, from what I could tell, but she was in baggies. She was attractive, though. I would.'

'That doesn't count for much. Anyway, I'll meet you there, it's time to play with her head.'

'OK. See you soon.'

DS Mark Sharman had been busy. He had found and groomed a possible new recruit.

They had a good thing going, it was proving to be very lucrative.

Guy couldn't concentrate. Normally he was adept at doing his books but his mind was racing. He had reached out to someone he didn't know hoping this stranger would save his business. He didn't even know the man's name. Guy closed the laptop and walked over to the window. It was grey outside. Not raining but he didn't think it would be long. He had tried a plethora of ways to try and take his mind off the perilous situation he had found himself in. TV. Music. Reading. But nothing worked; he was so close to losing everything.

When the wine bar had first started making money, he had got himself a nice, new car on finance, arranged through the business but that was now causing him sleepless nights. His credit card was heavily laden and normally that wasn't a problem as the cash flow from the bar would clear the bill each month. But now, at least four nights a month he still had wages and stock to pay for but with no income from those nights to actually cover it. He had fallen behind on the bill and now was struggling to make even the minimum payments. His dream, a business plan created on a blank piece of paper in his kitchen, was now a living nightmare. He went to the kitchen and took a beer from the fridge, twisting off the cap and leaving it on the worktop. His mind went back again to the stranger who was on his way to meet him, and how he had come to hear about him.

He'd been researching on the internet one night. It was after the fourth time he'd had his bar taken over. The till had been pillaged and his refined clientele had been replaced with rowdy men. The bar was a mess; chairs upturned and broken glass. He had been told in no uncertain terms that calling the police wasn't in his best interests, not if he liked walking, that is.

He thought back to when he'd first spotted them in his bar. Two big guys sitting opposite each other in suits, drinking bottled beer, in a wine bar. They had stood out. His customers were suit wearers, and a man could sit opposite another man, of course they could, but these two weren't courting; well, only trouble.

They had waited until the end of the night before they approached him, or rather he approached them to take their empties away. After a minute or so of chitchat they had got down to business and told him they would be taking over his bar a few nights a month and that it wasn't up for discussion. They reiterated that fact later that night. He had locked up and walked over to his car and had been jumped on; a knife held up to his throat.

It was after that fourth night, though, that he went in search of help. His own door staff were out of the question, they were employed for their etiquette, not for their brawling skills. He had asked around for a bigger firm to head up his door but when he mentioned what had been going on, they either didn't want the hassle or didn't want to upset whoever was behind it. And that was another issue, he didn't know who was behind it. He wasn't sure if it was the two suits who came for the money or if they were just puppets for some ruthless gun-toting Italian mobster with a tooth-pick in his mouth. He had been watching too much Netflix. But thinking about it didn't help. Nothing did.

He had heard of the black web, or dark web, not quite remembering what it was called exactly. He'd tried to find it but wasn't sure if it was just a figment of someone's imagination as whatever he typed into Google didn't seem to lead him anywhere. He had been awake all night, his head hurt and his eyes were stinging. He had resigned himself to the fact that his business was now being run by gangsters. He was too tired for tears and too frightened to fight. It was then that he'd had a notification come up on his phone.

It was a number, not a name, meaning it wasn't someone in his contacts.

He was unsure whether to open it; he couldn't take much more in the way of threats or stress. He was a broken, soon to be broke, wine bar owner living on his nerves. He clicked on the message: **It's Jamie, the driver from JB drinks: I know what's going on there. I know someone.**

Guy was unsure what he meant. He knew Jamie, he liked him. Jamie would arrive every Thursday morning with his order and would even help Guy put all the bottles away. But what did he know, and what did he mean when he said he knew someone? He messaged back: **You mean the trouble I'm having with the club?**

As soon as he sent it, it was read and Jamie was already formulating his reply. It took seconds to arrive: **Yes. It's happening to a few of you. Well out of order. But I know someone.**

Guy was intrigued. He typed back and pressed send: **A few? Know someone in what way?**

He looked at the thread, it said delivered, not read. *Shit, don't go quiet on me now, Jamie.*

A minute passed. Then two. Five. Seven. Eleven...

His phone pinged nearly twenty minutes later. Guy couldn't get to it quick enough.

Sorry, my bird called. Yes, a few places I deliver to are being hit.

Guy knew there were others but as sad as that may be, he wasn't interested. He couldn't afford to be. He *literally* couldn't afford to be. It was now a case of each man for himself. Of survival. His survival. His only interest now was with whoever it was that could help him. He sent another message: **You said you knew someone? Who is it? Could they help?**

Three questions. He hoped Jamie could answer them all.

He could see Jamie was typing, hoping his reply would answer his prayers.

I don't know this person personally but he is proper badass. Takes no shit.

First question not really answered. Hopefully he could answer the other two.

I don't know his name. He is a secretive guy, by all accounts.

Two questions unanswered. But it was the third one that mattered, could they help...

All I know is one of my mate's brothers is in one of those biker gangs, and this fella is sort of freelance. He sorts out trouble for people for a price. He's a bouncer, too.

Guy liked the 'He sorts out trouble for people'. The price didn't concern him. He would find the money. But right now, he just needed help. He replied: **Do you have his number? And mate, I really appreciate this.**

Jamie said he didn't, but that he would get it and text it

over. Guy got into bed that night, and for the first time in weeks, slept like a baby.

Harlan stopped off at a small roadside cafe for a Coke. He didn't like coffee and disliked the inflated prices coffeehouses charged, even more. Harlan was all for making a profit, but not for outright profiteering. He'd always thought it ironic that he, and his brothers, were labelled criminals when the biggest outlaws in the world were the ones who wore suits and shiny shoes and traded on the stock exchange. Legal gangsters pocketing other people's profits and losing other people's money. He didn't care that these big companies would be paying next to zero tax, though; he wasn't a taxpayer himself. His money was best off in *his* pocket, not the Government's. Harlan's philosophy was simple, the taxman didn't care about him, and as such, he didn't care about them. No, Harlan earned his cash his own way and he would be keeping it. Every last penny of it.

He stood outside the cafe, his helmet resting on the handlebars, and flicked the ring pull with a bitten fingernail. At the same moment, three sports bikes pulled into the car park, the riders tilting their heads as they rode past him. He watched as they parked just a few metres along and got off, each dressed in a rubber-looking onesie, looking like a trio of Power Rangers. They took off their shiny helmets and stared at him, mumbling under their breath. There was a cackle of laughter.

'Something funny, fellas?' Harlan asked, half inquisitive, half menacing.

The shortest of the three took a step forward, creating a taut triangle.

'Just amazes me that you guys won't let it go.' Shorty replied. There was mockery in his tone.

'Us guys?'

'Yeah, you greasy bikers trying to cling onto the seventies. Time AND technology have moved on, pal.' His two friends sniggered at the comment.

'There was one mistake you made there in your little summary. No offence, short stuff.'

'Oh aye, and what's that?'

'That I'm your pal.'

The short guy had just lost face and Harlan could tell that his ego wasn't going to let that go. Plus, there were three of them. If it kicked off, his mates would have his back. He would be banking on that. Harlan watched as the guy took another step forward. His swagger was evident. His soon-to-be downfall wasn't. Well, not to the Power Ranger. Not yet, at least.

'There is an invisible line just in front of you, dickhead, and if you cross it, you'll wish you hadn't. Up to you. Are you going to take one step forward or one step back?' Harlan said, giving him a chance. The sportster could back away now or forever wish that he had.

'I don't see no –' He never got a chance to finish what he was saying as he stepped forward before Harlan put his right fist into the guy's chin. He felt his knuckle strike bone and the guy's head snap back. Harlan caught him before he fell, grabbing hold of him by the collar of his racing outfit and lowering him to the ground gently. He wanted him out cold, but didn't want him banging his head when he fell. Harlan didn't hate him, he just needed to teach him some manners. Brutal, but effective. Shorty's mates both stood there, slack-jawed and wide-eyed, shocked by the speed of what had just happened; their friend laying spark-out on the ground.

'Fancy it?' Harlan said, standing back up and ready to go. No reply. They stood as if cemented to the spot.

'A piece of advice, fellas. Don't write cheques your chin can't 'cash.' They both nodded in agreement, not wanting to end up on the tarmac next to their friend.

Harlan drank the last of his coke, crushed the can and put it in the bin. Over his shoulder the guy on the floor was just coming round, rubbing his chin and looking startled.

Harlan felt bad, not for punching out the power ranger but because he had again resorted to using violence to end an argument. He wasn't a thug. Or a bully. He didn't throw his weight around and he didn't go looking for trouble. But years of working in pubs and clubs had shown him that all too often you needed to fight fire with fire, or rather you needed to put the flames out, fast. He had witnessed what happened when people procrastinate. The results were often ugly. And sometimes, fatal.

He knew first hand that if you believed an attack on you was imminent, you had two choices, one, hope that they wouldn't do it or two, strike first and with maximum force. One shot, delivered with power and precision would bring down the biggest of men and it would be game over. He knew too that, in this case, the short fella had set himself his own challenge. He had acted out, to show off to his friends and couldn't be seen to retract, for fear of losing face.

Harlan had given him a chance. He had made it clear that he could take a step back and that would be that, but he hadn't. Instead, through arrogance and stupidity, Shorty had ignored the advice and then felt the full force of his mistake. His own fault. Nothing left to think about.

4

Finally, she was happy. It was the fourth outfit she had tried on. The first one made her look too young, the second, too formal, the third, too friendly. By the fourth, she felt happy. Black trousers, white blouse and a pinstripe blazer. Just a light dusting of makeup and nude lipstick.

Her parents had questioned her when she'd walked into the lounge and said she was popping out. Her father had commented on where she was going looking all smart on a Sunday. Rihanna said it was a date, a half-lie, so she didn't feel quite so bad in telling it.

She got into her car and googled the postcode of the coffee shop. She had a rough idea of where it was but needed certainty.

The driveway was big enough for three cars. Her mum and dad's cars were guaranteed their space, the third space being a battle between Rihanna and her brother, depending who came home first that day. Her brother, Aaron, was away in the Lake District for the weekend with his girlfriend so she was on the driveway. She pulled the seatbelt across her chest and clicked it into place, took a deep breath and set off for her meeting with the man who was going to help her.

DS Mark Sharman was waiting. He had ordered himself a latte and was dunking in the caramelised biscuit that came with it. He knew today was payday and was looking forward to his envelope. He had already been paid once this month, but that was different. That was his salary; taxes and pension deducted. The envelope though, that was all his, to do whatever he wanted.

He took the long spoon and stirred his drink, white swirls appearing on the top. He blew on it before taking a sip. He had positioned himself at the far end of the shop, his back facing the wall so he could see everyone who entered. He wondered if that was the policeman in him, or the gangster. Rihanna arrived first. She stepped inside and looked around nervously trying to locate the policeman who had arrested her. She spotted him at the far end and made her way over. She started to sit down but he spoke before she had a chance. 'You may want to get a drink,' he said.

'Yes, sorry,' she replied, fumbling for the right words. 'Do you want one?'

She looked down and could see his cup was full.

'No, thanks. In fact, yes, get me a bottle of water, would you?'

'Sure. Still?'

DS Sharman nodded and Rihanna went over to join the queue.

The rain came as he'd predicted. It wasn't a downpour, more a drizzle. Guy couldn't settle. He was hungry but had only taken a bite from his crayfish sandwich before pushing it away. He had drunk a beer, a tea, a coke and another beer, none of which satisfied him. He knew he was on edge. He wished now he had a dog. At least then he could take it for a walk to clear his head. Instead, he was at home waiting for a phone call. It was like waiting for a woman to call to confirm a date.

He knew nothing about the bouncer apart from what Jamie had said. For all Guy knew, he could be a psychopath. He decided to call Jamie, to see if there was anything else he knew but it went straight to his voicemail. Shit. The unsettled feeling in his stomach went up a notch but there was nothing to do now but sit and wait.

A black 4x4 pulled up right outside the coffeeshop. The rear windows were heavily tinted and the front ones were a lighter shade, but not by much. Edward opened his door and stepped out. As always, he was looking dapper; Savile Row suit and an expensive looking leather bag. It wasn't a briefcase, more a satchel, but minus any form of strap. It spoke of Oxford. Or Cambridge. He told the driver to park across the road and wait. Edward opened the door of the coffee shop and spotted DS Mark Sharman and the back of a woman, her hair a tousled blonde. He started to walk over.

Rihanna noticed DS Sharman was looking over her left shoulder so she turned her head to follow his gaze. An elegant man with glossy black hair was approaching. He arrived at the table and spoke with aplomb. 'Afternoon, so sorry to have kept you.'

Mark moved across the burgundy bench seat to make room. The solicitor manoeuvred himself between Rihanna and the table to sit down, placing his bag on the floor beside him. DS Sharman gave the introductions.

'Rihanna, this is Mr Broadbent, the solicitor I told you about.'

'Please,' he interrupted, 'Call me Edward,' and held out his hand for Rihanna to shake.

With the pleasantries done, Edward Broadbent, QC, began. 'DS Sharman has informed me that he arrested you last night on drug charges?'

Rihanna nodded, then hung her head in shame, it was becoming all too real.

'Now, now. It's happened. No good feeling sorry for yourself, it's time to deal with it.'

Rihanna lifted her head up, he sounded like her dad, telling her to square her shoulders.

She looked over at the policeman, it was all a bit surreal. She spoke, her nerves and naivety all too evident. 'I don't know what happens next.'

'I know you don't, dear, but this is where I come in.'

He turned his head to speak to the policeman. 'Is it PWITS she is being charged with?'

DS Sharman nodded and Edward turned back to Rihanna. 'Do you know what that is?'

She shook her head. Up until now she knew she had been busted with drugs, but that was it.

'PWITS – possession with the intent to supply. A serious charge. Very serious indeed.'

She could feel her face getting red. Embarrassment was difficult to hide. She went to speak but her mouth was dry, she wished she had gotten herself some water, too.

'PWITS' is a custodial sentence. No ifs or buts. What you were caught with was considered too much for simple possession. No, I'm afraid, this is bad news for you.'

The solicitor was turning the screw, slowly, grinding through the lower gears.

He took a moment, more for dramatic effect, letting his words sink in.

She spoke first, realisation and fear in her voice. 'What happens next?' she asked.

It was time for DS Sharman to step in and play his part in the act.

'You come into the station, yourself. Today. If you don't, I will turn up at your house and arrest you. The full works, lights and cuffs. From there you go into a holding cell for a few hours whilst the case is set up. Then I formally interview you and then charge you. You won't get bail as drug dealers don't. The CPS wants people like you off the streets.'

'People like me?' she asked, unsure of what he meant, exactly.

'Yes. Scumbags. Dealers driving around making fast cash and being the root cause of crime in the city. Oh, you didn't see yourself like that, did you?'

Rihanna's eyes started to well. She shook her head. The shame was too much.

'The people you deal to, they beg, steal and borrow to buy your little bags of powder. They can't afford it, so they rob. Rob off their wives, girlfriends, their mums, their grannies, just to give you cash to fritter on designer goods and nights out. You people disgust me. You are the lowest of the low.' He said the last part through gritted teeth to scare her.

It was time for the solicitor to take over again, she was just a tennis ball now being batted between them. This was a well-practised act and she was fully caught in the bear trap.

'Prison isn't pleasant. It's not like it is on television. It's brutal, the weak are food for the strong. You would have another problem, too, if you don't mind me saying.'

Rihanna didn't speak, just listened. He continued.

'You're young, and pretty. Too pretty, really. In prison, you have women rapists, yes, there is such a thing. And gang rapes happen. And worse, you could be owned, meaning one of the nastier ones would claim you as theirs, a trophy, if you will.'

DS Sharman nodded his head in agreement. Rihanna sunk hers. The ploy was working.

The solicitor passed the baton back to the policeman.

'Not such a good idea now, is it, selling drugs? What are you, twenty? Twenty-one? And you'll soon become a bitches' bitch. Coming out with a criminal record. All for a few extra quid a week. I am not even going to push you to give up your own dealer. I'll settle for having you off the streets. My old boss used to tell me, 'Catch the rats and you'll stop the disease.'

Rihanna started to cry, the plan to break her had worked. It was Edward's turn.

He pulled a hankie from inside his suit jacket and passed it over so she could dab her eyes.

'As you can see, DS Sharman holds dealers in the utmost contempt. But he did call me to see if there was something we could work out to spare you jail time. Are you ready to listen, my dear?'

By the time Harlan arrived it was getting dark. The city was winding down, ready for the start of the working week that would arrive tomorrow. He had missed most of the rain. His jeans and vest were damp, but not soaking. Plymouth was a historical city, most of it maritime-based. He'd seen the lighthouse as he rode slowly through the back end of the city looking for digs. Over the years he had veered away from budget hotels as too much information was required, too many electronic trails. He'd gotten quite adept at finding a quiet Bed and Breakfast that didn't need much in terms of personal information and that was quick to accept cash.

As he rode through the cobbled streets, he noticed women brazenly resting up against lamp posts or partially hidden from sight in doorways. Ladies of the night, he knew, the oldest trade in any city.

The M.C. had their own hookers, or club groupies as they were also known. Whatever the title, those women were often seen as belonging to the club and as such, were protected by the club. These women tonight didn't have that safety net. At best they would have an aggressive pimp taking their pound of flesh, and often, quite literally. At worst they would be on their own, selling to men in need of sordid sex and hoping to God they wouldn't get roughed up in the process.

This was Harlan's world, the ass-end of towns and cities, dealing with the undesirables. Power drinkers. Steroid junkies. Drug dealers. Gangsters. He didn't particularly dislike them, if they behaved. But if they didn't, then hell would be set free.

He saw a row of houses up one of the side streets, each one with a canopy roof and lights on outside. Houses in need of guests. Paying guests. The first two had a sign saying *no vacancies* hanging from the window. The third said the opposite. He turned his Harley into the road and then walked it back into the space that was just big enough for a motorbike. He put the bike on the stand, walked in under the canopy and rang the bell. No-one came so he rang it again, holding his finger on the button a little longer. He saw the light come on in the corridor and then a few seconds later a young man walked into view. He opened the door.

'Good evening, are you looking for a room?' he asked. He was wearing glasses and had a wispy beard. Harlan thought it was a daft question, seeing that this was a B&B and he was standing there holding a rucksack.

'Yes.'

Harlan used to feel like Joseph trying to find an inn but now he was used to knocking on strange doors in strange towns. 'A double, if possible. And my own bathroom.'

The man with the wispy beard wasn't the owner. He was their son and he was covering whilst they were on holiday. 'You're in luck. It is facing the main road, though. Is that OK?'

Harlan said it was fine and followed the young man in and to the reception desk. The walls were woodchip paper painted a dark red and there were drawings of old ships in dark frames hanging on them. He watched as the young man took a laptop from under the desk and opened up the lid then heard his fingers clack on the keyboard, entering a password, no doubt. He watched as the man's fingers traced around on a small, grey rectangle just below the keyboard and pictured the cursor on the screen flitting around accordingly. 'OK. Here we are. So, a double you say, and how long for?'

'Not sure yet. I'll take it for two nights but can you keep it open?'

'Open?'

'Yes. Like an open-ticket. I may be here for two nights, maybe two months. Not sure yet.'

The young man looked at Harlan; broad and brash, a beard better than his own. The leather vest he was wearing had different words spelt out on patches in various positions. His jeans were damp, but not dirty. He had on a pair of boots, not quite cowboy boots but not far off. Clearly a biker, and clearly not someone to upset.

'That should be fine. Pay for the two nights now and then see where it goes?'

'Yeah.'

'That will be forty-pounds to pay then, please.'

Harlan pulled out some crumpled notes from his pocket and peeled off two twenties.

It was company policy to check any notes using the pen under the desk but he didn't want to annoy the burly biker standing across from him. He had heard the stories. There was a motorcycle gang in the city that had a bit of a reputation but this guy didn't seem to be one of them, he didn't have the Devonshire accent. He handed him the wooden key fob to Room 3. It had two keys on it. One for his room and one for the front door. He dropped them into Harlan's open palm and watched as he turned away and headed for the stairs. He couldn't help but stare at the large emblem on the back of his vest and the two menacing words: SATAN'S SECURITY.

The room was nondescript. They always were. A bed with a few clean towels on top. A desk with a half-sized kettle and two cups with saucers. Small pots of milk and sugar sachets. He counted the teabags: six, that wouldn't be enough. There was no fridge. On the wall was a cheap, flatscreen TV. The bathroom was pleasant enough. White tiles and clean grout. The sink had a monochrome tap and on the worktop was a glass. The room was there to serve a purpose. To eat, sleep, shower and shit. It was home. For now.

Harlan unpacked. Five black t-shirts and three pairs of black jeans. If he needed more, he would buy more. If he didn't, he wouldn't. Waste not, want not was his motto. He checked the time. A little after six.

He was hungry and didn't want to wait. He rang Guy. 'I'm here. Let's eat first. Got anywhere in mind?'

Guy thought about his answer and then said, 'Will a Steakhouse do?'

'Good choice. Text me the address.' Harlan hung up.

Less than a minute later his phone chimed. He put the postcode into his smartphone and then sent a text from his not-so-smart phone. **I'll be there in ten. Make sure you are.**

Rihanna was sitting in her car, overlooking the sea. It was cold so she had the heating on. Her friends had tried to get hold of her throughout the day but she had declined them all, just sending short texts to say she was fine/busy/having a bath, anything to deter them from hounding her further. She needed to think and overlooking the choppy sea was as good a place as any.

The detective had told her she was facing prison and the solicitor had told her there was a way out. They had started off on opposing teams but then had seemingly come together with a solution for her, or rather, an offer. She had two options and neither were good.

Guy had called to reserve a table although he needn't have bothered. It was quiet and he didn't have to look too hard to spot the person he had come to meet. There were eight tables in use. Four families; mums, dads and different denominations of children. Two tables with couples, a candle in-between them, some sort of date night. One table with three men, work colleagues, consultants, in town for business, a few beers before work the following day. The other table, right at the back, that was who he had come to see. He now had a face to go with the voice.

Guy took off his coat, scarf and tweed cap and hung all three on the coat rack that was just inside the door. The waiter spoke but Guy didn't hear. He was too distracted, a mixture of excitement, apprehension, nervousness and nausea. Guy was an emotional wreck because sitting at the back, with a beer, and a beard, was his saviour. He hoped. Guy had about thirty steps to compose himself before he would arrive at the table. He knew first impressions counted and couldn't afford to mess this up. As in, he literally couldn't afford it.

Guy arrived at Harlan's table but was unsure of the protocol. Did he sit or wait to be asked? Harlan spoke first. 'Sit down, you're making me feel uncomfortable.' His voice wasn't as harsh in person, Guy thought to himself. It was softer, more placid. His nerves began to settle, slightly. He pulled out his chair and sat down.

'Beer?' Harlan asked, picking up his bottle and putting it to his lips.

'Um. No, thank you. I'm driving.'

'So am I,' said Harlan, taking a long swig. 'So, from the top.'

Guy started at the beginning but just then a waiter came over, two card menus in his hand.

'I'll have the mixed grill, steak, well done. And an extra egg,' Harlan said, without even bothering to take a menu. The waiter scribbled it down onto his pad. 'And for you, sir.'

Guy took a few seconds before settling on a sirloin, medium rare. The waiter took the order and Harlan added another beer and a coke to the order.

Guy continued from where he left off. Harlan knew all this from before. He now wanted specifics. 'So, how much are they taking, or better still, how much are you losing?'

Guy took out his phone from his breast pocket and after putting his thumb to the screen, went into the apps and onto the calculator. Harlan watched as he hit some digits, erased them and then started again before finally saying, 'All in, £4k a night.'

'And this is now happening twice a week, so eight bags a week?'

Guy sat there, looking nonplussed.

'Eight grand, yeah?' Harlan changed the lingo to suit.

'Oh, yes, right. It's not every week they do it twice. But at the end of the month, it is.'

'Pay weekend.' Harlan said.

Guy nodded. He felt weak. Ashamed.

'So, you pay the wages for the staff that are working these nights, and these aren't your own staff?'

Guy shook his head. 'No, and they are all young, dressed up like Hooters girls.'

'Door staff?'

'Same. Not dressed as hooters, obviously, but two thugs on the door, yes.'

Harlan hated it when bouncers were referred to as thugs. He knew that some were, but not all. Most were husbands, sons, brothers, there to do a job that most people couldn't, and then go home to their families. It was a job where you were spat at, sworn at, punched, kicked and slashed. And all that for less than twenty-quid an hour. Thugs? Maybe some. The rest? Often someone's hero.

'And it's your liquor that's used?'

'Yes. And then at the end of the night all the cash from the till is taken. It's like I lay on a free party every week.'

Harlan could see the stress in his face. His eyes had no brightness and there were heavy bags underneath. The waiter arrived with the drinks which gave Guy time to take a breath and compose himself.

'They are hitting two other bars that I know of. Christ, for all I know this could be happening all over the county.'

Harlan took another gulp from his beer. 'It could. Thing is, it's actually very clever.'

Guy stared at him; these weren't the words he wanted to hear for someone who could help.

Harlan continued. 'As long as you have a reputation, it works. It's one step-up from the days of charging security fees.'

Guy was confused. 'What do you mean?'

'Tasty fellas would go into pubs and clubs and smash the place up for a couple of weeks, and then after, would tell the owner that it would stop if they paid a few hundred a week. Basic extortion and very easy to pull off if you had a name about town. This just seems more refined, and puts sex into the saucepan. Like I said, it is clever.'

The waiter came back, this time carrying plates. He placed the mixed grill down on Harlan's side of the table. The sirloin going to Guy. 'Sauces?' They both shook their heads.

'Clever aside, can you stop it?'

Harlan picked up his cutlery and began cutting into the thick steak. He raised his fork to his mouth. 'Yes.' He put the piece of beef into his mouth and Guy watched him chew it down.

'How, though. How do we stop it?' asked Guy, unsure of the next steps. The details.

Harlan put his knife and fork down and took the napkin from the table and wiped his mouth. 'We don't. I do. From now, until I walk, your bar is mine. It's my liquor they are nicking. My cash they are taking. My business they are ruining. That's how this works. OK?'

Guy wasn't sure what he meant. His bar? He needed clarity. 'So now you take the money instead? Is that not swapping one for another?'

Harlan knew right then he was dealing with a straight, someone who didn't know how the underworld worked.

Someone who probably still believed in the tooth fairy and Santa Claus.

'I will run your bar until it's safe enough for you to do it. Your name above the door, my rules. I say when we open, close and all that happens in-between. I'm the poison you need to rid your place of rats. You're in a world now that's unfamiliar to you, and I'm glad, as my world isn't nice. For this to work, it has to be this way. My world, my way.'

The restaurant had thinned out and Harlan lowered his voice accordingly.

'So, the question isn't: How do we stop it? it's: Are you ready for *me* to stop it?'

Harlan knew what he was doing, he had done it many times before. Was the owner ready to relinquish control, ready to do whatever it took. Were they committed to the cause and ultimately, were they ready for war? He had walked before at this stage. If the person sitting opposite him procrastinated, or didn't have the stomach for the fight, then the conversation stopped there and they were told to delete his number. He didn't need them to watch his back, but he did need them to have a backbone. He looked directly at Guy.

'Yes. I'm in. It's your way. Whatever it takes.'

Harlan prided himself on reading people. He knew Guy meant it. He could feel it.

'Eat your steak before it gets cold,' Harlan said, slicing into his sausage.

Guy felt a calm feeling come across his stomach, like the storm had passed, for now.

5

————

Harlan had decided not to see the wine bar. He was tired. It had been a long ride down to Devon and there wasn't much to gain tonight in seeing Guy's business. He waited on his bike for Guy to drive past and his rear-lights to disappear out of view. The rain had turned back to a drizzle and he felt his jeans dampen. The Harley roared into life, startling a tabby cat that ran from its hiding place, across the road and under a Luton van.

Harlan liked riding at night. Less time needed to concentrate and more time to think. Harlan was a skilled rider. His first bike belonged to his best friend at the time. Teenage years spent jumping over muddy puddles on dirt bikes, riding until dark. Carefree and already rebellious.

Times had changed. His best friend went on to join the family haulage business, swapping motorbikes for articulated lorries. Harlan went another route, swapping dirt bikes for choppers, ending up with his custom 1200cc; his best friends were brothers, not by blood, but bound by it.

He'd joined Satan's Security as a prospect at nineteen. For twelve months he had done what was expected; the grunt work. Fetching beers and washing bikes. He stepped up when needed and hung in the shadows when required. Being a prospect meant his metal was tested by some of the full-patch members but Harlan didn't suffer fools and although respectful to the hierarchy, if you crossed the line, stepping forward for a fight, he would end it as quickly as it started. One punch and then it would be over. The end.

His punching prowess and precision got him a reputation in the club. His probationary period wasn't fast-tracked, that was against club rules, but the menial tasks stopped. The day he became a full-patch member, when he got his colours, he felt at peace. He felt ... at home. Over the next decade he witnessed, encountered and experienced many things. Many memorable, and many he had tried to forget.

The space was still there outside. He walked his bike back and put it on its stand. The front door wasn't locked, meaning he hadn't outstayed the curfew. He wiped his feet on the coir matting and then walked up the stairs and into room number 3. He rested his helmet on the desk, droplets of water running around and down until coming home to roost on the veneered desk. Harlan grabbed a hand towel from the bed and rubbed it over his face and hair. He checked the smartphone that he'd left charging. As always, nothing. Harlan sat down on the bed, and then fell back onto it.

His mind went back to Guy and his problems. A man who had taken the plunge, sold everything for his dream. And by all accounts had done well. He wasn't a grubby club owner, a gangster wanting a club as an extension of his dick. He was someone who was proud of what he had achieved and wanted to give his customers a good time. He needed help. He deserved help. That was why Harlan had said yes. But there was another reason for wanting to spend some time in Plymouth. It was sentimental.

.   .   .

Harlan's father had been in the navy and some of his childhood had been spent in this city. Saturday afternoons aboard a warship, drinking a soda-stream whilst his father played cards with his mates. His parents had split up when he was young. It had been a bitter split and a messy divorce. His father had moved out and got digs in the naval base. It was more of a bedsit. It had a single bed, a small wardrobe and a black and white telly. No good if you wanted to watch the snooker. The room wasn't big enough to entertain an adult, let alone a child, so the warship was the next best thing. Harlan loved being shown around the control rooms. Dials and buttons. Levers and screens. Guns and missiles. The stuff of dreams for a young boy with a vivid imagination.

Harlan's father had since died. Cancer. He had been a big man but had been whittled down to nothing. Harlan was in Belgium on a club run when his father got rushed in and never made it back in time. It felt weird being back now. The city had changed from when he was a kid, but as he knew, everything changed. Cities evolve, he thought. The one constant is the people. People don't change. They try to, some even need to, but they don't. Harlan disliked people in the main but found them fascinating nonetheless. A good nightclub bouncer is many things, one of which is a skilled people watcher. As Sun Tzu once said, 'Know your enemy.' It was a tattoo Harlan had on his ribcage.

The shower wasn't as hot as he would have wanted. Harlan liked stepping into steam, his muscles unknotting in the heat. But it would do, for that night. In the morning, he would mention it at breakfast. He walked into the bedroom with a towel wrapped around his waist. Wet footprints on the floor. The duvet cover was grey with a white, cotton sheet underneath. The wooden frame creaked a little as he got in but the mattress was firm which he liked. Overall, not bad for the price. Providing breakfast was nice. He would stay here. The conversation about adding evening meals and doing his laundry could come later. He clicked off the lamp on the night table and closed his eyes.

Rihanna had tried to sleep but her eyes wouldn't close. She was yet to eat. The cheese sandwich her mum had brought up for her was still there at the foot of her bed, untouched. She had told her mum she was feeling under the weather which was why she wasn't down at the table for dinner. The only positive was that she hadn't needed to go down to the station. She hadn't been charged. Yet. But that was the only silver lining. The choices they laid out to her were simple: Prison or pole dance.

Rihanna wasn't a flirtatious dresser. She had a good body, which she maintained through Sunday morning jogs, and she had never suffered with bad skin. But she wasn't someone to hang out of her clothes. She was ample-busted, like her mum, but her cleavage was often contained, even on nights out her tops wouldn't be classed as low. How would she have the courage to dance around a pole? She hadn't been to a strip club but she knew the attire, which wasn't a lot. They had made it clear; 'Dance and the drugs charges disappear. Don't, and the book will be thrown at you.'

The lawyer had changed right in front of her. Going from saviour to sinister. His eyes had changed from a warm brown to black, like coal, burning into hers. He scared her.

It was quiet. No-one had driven past and aside from a fox poking and sniffing around for scraps, there hadn't been any sign of life. It was cold but the engine was off, so too was the heating. The person they were waiting for was late, but only by a few minutes.

'Casino after?' the driver asked, already spending his wages.

'Yeah, why not. Food first, though. I'm bloody starving.'

The driver nodded. Headlights came into view, getting brighter, and closer, then stopped shining altogether. Edward Broadbent was sitting in the passenger seat of the 4x4, his driver behind the wheel. Employed for his ability to not ask questions. 'Drive – don't talk' was what he was told when first hired to drive Edward and so far, he had proved to be a good recruit.

The passenger in the car in front got out, the taller of the two suits. He walked over to the 4x4 and tapped on the passenger window. He was wearing leather gloves. The electric window came down and he leaned in to speak. 'Evening, boss.' Respectful.

'Evening.' The reply, courteous but aloof. A clear line of distinction. A division of labour.

Inside the car remained dark, the interior light off.

The drizzle had gotten heavier. He didn't want to be out in the rain any longer than needed.

'I have a new dancer starting. She will need to be shown the ropes.'

'Yes, boss,' the suit said, nodding, trying not to show the cold.

'It was a good week. Any dramas I need to know about?'

'No. Nothing. No heads needed to be busted and both nights were busy.'

The sting has been run across the weekend. Two nights, two different venues.

'OK. Good. Well, no need to hang around. Here,' and the

lawyer pulled out two envelopes from inside his wax jacket and held his hand out the window.

The suit took both envelopes and knew not to count it. His boss was meticulous with their money. It was never light. Their pay was dependent on the takings. They got 10%. It was in their interests to make sure the club was busy and the bar was full. He put the envelopes inside his padded jacket, to keep the paper from getting wet and thanked his boss.

The electric window went back up and the engine started. By the time the suit had walked back to the Mercedes, the 4x4 had swung around in the layby and was making its way back out onto the main road. He opened the door and got in, wiping rainwater from his forehead.

'They feel fat?' said the driver.

'Like my stomach after a Sunday roast,' his sidekick replied, chuckling.

The B&B dining room was busy but there were two empty tables. One seating four, the other, two. Harlan took the smaller table. He liked its position, the far end of the room meaning he could see anyone who entered. Making enemies had made him this way. Cautious. Alert.

The room was nice but outdated. The same could be said for the rest of the building. The sign of tough times or a love lost. Harlan hadn't been there long enough yet to tell, but at a guess he would say the former. The young man who'd booked him in entered the room, spotted him and headed over. 'Good morning. Sleep well?' he asked, a formality rather than actual interest. Harlan knew this wasn't his preferred vocation. It wouldn't be his own, either.

'Fine, thanks. Can I just have tea and toast?'

'Certainty. White or brown?'

'White. No, actually, can I have two fried eggs on toast instead? No seasoning.'

'Two fried on white coming up. I'll bring you a pot of tea.'

Harlan thanked him and went back to scanning the room. No-one of any interest.

Harlan had arranged to meet Guy at lunchtime at the wine bar. It was shut the first three days of the week in the evenings ready for Thursday, Friday and Saturday nights. Leaving Sunday for the deep clean. It didn't need to be open more as those three nights could make a healthy profit and allowed Guy the time needed in the week to take care of the paperwork side of things. Guy was a one-man band. He was the bookkeeper, caretaker, cleaner, manager, and owner. He'd said he used to find it fun. Not anymore.

The young man arrived with a pot of tea. 'Would you like me to pour?' he asked.

'It's fine. Question, do you have anywhere I can store my bike, a garage? I'll pay.'

The young man scratched his chin. Thinking. 'We do have a garage, well, more a lock-up really, but not quite sure you'll fit your bike in. Bloody gorgeous bit of kit. Harley?

'Yeah. An iron, 1200cc. I had a soft tail before. You ride?'

'No. I want to though, but my old dear tells me not without stabilizers! It is lush, though.'

'It should be, the amount of money I keep spending on it. And if I could rent your garage, I would really appreciate it.'

'I'll have to check. Leave it with me.'

'Thanks. I didn't catch your name?'

'Michael. But most people call me Lenny.'

Harlan didn't ask why. None of his business.

The eggs were cooked just how he liked them. Runny, but not too much, on lightly toasted bread with plenty of butter. He cleared his plate and poured himself a second mug of tea. Three sugars. He checked his phone. 9.23. Plenty of time for a quick workout, a shower and some calls. He put his knife and fork together on the plate. His mum had told him that's when waiters knew you had finished your meal, regardless of whether the plate was empty or not. A knife and fork apart; meal still in progress. Knife and fork closed; you were done. He wasn't sure if this was true or not, but he had been brought up to believe that and had continued to do it to this day.

He walked through the room, now with only one other table in use, and back up to his room. He took off his tee-shirt and jeans, placing them in a heap on his unmade bed. He got into the push-up position. Legs straight and ankles touching, palms flat on the floor. He did a quick burst of fifty before changing his open palms for clenched fists and proceeded to do another hundred. These were slower, more controlled, concentrated breathing. Next came the sit-ups. He hooked his feet under the bed, curling his toes as if to form a hook. He rested the fingertips of each hand on his temples and then lowered his back until he felt the strain across his stomach. He held himself there for a second, then slowly brought his torso back up. He did this two-hundred times. By the time he got to the last twenty he was grimacing and the strain in his stomach had turned to fire. A burning sensation across all quadrants of his core. He hit the magic number and then fell backwards, unhooking his feet and splaying his arms out wide on the carpet.

He had forgotten to mention the shower at breakfast. He stepped in and washed and got out. He liked to stand in a hot shower, the bullets of water peppering his skin but, like last night, it wasn't hot enough to enjoy. He put on the same clothes that he wore for breakfast. He had also forgotten to ask about someone doing his laundry.

Harlan looked at himself in the mirror. The beard was getting to that itchy stage so he put his trimmer on charge. His hair, black with flecks of grey around the temple area, was wavy, like a very loose perm on a woman. Its length covered his neck but didn't go past it. He had it shoulder length before but he had been teased by club members that he resembled a certain Chippendale male stripper so he had it shortened. Slightly. He stood at 5'11 but looked taller, his physique was masculine. Big arms. Slight waist. Strong legs. Steely eyes. He had made his calls and decided to lay on the bed and watch some daytime telly to while away the time before he needed to leave.

Her mobile phone shuffled across her desk. It was set to vibrate and was doing exactly that when it started to ring. She glanced down at it: Unknown number. She couldn't answer it as taking calls at work wasn't allowed. It rang off. Then it rang again. Her colleague looked up at her, over her monitor.

'Sorry,' Rihanna said, in a whisper. The vibrating stopped.

Then it started again. She knew she needed to answer it. She lowered her head down to her desk and accepted the call. 'Hello?'

DS Sharman was on the other end. He sounded like he was outside. She could hear traffic.

'Decision time. What's it to be?'

Rihanna knew her answer but the words wouldn't come.

'I'll ask one last time. If not, I'll send some constables over to your work.'

She didn't know he knew where she worked? But he was a policeman and they could run checks on her, she guessed. She had watched the telly, seeing how they operate.

'I'll do it. I'll dance.'

'Good girl. You know it's the right call. Someone will contact you soon. Get yourself something sexy to wear. Hey, you never know, you just might like it...'

Rihanna knew she wouldn't. Even the thought of it was making her feel sick. Stripping off in front of drunken men. And stripping off to what? Underwear? Topless? More...?

'When do I start,' she asked, stuttering; the reality of what she had agreed to setting in.

'Soon. In the meantime, start learning how to shake your ass, they love that. You might earn more money doing this than you were, being a little Escobar!'

His little laugh at his own joke turned her stomach. She hated him.

Mark Sharman tossed his phone through the open window of his car. Cars and trucks were hurtling past as he waited for his bacon bap to cook. The roadside van was a favourite of his. The owner, Micky, knew he was a copper and every now and then it would be 'On the house.' Micky, like so many, knew being nice to a policeman could have its benefits, although to date he hadn't needed to call on him.

'Ketchup?' Micky asked, the sauce bottle already in his hand knowing the answer.

'Yeah. Ta.'

Micky shook the bottle and a dollop landed on the centre of the top rasher. He pressed down with his fingers on the top half of the bun to spread the sauce and then handed over the bap, a serviette wrapped around it. DS Sharman took a large bite, chewing it with his mouth open, the fat sticking to his back teeth. It didn't take him long to demolish his breakfast. He wiped his hands on his jacket, leaving faint fingerprints of flour. He ordered a coffee to take with him. He had been a dedicated detective but after being lured with easy money, and now, enjoying what came with it, his day job was becoming irksome. He knew he still needed to be seen to be doing his job so as to preserve his pension, but still.

He sat in his car; the driver's door left open as he fumbled around for his cigarettes. He rolled his thumb down over the wheel of his lighter, held the naked flame to his fag, and inhaled to set it alight. The first plume of smoke from a fresh cigarette was always his favourite. It was like his whole body exhaled, not just his lungs. He knew only too well why they were referred to as stress-relievers.

He was a serving policeman. A detective. Someone people turned to when there was a crime, a sleuth searching for clues to put away the bad guys. But now he was a bad guy himself. And he enjoyed it.

It had been Edwards' idea, told to him one night at one of the gentlemen's clubs Edward frequented, clubs that your average copper wouldn't be invited to. Not unless you were the Chief. Or a mason. Edward had invited him and after feeling out of his depth to begin with, the brandy and the cigars had helped him to relax and by the end of the evening he was feeling at home and wanted more of how the upper-ends spent their nights.

Edward hadn't mentioned his scam the first night. Nor the second. It was on the third night when they sat in big Chesterfields with a little table in-between them that had a huge lamp on it that he'd brought it up. It was so easy. Genius, even. Edward knew the law. He was the law. Edward had a naughty black book from some of the people he had helped so muscle wasn't a problem. All Mark had to do was provide the fodder. Groom potential prospects using fear, and Edward would be the knight in shining armour, their saviour. When they were on the hook; they'd work together to reel them in. Like they had with Rihanna. Girls due to go to court without the means to pay for proper legal help would be offered an alternative. 'Dance for us, you'll even be paid,' was their offer. But it wasn't an offer - it was an order.

Selecting the clubs to take over was also easy. Mark knew the main players in the city, which gangster may have an interest in what clubs, so they were avoided. Instead, they went for those whose owner would be gullible. Those who could be easily intimidated. Those who didn't have anyone to help them. It was such a simple, yet brilliant plan. The girls wouldn't talk, fear of repercussion would put paid to that. The owners wouldn't talk, fear of violence would put paid to that. He would get 25% of the profits after costs. Their tumblers had met and chinked. The deal had been done. DS Sharman would get to work on the grooming, not realising he had, in fact, just been groomed himself.

The wine bar was situated within the old naval yard. Big stone buildings that would have once been used as surplus stores had been sold off and developers had created luxury apartments and spaces for businesses to sprout. The row consisted of an Italian restaurant, one of a chain, a boutique coffee shop, an upmarket deli and Guy's place - a wine bar, but with a 3am licence. Each business complemented the others. It was all very chic and different to what Harlan was used to. He was more likely to be found in a run-down pub at the council end of the city. Or in a nightclub on the main strip. This was different. Very different.

The constellation of businesses had a large parking area outside on cobblestones. The whole complex sat at the foot of the marina, too narrow for boats to actually moor, meaning the view of the sea was unspoiled. Harlan could see why Guy had chosen this location. Good choice, he thought, a smart move and far enough away from the main drag. His whole body vibrated as he drove over the cobbles and into a space reserved for motorcycles. Guy was standing outside waiting for him, a cup of coffee in each hand.

'I got you a flat white,' he said, holding out a cup as Harlan approached.

'No, ta. I don't drink coffee.'

Guy put the polystyrene cup up to his lips and sipped, trying to hide the rebuttal.

'Nice place. Bet the rent stings each quarter?'

Guy appreciated the compliment and acknowledged the question. 'You're right. It's a lot.'

Guy put the two cups on the floor and then took a set of keys from his pockets to open the door. The alarm sounded as soon as Guy pulled on the handle but he was quick to step inside and silence it. He flicked his hand down through the bank of switches on the wall and the bar lit up.

'Very nice. Very nice indeed,' said Harlan, his eyes scanning around the whole building.

'It was,' replied a dejected Guy, his love for his business waning by the week.

'And it will be again. Correct?' Harlan shot back.

'Yes. Correct,' said Guy, although a little more lacklustre than Harlan would have wanted.

'First off, we need to replace the earnings you're losing.'

Guy found his head tilting. 'What do you have in mind?'

'We are going to open lunchtimes. 12-3. Wine and olives.'

'I'm not so –'

'I didn't ask if you were sure. You are a wine bar but you're missing out on boozy lunches. That's easy money you can be banking. You can push different bottles on different days.'

Guy had toyed with the idea before but that's as far it went. The evenings were enough.

Harlan continued. 'You should be doing a monkey a day at lunch.'

'A monkey?' asked Guy, still not au fait with the street slang the biker was using.

'£500. In the summer that should easily become a bag. A couple of waitresses and you.

Minimum costs for a healthy reward. Money you can't afford to be turning down. Agreed?'

'Well, yes, I am not going to say I don't need the money.'

'Right. That's your gig – I want this to be up and running from next Monday.'

Guy was taken aback by Harlan's business focus. He had hired him for his brawn, but he clearly had brains, too. Never judge a book by its cover was the thought that came to mind.

'You got good deals on the stock?'

'I... I think so?'

'Think? We need to know, not think. Get the costs up on your computer. I want to see your margins. Are the door staff agency based or paid directly? Staff, contracts or cash?'

The questions came in thick and fast. Harlan wanted to dissect the business and Guy felt like he was in some sort of tornado. 'Um. Cash. Sorry, what was the first question again?'

'Margins.' Harlan then pointed over to the bar. 'Bacardi, what's your GP on that?'

Guy knew his numbers inside out but he was spluttering like a novice under the interrogation. Harlan wanted answers off the bat and Guy was struggling to keep up.

'Let's go to my office. It's all on my computer.'

'Lead the way.'

Guy's office was neat. There was an in/out tray for invoices on his desk and box files in month order on a shelf above it. The chair was leather, a swivel one, half-price if he bought the computer that was on offer that month. The CCTV monitor sat at the far end of the desk; a screen split into eight quadrants.

'Is that recording now?' Harlan asked, pointing at the screen.

'Yes, why?'

'What's the roll-over. 24hrs, 48?'

'48' Guy answered.

'But I take it on the nights you get taken over it's not recording?'

'Correct. They come in and do something to it. They don't unplug it but they log in somehow and then it doesn't seem to record.'

'Thought as much. They disable it, through the VPN.'

'Bastards.' The anger Guy felt showing through his snarled comment.

'It's OK. We won't be wanting cameras anyway for the next couple of weeks.'

Guy looked over at Harlan but he was met with a steely stare. This was the brawn that went with the brains, he thought. Guy could tell Harlan was a force to be reckoned with. He was a gift from God here to help him save his fledgling business.

'You said other venues were being turned over?' Harlan asked, whilst waiting for Guy to bring up the company accounts.

'Yeah. At least two. One of them is a sports bar. Two brothers own it. Andy, and I forget the other one's name. I know Andy fairly well, nice bloke.'

'Who is up next. Do you know?'

'I think Andy. I can soon tell you.' Guy took his phone from his pocket and scrolled and swiped before answering, 'Yes, the sports bar. He has put it on his social media.'

'He has?'

'Yes. We have to advertise it. To get the customers in. I think I told you, if we don't get enough people through the door then we are expected to make up the shortfall.'

'Door money?'

'Yes. And the coat stand. That's a fiver just for that. It's just about how much cash they can take and that's without their side hustle of charging a tenner to actually get cash if you don't have any on you.'

'Why do people still come then if they are being blatantly extorted?'

'The girls. The promise of extras. And even if the girls dancing won't go home with them, it's known that other girls can be brought in at a moment's notice. My bar is now basically a brothel. It's all disgusting. Turns my stomach.'

'And it's the sports bar turn this weekend?'

'Saturday, according to this.'

'OK. Anyway, back to your books.'

Harlan got himself a can of coke from the little café. It was no more than a portacabin but it was the only one about, so had a captive audience. He liked their thinking. The café was empty except for a couple of dog walkers getting their coffees to go, but he knew in the summer months it would do serious numbers. He walked across the field to the clifftop and looked out, across the sea. In the distance was a warship which took him back to his childhood, sitting in the officer's mess watching a grainy video whilst his dad laughed and joked with his mates. Happy times. There weren't many.

His mind came back to the present day and to Guy, Andy, and whoever else was being robbed. He had to admire the gang, though. It was a polished plan and the reality would be not too much jail time. It wasn't as if they were going in with shooters and masks, robbing the place. In fact, a good barrister could argue you were running your night with the consent of the owner, like a concession stand in a department store. But Guy was getting turned over and customers were getting ripped off. He had a reputation for sorting out trouble and Guy was definitely in trouble. The books told him that he was probably a month or two away from being bankrupt. Three months, max. Guy hadn't been trading long enough to develop deep enough pockets to withstand losing the amount of money that was being taken. Like Harlan, he too was on a cliff edge except Guy's was more metaphorical than literal, and the difference was that if he didn't stop these thugs then Guy was going to fall off, hitting financial ruin at the bottom.

Harlan found a bench. He had nothing more to do for the day so he sat down and reminisced.

6

_____

Harlan walked back to his bike. He liked his leisure time but got restless easily. The car park had started to fill. Young children were getting their coats zipped up and their gloves put on. Dogs were barking excitedly in the boots of cars waiting to get out and start sniffing. Teenagers had put down their jackets to form makeshift goalposts. Early evening fun. The roar of the exhaust made one young child cry and got a shake of the head from the disgruntled parent. Harlan didn't care to acknowledge, he didn't set out to make the kid cry so no harm, no foul.

He knew his colours would make people stop and stare. A leather vest with SATAN'S SECURITY stitched in bold letters above an image of Hell. He also knew it would attract the attention of other MCs. Most respected the club, revered it even, it was the second most prominent club in the country and as such, beefs with other clubs were few and far between. In the outlaw world, Harlan was well known by the upper echelons and rightfully feared as an enforcer. But he was also known as a strategist, a tactical thinker. He had done his club proud as a charter member and was still fiercely respected as a nomad.

He decided to take a drive through the rougher end of town. He felt more at home there. The city wasn't as affluent as others he'd worked in and its biggest employer was still the naval dockyard. It was kicking out time as Harlan drove past one of the many entrances. Men in boiler suits were leaving en masse, many heading to the pubs that had sprouted up in the seventies to catch the blue-collar trade. The light was red at the crossroads and to his right was a pub. 'The Trafalgar' read the brass letters high on the building. The white paint on the brickwork was flaking and one of the lamps that hung over the doorway was out.

He decided to stop and have a drink. He indicated, waited for the oncoming traffic to pass and then cut across the road, mounting the kerb and pulling up outside just in front of one of the three stained glass windows. The door dragged on the carpet as he pushed it open and stepped inside. A quick headcount, sixteen punters. One barmaid. Out of the sixteen, two were playing pool, with one watching. Two playing darts. Two sat together on a table under a window, six at the bar and one each at the three fruit machines. Sixteen.

Out of them all, only the three at the pool table looked lively. They weren't from the dockyard. No boiler suits. Instead, they were wearing baggy shorts with legs disappearing inside tanned rigger boots. One had a tattoo on his calf. Their jumpers were baggy and grubby. There was a pile of fluorescent vests on a stool. Scaffolders, Harlan thought.

He had grown accustomed to scanning for threats. A pub can be a dangerous place with weapons easily to hand; bottles, pool cues, darts. Each one capable of doing some real damage, especially if fuelled by alcohol. He had been stabbed a few times, superficial mainly, but regardless, it wasn't pretty and he preferred his own blood on the inside. Theirs? He didn't care where that went.

He got a few looks but none were threatening. He ordered himself a beer and stood at the bar to drink it. The pub was doing a decent trade. He had seen worse at this time of day. He liked pubs to do well, too many had gone under or been taken over by the chain brands wanting to serve cheap food at gourmet prices, replacing a decent landlord with cheap, young labour. Pubs had become faceless. A way of life, he guessed, but sad none-theless.

'Fancy a game, pal. Doubles if you're up for it?'

Harlan turned his head to put a face to the voice. One of the lads playing pool had just potted the winning black and shouted over if Harlan wanted to make up the numbers for doubles.

'Aye, go on then.'

'Good man.'

He heard the clunk as the silver receptacle was pushed into the body of the pool table. The red and yellow balls dropped and started rolling down. The one who had been standing watching was already at the head of the table and had the plastic triangle in his hand, eager to rack up and get going.

The one who had lost handed his cue to Harlan. 'You can break, big guy.'

It was said with a flat tone. No menace. Not a compli-ment, more a recognition.

Harlan seemed bigger than he was. He wasn't small, but he wasn't an NFL line-backer, either. Harlan chalked his cue and then bent down to break. Thwack. He hit the pack with force and two balls, one of each colour, found their way into the pockets.

'Red,' Harlan said, nominating the colour for him and his pool partner.

'Haven't seen you here before,' one of the three said. He was around thirty, with leathered skin, rough stubble, no more than a day old and two faded tattoos on his forearms.

'First time. Seems a decent boozer?'

'Yeah. It's not bad. Get some fit birds here on the weekends and the beer is cheap enough.'

'Well, that constitutes a good boozer to me,' replied Harlan and they had a laugh at that.

'I take it that's your bike I heard pulling up?'

'Yeah. Twelve hundred Harley. You ride?'

'Nah, not me. My brother does though, and my old man.'

The game fell silent. Shots and pots taken. No side wanting to lose. Harlan potted the black and pulled a pound-coin from his pocket to signal another game.

'You know if there are any good strip joints around here?'

'Ah, you like the titties then?'

'Don't we all?' replied Harlan and got another round of agreed laughs.

'You're in luck. There's a company going around doing, like, pop-up strip nights'

'Pop ups?' Harlan acted dumb.

'Yeah. We used to have a few strip clubs but they all went. Now there are a few places that once or twice a month have strippers in. It's weird though as they aren't the type of places you think would have birds walking around with their jugs out.'

'What do you mean?'

'Well one place is this fancy wine bar. It's an upmarket place, somewhere you would take a classy bird you wanted to impress. It's not cheap, mind, bottles of bubbly for fifty quid a pop but lately it's having strippers in there a couple of times a month. All a bit mad, really.'

'Really. Seems odd?'

'Yeah. I think it's dodge, though.'

'What do you mean, dodge?'

'Dodgy. It's all cash when you're in there and if you haven't got any there is this huge fella sat with a card machine and he has a wad of cash on the table. You pay him fifty quid on your card and get forty quid back in notes. And you need the dollar as the bar only takes cash on the night.'

'So why don't people leave and go and use an ATM nearby?'

'If you leave you don't get to come back that night. It's funny, they stamp the people who leave, not the ones who come in. It's all ass about face, really, but the birds are banging. We go there because the place just feels edgy, know what I mean? A proper G's evening.'

Harlan did know what he meant. Straight goers liked to mix with gangsters. To be seen in places that had a criminal element and the criminals played on it. Harlan knew that even men could be gangster groupies, fellas wanting that kind of life even if they knew they couldn't actually live it. The more he heard about their enterprise the more he admired it. It was something the club would get involved with. The only difference being the owners would be cut *in*, not cut *up*.

'It can get rowdy though. Bit of a zoo at times. But the birds are fit and the word is they will do some extras, if you get me.'

'I get you. Is there one happening around here soon?'

'You're in luck. The sports bar is having the girls there this Saturday.'

They carried on playing the frame and Harlan made the winning pot again. He thanked them for the game and left the pub. A minute later they heard the thundering sound of his bike starting up. 'Seemed a decent bloke,' one of them said, and the other two agreed.

Rihanna stood looking at herself in her underwear. She had a voluptuous figure but like all young women, had her hang ups. Her stomach was taut, her chest fairly large and her legs, although not long, were shapely. Her mates said she was hot but she also knew a few in her circle were hotter. Hot, or not, she was quite prudish that way and stripping down to her bra and pants scared the shit out of her. The alternative was worse, though. They had made that clear.

That first night she'd agreed to deliver the little packets of white powder had been so easy. Driving around and stuffing cash down her bra. Child's play. Now the game had changed, it was her bra that was coming down. Not a game for children after all. She wanted to tell her parents. To come clean. For them to fix it. But she couldn't, she was an adult and needed to deal with it like one. She started to weep, and not for the first time.

Lenny was alone in the dining room when Harlan walked in. There were still plates on some of the tables that needed clearing. Harlan helped carry them through to the kitchen and Lenny loaded the dishwasher. The kitchen had stainless steel worktops and cheap white appliances. Pieces of paper were sitting inside plastic wallets on the walls. Cleaning tick-sheets and stock forms. The engine room of the establishment. Lenny was busy but still looking laidback. 'Oh, I spoke to mum and dad. There is some space in the garage, they said.'

Harlan thanked him. The winter months played havoc

with the chrome work. 'Can I ask something else? I will be staying for a bit, so can I use your washing machine?'

'Yeah, sure. You here for work?'

'Yeah.'

'What do you do?' It was an innocuous question but Harlan gave a wry smile.

'Pest control.'

His fingers were long and thin. White collar fingers. Manicured fingernails. He pressed the buttons on the keypad and waited for the door to release. The safe revealed success. Cash. And lots of it. Next to the cash, a passport. On top of the passport, a memory stick.

He didn't need anything from the safe, he just liked looking inside it. It made him feel powerful. He came from good stock. Privileged. Respected. He had been privately educated and had left university with a first-class honours degree, determined to take the profession of law by storm. He had been a partner in the firm at just thirty, unheard of at the company. Then came the sports cars, the parties and the party drugs. It didn't make him happy. Law bored him. The criminals he defended, those breaking the law, that was what excited him. He wanted to be like them, but better. And he was. It wasn't the money. Not really. It was the fact that he now had respect. When he wanted things done, they got done. People were afraid of him. He liked that. Power felt good.

He went into the study and poured himself a brandy from the crystal decanter. He gently swirled the glass, the aromas warming under his nose. On the mahogany desk was a case of hand rolled Cuban cigars. He had grown accustomed to the finer things in life and had people in place to ensure they continued. He moved the mouse, just a little, just enough so the screen awoke. A faint clack on the keyboard as he typed in his username and password to gain access to his portfolio. A devilish smile came over his narrow face. He had pencil thin lips and drawn in cheeks. There was no fat to his frame. He could appear gaunt to those who didn't know him. He didn't need an impressive physique though, only an impressive bank balance. Money bought muscle. His portfolio revealed what couldn't be traced. Bitcoin.

The plan he had created was simple. Move into venues whose owners could be easily intimidated. If they did protest, they were roughed up. Not too much, but enough, enough that the fear of more would weigh so heavily they would end up beating themselves up. And that was the power of fear. It was a debilitating disease to those who suffered at the hands of it, and a powerful tool if you knew how to wield it.

He also knew that fear, left unconfronted, only grows. He understood fear well. Too well.

Once the venue was secured, he would insist it was to be a cash affair. The cash itself didn't concern him; it was no more than turnover. Simple business economics. It would pay for the protection. The hired muscle. It also paid for DS Sharman, a pivotal part of the plan. All good criminal enter- prises require a bent copper if there is to be any longevity and DS Sharman was easy prey. He wanted cash. Lots of cash. And cash without questions. Edward had told him he could make all that happen but he needed something in return if they were to be partners. He needed girls. Girls who would dance, strip or serve. Girls who would do this for free because the alternative would be too incomprehensible to consider.

He knew DS Sharman well. They had sat on opposite sides of the table when he worked with the vice squad, and then the drug unit. They would argue in an interview room, the suspect being no more than the pawn in the game of criminal chess but he could tell Sharman was a kindred spirit, disillusioned with his chosen career and wanting more from life.

Edward had slowly, but surely, opened the door into his life and let Mark take a peek inside. DS Sharman soon found himself being invited to private members' clubs and sex parties. He made it so DS Sharman could taste the finest malts and sample the most seductive of escorts. Sharman had started to live a champagne lifestyle on a Budweiser salary. He was ripe for the picking when Edward made his move to recruit him fully into the fold and make him yet another one of his many yes men.

What excited him the most was the laundering. The plan was elaborate but low tech. He knew enough about the law to know that the police often pursued complex theories when it came to money laundering and ignored the simpler ones. They gave criminals too much credit for ingenuity. His own plan was simple. Create a chain of companies so that when the money from the card machine came into company one, it bounced immediately into company two, and so on. The only thing being, none of these companies existed. Not in the bricks-and-mortar sense, anyway. They were no more than domain names and online bank accounts. There would be a token email address but that was just to pass security checks, they would never be manned.

Money would flow in on a Monday from the Friday and Saturday scam, unsuspicious to any bank manager. Just a tranche of small transactions from customers at a busy restaurant, which was the ruse of company number one. From there, it would be collated into one large amount and sent across the matrix of companies until landing, cleaned, in a bank account in the Cayman Islands. Once safely there and away from the prying eyes of the HMRC, it would be used to purchase Bitcoin and hidden safely in his virtual wallet. It was swift and simple. The best laid plans always are.

Edward logged out and left the study. His guard dog got up and followed.

7

The deal had been struck. Although it wasn't really a deal because there was no negotiation. Harlan would help him, would return his business to its original state but for that he wanted two grand a week. In cash. Overall, it was a small price to pay if it worked. Guy was haemorrhaging money at an alarming rate trying to stay afloat and it was either this or face ruin.

'I never said I was cheap,' Harlan said, as he and Guy went over the plans to open up during the day. Guy was dressed in a pair of grey suit trousers with a pale pink shirt. Harlan noticed his watch was missing.

'Where's your kettle?'

Guy looked confused. 'My what? Oh, you want a drink?'

Harlan kept forgetting Guy wasn't fluent in slang. He hadn't been raised in the streets.

'Kettle. Your watch'

'Shit. Sorry, I thought you mean my actual kettle. Why is it called a kettle?'

Harlan started to explain but got bored so reverted to the original question. 'Where is it then?'

'I left it at home. If I'm being honest, I think I am going to have to sell it. Or pawn it.'

'To pay me, you mean?'

Guy looked down at his feet. He felt embarrassed. To the outside world he was a successful wine bar owner. His business overlooked the sea and he could name other successful business owners, professional footballers and other high-flyers from around the city as his clientele but the reality was that he now needed to sell his watch to pay for the bearded biker.

'Rolex, right?'

'Yeah. A Submariner.'

Harlan knew about watches. Living off the grid for as long as he had and making money the way he did, he couldn't exactly deposit large chunks of cash into his no-frills bank account.

Instead, he invested in watches. But only if the price was right. He did the math in his head and then outlined his new plan to Guy.

'I'll tell you what, I'll help for four weeks. That's eight large. Two bags a week. But, I'm gonna offer you a deal. I won't take a penny now, nothing except that you cover my living expenses. Then, at the end, when it's over, and trust me, it will be over, you pay me the cash.'

Harlan watched Guy's eyes as he processed what he had just been told, to see if there was some sort of tell to what he was thinking. There was. The squint, barely noticeable, told him so. Harlan knew what it was. 'I know you are struggling financially, let's have it right, so, I have another offer for you instead. You can pay the eight grand in cash, or, you can give me your watch. I know it's a ten-grand kettle, but you may need the money more than you need to know the time by then. Deal?'

Guy knew it was a fair offer. Whoever it was, standing in

front of him, was fast becoming his hero. 'OK. Deal.' They shook hands and got back to work.

Andy was busy in the back room when he heard the thud. He had come to recognise it. He wanted to ignore it but with these two, ignorance was far from bliss. He put the crate down on the floor, his back pinching, and walked over to the door. He opened it and before he could take a step back, he felt the door strike his chest as they barged past and into his premises. The force of their entry had taken him by surprise and he was rubbing his chest when the taller of the two stepped forward, almost nose to nose.

'We better be good to go?' It wasn't a question, rather, a threat.

Andy was a game guy. 6ft and muscular, he worked out and didn't suffer fools gladly but these weren't fools. These weren't two drunk customers who needed kicking out. These were two men with a CV of violence. Andy would know. He had the scars to prove it. They had visited the bar six months back. They had sat and watched the game, drinking no more than two bottles of beer each. Then, when it was time for everyone to leave, they had hung around until they were the last two in there and that's when it had happened.

Before he even knew anything about it, Andy had been headbutted and then his left leg swept away from under him. He had fallen to the floor and taken a series of kicks to the ribs until they broke. In the space of three seconds, he was bleeding and suffocating. It was then that the idea was put to him. Agree or this will happen to you regularly. There wasn't much of a choice. His business partner had come off worse. He'd had his leg broken and spent two days in hospital with concussion.

'Yes. I've put it over social media, too.'

'Good lad.' Andy hated being referred to as a lad. He was a grown man although right now he didn't feel like it. Perhaps lad was apt.

The taller one was still close to Andy's face, his cigarette breath repulsive.

'You better do some good numbers here. Last week was a little... lacking.'

It wasn't. Every time was better than the one before but they kept increasing the target. Like payday lenders increasing their penalties. Andy knew they were in a vortex and would be bled dry. He felt his fists clench.

'I wouldn't,' came the sneered reply, as Buzzcut flicked his coat back behind the right side of his waist to reveal a carved handle protruding from his waistband. Andy's fists loosened.

'Good lad.' The condescending comment cut deeper than the knife would have.

'Anyway, back to it, don't let us stop you.' and just like that, they left.

The fear left his body as soon as they left the bar. He felt lightheaded. Sick. And then came the self-loathing. He was being emasculated and he hated himself for allowing it to happen. He ran to the gent's toilet and wretched.

'Looking good, boss.'

'Is he still compliant?'

'Oh, very!' Edward heard them laugh at this. He smiled too.

'OK. Good. There will be a new girl dancing this week. Let her know the score.'

'Will do, boss.'

'I'll see you on Sunday. I'll let you know where and when.'

'No prob –'

Edward cut the call and went back to reading a police interview transcript regarding his client. To the outside world he was still an in-demand criminal lawyer with a busy practice.

Harlan took his hoodie off. It was hot in the club. Guy couldn't help but notice his thick forearms and a glimpse of his triceps. Guy knew this wasn't down to gym work, this was natural brute strength. The sort of strength you see on farmers. Harlan was deft with his fingers on the computer, almost piano-like. There were tattoos on his arms and Guy found himself trying to make them out without being noticed. There were some relating to his MC, honour and brotherhood, but there was also a girl's name. It was too obscured under the sleeve of his t-shirt to make it out fully. L, something. Laura. Lisa. Lucy?

Harlan had a flat stomach and Guy found himself looking down at his own slight paunch, covered in pink shirt. He wasn't fat, but the wine had caused him to now buy trousers one size up. He felt inferior to the biker standing beside him. Harlan was rough and rugged. Taut and tattooed. Hard and fearless. Everything that Guy wasn't.

'The numbers add up. Time to advertise,' Harlan said, happy with the costings.

'Yes, agreed. I think I was just lazy not doing it before.'

'Don't be hard on yourself. The numbers say you didn't need to before. But now you do.'

Harlan was right. The wine bar had been profitable enough in the evenings that Guy could have the days to himself. He worked hard on those nights. He was often front of house but would also help out behind the bar when it was busy. He enjoyed talking to his customers; advising them on different vintages and checking they were being properly catered to. Behind the scenes it was different. Guy was heading up all aspects of his business, going so far as bleaching the toilets, but to his customers in the evenings, he was charming, calm and conscientious. Harlan liked him. And that was saying something.

The satnav in Rihanna's car told her she had arrived. It had taken her down a back alley and into a dead end. There were a few houses on either side. Not derelict, but not far off. The street she was in was minus any form of illumination. The council didn't spend money on this part of the city. It was an eyesore by day so why brighten it at night? The darkness she had found herself in wasn't helping. She could feel herself trembling. The text message had been clear: **Be there for 9pm. Wear loose clothing.**

It was from a number outside of her contacts but she knew it was related. She arrived wearing a velour tracksuit. It was burgundy in colour. Her hair was pulled back into a ponytail. Her phone said 20.56. On time. The house was the last one down on the left before the street ran out of houses. Rihanna got out and pressed down on the fob to lock her car. She pressed the button again, just to be sure. It was spitting rain and cold.

Rihanna ran across the road and over to the house. There was a light on in one of the rooms upstairs. She rang the doorbell and waited, her body starting to shiver, due to the cold, and the fear. Rihanna saw a shape through the frosted glass in the door. She couldn't make out the sex. The door opened and a woman with a svelte figure wearing leggings that stopped at the shin and a white t-shirt over a gym vest, stood there.

'You must be Rihanna,' she said and held out her hand.

'Um, yes.' Rihanna shook her hand gingerly.

'I'm Carla. Come on in.'

Harlan went back to the Trafalgar pub before heading home. He liked the feel of the place. Unpretentious. Unassuming. It was a spit and sawdust affair. He stepped inside and counted. Twenty, on the nose. Blue collar workers catching a beer on the way home. The backbone of British pubs. It was the same barmaid as before. She smiled.

'Same again?'

'With again being?' Harlan replied, a grin on his face.

'A bottle of Bud. Correct?'

'Correct. Well remembered.'

'I don't tend to forget a face, or a body.' There was a tease in her tone.

'Likewise,' he replied, playing his part in the friendly flirting.

She bent over to grab a bottle from the fridge, making sure her ass was in full view.

Harlan appreciated the gesture. He wasn't an ass man, per se, but he knew never to look a gift horse in the mouth. She wanted him. It was written all over her face. And her ass.

He sat at the bar and took the first mouthful. Harlan had a thing of finding a pub when arriving in a new town and sticking with it until he left. He took out his two phones and put them on the bar. He tapped the screen on the smartphone. Nothing more than the screensaver to look at. He knew there wouldn't be. Only two people had this number and neither of them ever rang. He wasn't sure they ever would.

Rihanna was exhausted. Sweat was running down her back and strands of hair were sticking to her face. Her inner thighs hurt. Everything hurt. Carla returned to the room with a bottle of water in each hand.

'Here.' Carla offered her a bottle before sitting cross-legged on the floor.

'Thanks,' she replied, twisting off the cap and chugging the water down her throat.

'You did good,' Carla said. 'Not as easy as it looks, is it?'

'Not in the slightest. You make it look so easy.'

'The trick is to look like you're making love to the pole.'

The pole was dead-centre in the bedroom. It was sitting inside two circular plates, one screwed to the floor, one to the ceiling. The carpet had been taken up and the floor-boards had been varnished. There was a stereo on the floor which Carla had turned off now the session had finished. Apart from that, the room was bare. It was the only nice room in the house, which was saying something.

'Do you live here?' Rihanna asked after apologising for her belch.

'No. Of course not. But this is where I train the girls.'

'The girls?'

'The other dancers.'

'The strippers?'

'We prefer dancers.'

'Sorry.'

Carla smiled. There was no offence intended so none taken. Carla was tough but the young girl sat opposite her, panting, was far from it. A newbie, here against her will. She knew the feeling.

8

———

By the end of the week, Harlan had dissected Guy's business, financially, and rebuilt it. Some suppliers had been changed and credit terms had been extended. The 'taster' wine brochures had been printed ready for the following Monday's lunchtime grand opening and new software had been installed in the tills. Harlan had been hard at work. Guy had thought he was hiring his own thug. Instead, he'd also gotten his very own business guru.

Harlan had taught him the finer points of running a bar. How to maximise the margins and how to turn breakages into tax losses. Guy had thought he had a pretty good idea of how to run his business but he was in awe of Harlan's acumen in accounting. Harlan was going through the ancillary costs next. He was sitting at the bar on a stool, his hair back in a short ponytail and he was wearing glasses. The frames, like the rest of his attire, were black. Black boots. Black jeans. A black tee and a black braided bracelet. The Grim Reaper would be proud of his dress sense, Guy thought, although refrained from saying it out loud. Harlan scared him, but he guessed that was the point. Harlan sipped the hot tea from the mug. Guy had gotten used to how he liked it. Light brown in colour and with three spoons of sugar.

'What is this bill?' Harlan asked. Guy was at the far end of the bar tinkering with the ice machine that had always been problematic. He threw the tea towel onto his shoulder and walked over to where Harlan was sitting. He turned the laptop to face him to understand the question. 'That's for the bins.'

'Really? You could lease a Bentley cheaper. Why haven't you questioned it?'

'It's a touchy subject.'

'Go on?'

'The gentleman who does the bins does them for all the businesses here. He is... how do I say it, um, a character and if you don't use his bins, he makes life... difficult.'

'Does he now?'

Guy saw Harlan's eyes and posture change. He watched as he pushed his glasses up the top of his forehead. 'What's his number?'

'I don't think we should do that. He is quite tasty, apparently.'

'Good. I'm feeling peckish. Number.'

Guy sensed he wasn't asking and went into the office returning with a box file labelled INVOICES. He flicked through until he found what he was after, lifting the lever to release the invoice from its retainer. He passed it over to Harlan.

Harlan perused the invoice. He had seen enough. 'And he does everybody's bins here?'

'Yes. It is kind of an unwritten rule that we all use him.'

'Rules are there to be broken,' he replied, already typing the phone number into his phone. It went to voicemail. Harlan left a message: 'It's the wine bar at Cedar Yard. I won't be needing your services anymore. You got a problem with that, then call me back. Think twice though before you do.'

Harlan ended the call and went back to the computer as if nothing had happened.

'Was that not a bit –'

'A bit what?'

Guy lowered his tone before replying. 'Harsh?'

Harlan stood up from the stool and rolled his shoulders. Guy noticed the size of them.

'Whoever this prick is, he is charging easily 200% more than any other commercial refuse collector that I have come across. Ever. That's 200% you don't have and he has gotten fat enough from you. It's time I cut back his carb intake.'

'He won't like it.'

'I couldn't give a shit.'

Harlan's phone rang. It was the same number he just dialled. He answered it. Agreed something. Then put the phone down.

'Well? What did he say?' asked Guy, the conversation too quick to get a gist on it.

'He is on his way to see me.'

'Shit.'

'No thanks,' said Harlan, sitting back down and taking another sip of his tea.

An hour had gone by and Harlan was getting restless. As this wasn't a pub, there was no pool table to pass the time. He didn't like waiting for people at the best of times, even less if he didn't like them.

Guy was pacing the bar. His nervous energy was palpable. It was grating on Harlan.

'Will you sit the fuck down. Or go home. Anything but wear out your shoe leather.'

'This guy is a boxer. Bare-knuckle. Traveller type. Shall we not just continue with him?'

Harlan's patience with Guy was thinning. He needed him to start growing some balls.

'I made it very clear from the beginning. My club. My cash. My business. If not, I walk.'

Guy's mouth went dry. He went to reply but stuttered before finally speaking, 'OK.'

Harlan glanced up at the CCTV monitor and saw a flatbed transit van back up outside.

'That him?' he asked, pointing.

Guy looked up at the grainy image on the screen. 'Yes. That's him.'

'OK. Wait here.' Which were just the words Guy wanted to hear.

Harlan had swapped a cup of tea for a bottle of beer during the wait and emptied the last of it into his mouth before putting the empty bottle on the bar. He took his glasses off, folded them up and left them propped up against the bottle.

Guy watched Harlan walk out through the bar and waited a couple of seconds before seeing him again on the monitor pushing open the back door and walking out into the loading bay reserved for the four businesses. He wished now his system had sound.

The guy was standing at the rear of his van. His arms were crossed, his forearms resting on his gut. He was broad, squat and stern. 'You the new gaffer then?' - his tone confrontational.

'That's right,' replied Harlan, no hint of concern.

'I see. You don't know how this works, do you? I'll explain it to –'

'Let me stop you there. I don't care how it works.'

Paddy uncrossed his arms and then tilted his head from right to left and then back again and then rolled his shoulders.

'What's next, someone ringing a bell?' Harlan said, unimpressed with Paddy's act of intimidation.

'This isn't Queensberry rules, son. There are no rules.' Paddy growled.

'Just the way I like it,' said Harlan before unleashing a thunderous cross straight into the face of the traveller. It caught him just above the eye causing the skin to split and blood to seep. Harlan was impressed, it was a good shot and he had taken it well. Normally he would aim for the jaw. Breaking it first time, every time. But this man wanted to dance and Harlan was more than willing to tango.

The traveller brushed the blood away with the back of his hand and put up his guard. His stance, southpaw. Unorthodox. Harlan switched accordingly, both now ready to lead with their right arms. Paddy threw first, a feint, hoping Harlan would take the bait so he could land a left hook but Harlan was ready for it. He parried the jab and stepped forward, closing the gap to neutralise the hook and dropped his head hard on the bridge of the traveller's nose. Guy winced; he felt the bone crack from the safety of his seat. Paddy staggered back, his hands over his face and blood seeping through his fingers. He was back where he started, up against his van.

'Now would be a good time for you to stop,' Harlan said.

The traveller's face was covered in claret, his nose already swelling, his right eye puffy, turning purple and half closed.

It was now pride to fight for. He wiped his hands into his grubby wifebeater and took a step forward but with less conviction than he had a minute earlier. He threw a jab but it lacked direction and guile and Harlan slipped it easily.

Another aimless jab, his vision was impaired by both blood and bruising. Harlan knew it was over and it was just a case of how much pain he wanted to administer. Paddy tried a one-two combination, a jab followed by a right cross but Harlan was too experienced a brawler to be taken out by such an amateur attempt. It bordered on the insulting. The traveller left his chin exposed for less than half a second and that was all Harlan needed. His chin was in Harlan's crosshairs and he swung his hook like he was hitting a home run.

Harlan saw Paddy's pupils go up under his eyelids as his head cranked hard to the left causing his upper torso to twist. Harlan took him off his feet and dropped him like a bad habit. Paddy looked a sorry sight. Like a once mighty oak tree now wilting sorrily on the floor.

Harlan had the urge to hoist up the bin man's unconscious body and place him inside one of his own bins, like the piece of trash that he was. He decided against it. Five years ago, he wouldn't have thought twice. He liked to think he had mellowed with age.

Harlan looked around. No-one had seen. He stepped back inside and shut the door and a few seconds later he emerged back in the bar.

Guy's face spoke without the aid of his lips. 'Get the tape wiped,' Harlan snapped. He knew those sixty-seconds caught on camera could very easily multiply to a 3yr stretch behind bars. Harlan had been lucky so far as prison was concerned, but he knew that luck had a funny way of running out.

Guy nodded, still unable to speak. He had been in the

trade long enough to know fights occurred but normally there was either wine or women involved. This was over his bins. He had never witnessed anything like it. His hired help had just pummelled someone into unconsciousness in less time than it took him to make himself a latte and he hadn't even broken sweat. Guy was sure that if Jamie, the delivery driver, walked in, he would kiss him there and then.

Harlan sat on the bed. His knuckles were red but overall, it had been a quiet week; 3 fights. There once was a time it would be three an hour. He had learned to beat people with the threat of violence rather than the use of it, and that was what made him a good bouncer. But he also knew that when he arrived in a new town, he had to let it be seen that he didn't suffer fools gladly. It was psychological. In the dog-eat-dog world of problematic pubs and clubs, he had to be the alpha. Maybe one day he'd meet someone stronger, but he hadn't come across that someone yet.

9

Andy was balancing precariously on the step ladder lining up the pole into the fixing. The bar was a large, perfectly formed square and a bank of TV screens ran high up around the walls. The feature wall was where the large projector would drop down and draw in large crowds watching live football or the Las Vegas fights. On these occasions, the half-back leather chairs would be brought out from the back and the centre floor would be full. Andy offered 'chair service' on these nights and his bar staff would work in-between the chairs taking orders and delivering drinks, a card machine hooked to their trousers for payment. It was little extras like this that made their sports bar stand out from the rest and it had grown into a very busy and very profitable business for the two partners. That was until the pole arrived.

'I hate this. We are literally like two bitches,' Andy said, getting frustrated as he tried to secure the pole to the ceiling.

'I know, but what do we do? I like breathing if I'm being honest,' replied Jake, his younger business partner.

Jake had suffered worse at the hands of the two suited thugs. He was knocked to the floor and his leg was held out straight and then broken. The limp was still there. Jake's comment was delivered with wry humour but the reality was he was scared and suffered PTSD from the attack. Jake was younger, slimmer and sweeter than Andy. Shy, too. But he was adept at admin and took care of the back end of the business. They made a good team. But now their business was a once-a-week brothel and their takings were taken.

'The women will be arriving soon,' said Andy, climbing back down the ladder.

'Oh goodie, our resident Hooter girls,' Jake sarcastically replied.

Rihanna checked the time. She was hoping time would go backward, to a week ago, or even better, a decade ago. She had two more classes with Carla and had got the basics of pole dancing down but she couldn't, as told, 'Look like you're making love to the pole.'

Rihanna had slept with boys. She had been in two relationships and had had two hook-ups. She liked sex, but with boys. Not poles.

She had hidden her outfit in her gym bag. The short skirt had been delivered the day before from a cheap online store and it was as seedy as the picture portrayed. The underwear wasn't new. A black push-up bra and a thong. Carla had said to wear a bra that added 'bounce to your ounce,' which translated into showing them what was on offer and making them pay to see it. She hadn't eaten all day. She was too afraid she would throw it straight back up. It was time to leave. She wanted to die. The thought had crossed her mind.

· · ·

Harlan stood out. The wine bar had been open for an hour and it was already busy. Men in blue jeans and crisp white shirts, sockless and with gold watches. The women were in tight dresses, accentuated curves, and high heels. Harlan stood at the far end of the bar dressed in black jeans, a black club hoodie, and his scuffed boots. His attire spoke for him; rough and rugged and he was already attracting interest from some of the women there, who liked what they saw. Something different is always something sexy.

He knew the sports bar was a few hours away from being rowdy but he felt out of place at the wine bar and he wasn't needed there tonight. It didn't need protecting; the wine would flow and the till would be full. And more importantly for Guy, he would get to keep it. It would be a good night for him.

The Harley was parked around the back, in the loading bay. He found Guy and told him he was leaving but if he needed him, to call. Guy was dressed in a three-piece boss suit and shiny shoes. He looked good in what he was wearing. This was why he had opened his bar. For nights like this. To be the well-dressed, well-versed host. Anyone could hide their troubles if their smile was wide enough, Harlan thought.

The bike fired into life and he let it idle for a minute, the exhaust growling with intent.

He walked his bike back and then flicked it into gear, pulled out of the loading bay and into the road. It was early Saturday evening so the road was busy with black cabs and private hires. Taking people to places sober and hoping to return them home drunk. Taxi drivers lived for Saturday nights. So too did people like Guy and Andy in the past. But now they had come to dread these nights. He was here to change that. He was here to bring the good times back.

The Trafalgar wasn't far from the wine bar. It was

walkable but why walk when you could ride? One of the rules of the club was the number of miles you needed to put on your bike each year. There was a space under one of the stained-glass windows. Like before. Harlan mounted the kerb and parked his bike under the window. Like before.

The Trafalgar was more to his liking than the wine bar. More what he was used to. Men in tight jeans and expensive trainers. Tight t-shirts stopping at the triceps, shaded tattoos running the full length of their arms. Fake tan. Women in low-cut tops or short skirts. Tattoos on wrists or thighs. Red lipstick on enhanced lips. More fake tan.

This was pub life now. The pre-drinks before the clubs. Pubs had become places for the forties and under and it had saved the industry. The problem now was the element of chemistry that had entered into pub culture. Lines of coke being done on top of toilet cisterns. Or off the back of hands in the car park. The problem for Harlan was it made a regular dickhead an egotistical one. It made the stupid, stupider. But this wasn't his pub to police. He was just here to pass a couple of hours.

The same barmaid was behind the bar as before. She looked up, saw him, and smiled. He returned the smile but he didn't do more. She was too young. A girl in women's clothing. She was pretty and he hoped she found a nice man to treat her well.

Rihanna watched as the other girls went in. Blonde. Brunette. Busty. She felt out of their league. The knock on the window spooked her. It was Carla. Rihanna hit the button to bring down her window. Carla leaned her head in, her cleavage ample, her perfume heavy. 'Ready, hun?'

Carla was seen as the mother figure of the girls. She was

in her thirties and had a 5yr old son named Connor whom she adored. His name was tattooed on the nape of her neck.

Rihanna wanted to scream at her, *'No I'm not ready. I'm not ready to strip off in front of drunken strangers screaming at me to get my boobs out.'* Her spoken reply was different, 'I guess.'

'You'll be fine. The first night is the worst but the end justifies the means.'

Rihanna knew she was referring to the cash. Easy cash. But it was that easy cash that got her into this mess in the first place.

Rihanna picked up her gym bag from the passenger seat and got out of her car, locked it, and followed Carla into the sports bar. With each step she took, the feeling of nausea increased. By the time she got to the door, she was visibly shaking. Carla noticed and held her hand as they stepped into the bar. 'You got this, girl,' she whispered. Rihanna wasn't so sure.

Harlan took his drink over to the table and sat down. He scanned the room and it was like any other pub, a large group of people split into splinter cells. Small groups of common social standing. Like a school playground. Hot chicks with hot chicks. Cool guys with cool guys. Dads with other dads. Mums with other mums. People mixed with people their own age. Their own kind. You dressed the same as the group. You talked the same as the group. You were the group and the group was you. It was the same at his MC. Or any MC for that matter. You attracted your own.

The pub was busy. There was a large crowd around the pool table with pound coins dotted around the wooden edges and there was football on the big screen. Harlan knew it would do good trade tonight.

A woman from across the bar was giving him the look that he had seen a thousand times before. She was all ass and tight curves. A teenager's wet dream and a rich man's mistress. She could be with any one of the men in there but she kept staring at him; her eyes trying to lead the bee to the honey. Harlan had been in this situation so many times it had become old, women drawn to the new man in town, the bad boy. But he wasn't a boy, he was a man. He was an outlaw, a loner, and he liked it that way. He knew he wasn't nice. Kind, but not nice.

She was still looking over, smouldering. He returned her gaze. He might be kind but he never said he had a halo. The lingering, sultry smile she'd given him vanished as a glass smashed, immediately igniting his senses. The sound that meant it was on. The only thing now was to determine if the glass had been broken by accident or in anger. It was the latter.

The guy waving the broken glass looked like a waste of skin, a nobody who, with a belly full of beer and a nostril full of narcotics, wanted to be a somebody, and the jagged-edged bottle was his way of achieving that.

There was only one doorman working, normally a pub this size would have two. One might be late, Harlan thought. Or the landlord had stood him down to halve the expense. Harlan looked over at the doorman, hoping for a lightning-fast reaction. The fight was imminent, no two ways about it, and the doorman needed to step up and earn his pay packet.

The guy holding the broken bottle swiped at another man and although he missed, the unarmed guy came close to being slashed.

The hired help was now at the scene. Harlan stood near the bar; his eyes fixed on the three men whilst his peripheral vision was attuned to anyone coming into view from the wings. The pub has come to a standstill, the live game was on but that was merely now a side-show. Harlan gave a split-second glance over at the two-bar staff; two young girls, frightened and fearing the sight of soon-to-be blood. The doorman had become static, his feet had set like concrete, turning from saviour to spectator. Harlan knew this was about to go bad. Very bad.

The next sound was identical to the first, a glass shattering on the hardwood floor. This time not made out of anger, but out of distraction. Harlan had picked up his glass and hurled it at the attacker, close enough to him to startle him, far enough away to miss. He was now invested in the altercation. He didn't care about the reason behind it, only about the outcome. Harlan knew one thing and hoped for another. The thing he knew was that it would end as quickly as it had started. The second, that the pain would be minimal. The first part he could guarantee, the second, well that was down to the guy holding the broken bottle.

'Your move.' Harlan had used this ploy many times before. A statement of intent. Designed wholly to disorientate. The ante had been upped, so too, the stakes. He waited for a reply.

'This has got nothing to do with you, pal,' came the reply. A reply without conviction.

Harlan had him. He knew it, it was just a matter of seconds before broken bottle guy did.

'Too late, I'm afraid. I'm here now. Only question that remains is are we doing this here or outside. I'm really not bothered either way.'

Harlan's nonchalant comment was designed to defeat his foe without the need for force or fury. Harlan was a master fighter but had learnt to be an even better manipulator.

'Make your mind up, before I do it for you.' The last

chance he would give him but he already knew his fish had taken the bait.

Broken Bottle Guy was now lacking in both posture and presence. Harlan had done this so many times before, he had taken the air well and truly out the guy's bravado balloon. His ego has been smashed just like the bottle moments before. Harlan went again, this time for the fun of it.

'Last chance at choosing. Where do you want it to happen? And it will happen.'

Harlan could see Broken Bottle Guy thinking, weighing up the odds. He had nowhere to go. All eyes were on him. Did he really want to fight this bearded stranger? No, was the answer. He threw the remains of his self-made weapon onto the floor and barged past the few drinkers that were in his way and was out and into the night. A good result, thought Harlan.

The doorman, the one paid to do what Harlan had just done, came over wanting a word. With the issue now dealt with and his fear no longer exposed, his confidence had returned in earnest judging by his puffed-out chest. He seemed to have forgotten that just a few minutes earlier his ass had fallen out of his trousers.

'Hey, man. I had that under control. Next time, leave it to me.'

Harlan looked at him and without blinking replied, 'No, you didn't.'

And with that, he too walked through the drinkers and out into the night and to his bike.

The girl with the eyes could wait. They always did.

'Who's that?' Rihanna asked.

She was referring to the huge guy standing at the bar

with a gold necklace the width of her forearm hanging around his neck. Rihanna had never seen anyone as big.

'He provides the cash. The guys over there, in the suits, they provide the girls, that's if you want to earn a little extra tonight?'

It took a second to comprehend but then she got it. 'Pimps?' she said.

'Don't think about it. It's a slippery slope. Dance, get your cash and go. Don't engage.'

This was the first time Rihanna had heard Carla sound serious. Like she was talking from experience. Or regret. Or both.

She watched as the biggest man she had ever seen went over to a booth, sat down and opened a grey holdall. She stared as his bear sized paws pulled out two large stacks of cash, held tightly by an elastic band, and placed them on the table. She shook her head in disbelief and then got caught staring.

'Hey, you, newbie. Eyes off the prize. Unless it's this prize you're wanting,' he said, groping his dick over his trousers. The crude comment had come from one of the two men wearing suits. He had a buzz cut. Rihanna felt small, weak and unwelcome. Rihanna felt Carla grab the top of her arm, digging her long false nails into her.

'Don't stare. These aren't nice people, babe. Trust me on that.'

Rihanna could see the truth in Carla's eyes. 'Sorry.'

Harlan had seen enough faces cut like fruit to detest anyone pulling a knife. Same for bottles. But he knew this was the modern-day weapon now. The days of having a bare-knuckle straightener were long gone. In the nineties, doormen would carry knuckle dusters if the numbers were stacked against them, and Harlan had a pair gifted to him by the club a few years back. A solid brass bone breaker. But nothing prepared you for steel. The club had lost a member in a knife attack. Someone had come up to one of his brothers when stopped at a red light late one night and plunged him twice in the back. He had bled out right there at the scene. He left behind a wife and a young son. Blades aren't forgiving. The contract was still out on the attacker but intel had told the club he had fled overseas. The score *would* be settled, the death of a brother *would* be avenged. His time *would* come.

He was still riled. The pub should have had two doormen working. Two decent doormen were normally enough to control a venue that size. Unless it was a notorious pub that was seeing fights nightly or if it was a known watering hole of a local gang and there was some street beef brewing. That was when you upped your number of bouncers and tooled them up. One guy could control a pub but only if that guy was capable of extreme retribution. Harlan was a lone wolf, but like all lone wolves, he belonged to a pack.

Harlan missed the club runs but missed the camaraderie more. You trusted your brothers with your life. The club was a criminal enterprise. It had turned from a band of brothers on bikes to a business. Drugs were trafficked. Places were protected. The club was into counterfeit cash, fake goods and loan sharking but it also protected its own. It helped the down and outs and took care of the families if a brother went behind the door for a while. If you had a problem with someone and you knew someone in the club, and the club thought a liberty was being taken, your problem would go away. But business aside, it was a family. His family. If you stayed loyal, loyalty was returned. If you betrayed the club, it was time to leave town. Harlan had entered the club as a kid but had left a man. He had been beaten, shot at, and had shot back. He had screwed hundreds of women but loved just one.

It had been a brief love affair. Nothing more than a ripple in the sea of life but sometimes a few months can impact a lifetime. Every day he missed her. She wasn't part of the club and wanted no part of it. She didn't make him choose but she didn't make it easy. She had wanted him to change but he knew he couldn't. It wasn't that he wouldn't, he just couldn't. People don't change.

The position he held at the club came with responsibilities and with that came a lifestyle that she couldn't, or wouldn't, understand. All he knew was that when he was with her, when his vest was off and his pocket phone was set to silent, he could step into her eyes and get lost for a few hours. She took his heart and he hadn't gotten it back. He didn't want it back. Harlan wanted her to keep hold of it. Wherever she was.

She had his number but she never rang. He didn't blame her. To the outside world he was a gangster. Violence was his profession. He would ride his bike behind an unmarked van with high-end drugs stashed inside to ensure the safety of the cargo. He would leave suddenly if the club rang to say there was a problem. This wasn't the life for someone as sweet as her. Then there was the job. The one that paid. Working as a bouncer took away their weekends. She only came once to see him at work and she didn't like it. Bouncers are seen as saints or sinners. She hated how alert he had to be. How his eyes were always scanning. Scrutinising. Second guessing. She hated how other women looked at him. Wanting to sleep with him. Wanting to be a notch on his bedpost. She hated how other men looked at him. Wanting to take him on, wanting to be the one that beat the bouncer. It was no way to live. What she didn't understand was that pubs and clubs needed people like Harlan. People who protect your sons and daughters, your wives and husbands, from the sinister side of society. People who would risk their life and liberty for a stranger. Harlan wasn't a hero, nor was he a mindless thug. But he *was* difficult to love.

10

———————

Harlan rode past the sports bar and parked up on the opposite side of the road. There was a taxi rank parallel to the bar that would be busy later. It was a good spot for a bar and the taxi rank would only help. The boys had done well, Harlan thought. He knew that in the pub and club trade, location played a pivotal part in a company profits.

He wasn't wearing his cut. He couldn't change the fact he was a biker, but the wine bar didn't need it shouted from the rooftops earlier. Nor did the Trafalgar pub. And now the sports bar didn't need it, either. He was there on a recce. The bar sounded loud. And busy. He watched for a few minutes. He was far enough back from the bar to observe without arousing suspicion. A minute later a Mercedes came into view. It drove slowly down the street. Too slowly. Harlan watched as the driver reversed into a tight space, got out and walked across the road with his passenger, and into the bar. They were wearing suits. He knew these two would be involved somehow. Their walk spoke of arrogance. Taking on Harlan spoke of stupidity.

He waited for them to go in. Then waited another five minutes for them to get comfortable. He saw a group of guys walking down towards the bar. He knew they would be a stag-do. Normally these groups were harmless. You may have one in the group who couldn't handle his drink and start trouble but they would be spoken with quickly, told in no uncertain circumstances to behave and then they generally would for the rest of the night. No need for violence. But Harlan didn't care if this was the stag-do from hell. Not his bar, not his problem.

Rihanna was in the ladies. Behind a closed cubicle door. She was on her knees and looking down at the little well of water at the bottom of the toilet but there was nothing to bring up. She hadn't eaten all day, she couldn't. The music was thumping so loud the cubicle door was rattling inside the lock. But it wasn't as if she would be disturbed. Aside from the girls that were either dancing or serving, the clientele were all men.

Seedy men wanting to see naked bodies. It was little more than a cattle market. She would be up soon. Writhing around a pole, trying to look sexy, trying not to look scared. She heard the door open and the sound of footsteps walking towards her. It wasn't the sound of heels. First there was silence. Then there wasn't. A clattering thud on the cubicle door. Three hard slaps from a flat palm. Her whole body froze with terror. The worst thoughts imaginable entered her head in a flurry. Her worst fears were outside the door and were about to come in.

'Newbie. Let's be seeing you. NOW'.

The two men in suits wanted to see the new addition to their portfolio close up and personal. The boss had told them to let her know the score and the boss always got what he wanted.

'NOW.' Another slam on the door.

Rihanna rose to her feet. The thought of being raped in the toilet was all too real. Her fingers were shaking so much she struggled to slide the latch. The taller one pushed on the door gently, just enough so it opened inwardly to reveal the new girl. They both looked her up and down, like she was some sort of second-hand car, checking for faults on the bodywork.

She had never felt so dirty. So degraded. She stood there, shivering. She pulled her baggy t-shirt down over her panties and held it there, her legs slightly crossed.

'Take off your top. Let's see those titties.'

She did as she was told. She wasn't being raped, not physically anyway. She clutched her top in one hand, the other hand resting on her stomach, not knowing where to put it. Her ample chest was rising and falling with each breath.

'Yeah, nice rack. You'll do.'

The throwaway compliment repulsed her.

Harlan walked past the two bouncers on the door. They had paid him no interest. The same couldn't be said for Harlan. He had already made a mental note of them. He knew they were not there to police the place, but to fill it with as many punters as possible. He doubted anyone would be turned away at the door. He had been inside many a strip club, either as a guest or guard. They all looked the same. They all smelled the same. A cesspit of drunken men believing their cash was an aphrodisiac. But the women who stripped were strong. Master manipulators. And good on them. If treacherous men wanted to leer at their half-naked bodies, why not milk them for the privilege. He knew some women did this as it was safer than selling themselves on the streets. Others did it to pay for college or for the finer things in life. Some though, some did this because they were told to.

There was a redhead on the pole. She had on knee-high boots, gold sequined hot pants and nothing else. She was slim bordering on skinny and her fake breasts didn't sit well on her thin frame. Harlan looked into her eyes. They were vacant. She was stoned and the dance, unbeknown to the uninitiated, was simply being done on autopilot. She caught his stare, there was a slight smile, barely noticeable to the human eye.

'Can I get you a drink?' The girl looked barely old enough to be served herself. The skirt was shorter than it needed to be and her red t-shirt was a size too small to make her look bustier than she was. This wasn't the attire she would choose herself; he knew that, like he also knew that this was down to the two in the suits. Just like he knew already that he didn't like them.

'A coke, please.'

He noticed her nervousness. 'What's up?' there was sincerity in his tone.

'I don't think I can serve just regular coke.'

'Don't think?' Harlan's eyes narrowed.

'I mean, I think we are only supposed to sell alcoholic drinks here. They get funny.'

'Who gets funny?'

The waitress leaned ever so slightly to her left, so Harlan could see behind her and over to the two in the suits. So, he was right. This was their show. His dislike for them had gone up a notch.

'It's OK, I don't want to get you in trouble. I'll have a Jack and coke, thanks.'

She gave a smile. She had covered her freckles with

concealer. Harlan thought it was a shame. He watched as she walked over to the bar, ensuring she got there safely and away from wandering hands. He took a spot to the side of the stage, his back close to a wall. He avoided sitting at one of the few empty booths. Past experience told him to avoid being sat down if something was about to kick off. Everything was at a disadvantage when you were sitting down; you could be blocked in. You were half immobilised. And you couldn't twist from the hips to maximise your punching power. It was one of his rules: never sit down in an unfamiliar place.

He looked through the crowd at the three men; two stood together, suited and booted. The other man, alone and in a booth, surrounded by stacks of cold-hard cash. Three men; three antagonists. Three assholes. They would meet their downfall; they just didn't know it yet. The first was as Guy described: huge. Harlan couldn't tell exactly how big, as he was sitting down, but his guess would be 6'4/6'5 and probably close to twenty stone. He looked like he had been carved from granite. The other two looked just like wannabe gangsters. Harlan had come across enough fakes in his time to spot the real deal from the frauds. The waitress returned with his drink.

'I'm so sorry,' she said, placing the glass down on the table and a serviette.

'It's fine. It's not a bad upgrade,' he replied, making her feel better. 'How much?'

'£10 pounds, please. They gave you a double. They always do that.'

'They choose what you drink and what size?'

'Yes. Sorry, again.'

'Don't be, you don't set the rules.'

'I know, but I get the flak from the customers.'

'Much trouble here?' he asked.

'No, not really. It's just us. They can't touch the girls dancing so we get groped instead.'

'Card or cash?' but he already knew the answer.

'Cash only, sorry.'

'No need,' and he reached into his pocket and pulled out a crumpled ten-pound note.

He watched again as she made her way over to a table that was waving for her attention.

The redhead had been replaced by a blonde. She looked more together and was working the crowd well. She had strong thighs. Her breasts were natural and heavy. Notes were being thrown at her as she ran her index finger across the edge of her pants. Some of the men were standing up and cheering. Shirts were sweat-stained and ties had been loosened. The group of guys that Harlan had watched walk in were patting each other, their beer spilling in anticipation of what was to come. Harlan's eyes scanned the room as grown men turned into rampant teenagers and it was then that he noticed one of the two-suited men was making his way over to him. He counted the steps: twenty.

Harlan didn't move from where he was standing, his posture nonchalant. It was for the suit to start the conversation; it was for Harlan to decide when and how it would end.

'You sure you're in the right place, mate?' the suit asked. He hadn't stepped over Harlan's imaginary line, but he was pretty damn close.

'Meaning?'

'There's wall to wall women here and you don't seem all that interested, big guy.'

'Is that so?'

Their eyes locked. The suit was seasoned, but Harlan was a pro in dick measuring.

'Just wondering if there was something wrong with you? Bare flesh here. Prime pussy.'

Harlan took a sip from his drink before taking a step forward and closing the gap.

'If I wanted to paw at a pussy, then I would buy a cat.'

Harlan tipped the last of his drink into his mouth, his eyes not leaving the man in the suit.

'Think you're smart, huh?'

'No. I know I'm smart. But the question isn't if I'm smart, it's, are you?'

Harlan had been in this situation too many times before, the stare-off. Two tough men not wanting to break first. Harlan pulled a smirk. 'Question too difficult?'

He could sense the suit start to stiffen, the man stood inside of it tensing his muscles, another act of male pride. Harlan had been confronted by every type of ego before, and had dismissed each one.

The suit broke his stare first. He tugged at his lapels, gave a wry smile and spoke.

'I will give you a pass, putting it down to being pussy drunk. But buy a drink, or leave.'

Harlan's top lip curled at the suit's feeble attempt at being menacing. It takes more than a cheap suit and shiny shoes to make someone a gangster, and as far as Harlan could tell, his suit was made of nothing more than plastic. But he wasn't here to tear the guy's head off, that would wait. He was here to observe. The suit believed he had made his point and turned around and walked back over to where he had come from. Harlan watched him, wishing now he had driven his head into the table and out through the other side. But he could wait.

The blonde had finished her dance and she picked up her panties from the floor alongside the raft of notes. She looked pleased; it had been a good haul for her. Harlan watched as she disappeared from view to lewd chants of an encore. Harlan gave a quick headcount. It was a profitable scam they had going on. He didn't like them, but he couldn't argue with their criminal prowess now that he had seen it for himself. The crowd in the middle had started to settle. The blonde had gone and this was the calm before the next stripping storm. Some of the booths had scantily clad girls sitting on men's laps. Harlan watched as hands wandering up thighs and proposals were whispered into ears. Sex sells, Harlan knew, and right here it was selling well.

His stare was broken by the sound of cheering and he turned to face the stage. A young girl had come into view. The crowd could see her figure, Harlan could see her nerves. It was faint, but it was there. She was shaking, her fingers. Little tremors. This was more than stage fright. He knew only too well what was causing her fingers to tremble. Fear.

Rihanna stood frozen. Like a deer in the headlights. She was desperately trying to remember her steps, her moves. She could see the two men in suits grimacing at her. The man made from granite, the man with the stacks of cash, started to shake his head. She tried to move her legs but they wouldn't work. She could feel herself shivering but the glare from the spotlight had made her forehead sweat, a bead trickled down her temple.

'Get on with it. Get your tits out.' Harlan turned to see which face had spoken. It wasn't clear, there were too many rubberneckers. 'What are you waiting for? Dance, stupid bitch.'

Rihanna felt robotic. Her arms and leg, heavy. She didn't feel in control of her body, it was fighting against her, not wanting to participate in this act of public indecency. She had been told by Carla to be topless within the first two minutes. Fully nude within four. But she wanted the seconds to slow. For time to stand still. The crowd sensed blood. They wanted flesh and didn't want to wait much longer. She needed to do something. She needed to dance. She had never felt so alone. So vulnerable. She tried to move, to shake her hips, but she couldn't. She was caught in a bear trap, paralysed by her own fear.

Harlan was watching a car crash. This was someone's daughter. Someone's sister. This was a young frightened girl, desperate to stay dressed. He had had enough. This wasn't his venue or his punters or his money, but he wasn't going to watch a young girl lose her dignity to please a baying crowd. He made his way through to the centre, jostling people out the way, bottles and glasses hitting the floor in his wake. He was going to get her out of there, and nobody was going to stop him. He got to the front of the baying, booing crowd and held out his hand for her to take. Rihanna could see warmth in his eyes. He was there to help.

Harlan felt someone angrily grab at his shoulder, instantly igniting his instincts. Without looking, he thrust his elbow high up behind him, driving it backwards through a small twist of the hip and felt it break bone on impact. 'Quick. Let's go.'

Rihanna took his hand, hoping it would be a safe decision. He drove himself hard through the crowd with Rihanna hanging on behind him. His grip was hurting her. The DJ had put the music on, trying to reclaim some order. They got to the entrance and were confronted by the two doormen. One of them holding out his arm, palm facing outward. The universal language of stop.

'I don't think so, mate. She belongs to the club,' the

wider of the two men said. The other doorman stood next to him; his arms crossed, a show of strength for his oppo. Classic bouncer tactics. Strength in numbers. It works well on the average guy, but what they didn't know, yet, was that Harlan wasn't your average guy. Harlan started to snarl. His jaw, tightening. His muscles, tensing. Time to see if these two in front of him, who were trying to block his path, really wanted to earn their wages. The decision would be theirs; the outcome, he knew, would be his. 'I'll bury you both right here. Move, now, before you can't.'

The two doormen looked at each other. There was a big guy holding a woman, looking more than ready to fight. And more than capable of having one. They could see their employers in the background, in their suits, shouting at them over the music to stop them from leaving. Decision time. The wrath of them versus the wrath of him. They were over there. He was here, inches away and looking ready for it.

They did what he knew they would do. Deal with the now, the later would wait. In front of them was 15st of fury, clutching a girl and in no mood for small talk. He was the immediate threat.

'Want it?' Harlan asked. His mind was fixed on doing maximum damage. He was getting her out of there, no two ways about it. If they wanted to try and stop him, he would hurt them.

The wider one's bottle went. He stepped aside and then his partner did the same.

'Good choice,' Harlan said, grabbing for the handle. They were out. As they started to walk away from the club a group of men approached the venue, ready to enter.

'They do a takeaway service then, mate?'

It was meant as an off-the-cuff comment but Harlan was in no mood for glibness.

Harlan grabbed the man by his collar and put his face into his. 'She's not on the menu. But I am.'

Harlan could see the panic in the lad's eyes. He had made a witty comment to impress his mates but now had someone holding him by his throat, eyes dilated and talking through gritted teeth. Harlan relaxed his grip, letting his own anger go at the same time. It would have been easy for him to have destroyed this guy as collateral damage, and years ago he would have done. But maturity had taught him some valuable lessons and now he was able to direct his temper to those who truly deserved it. This one didn't, but he did need to learn some respect for the opposite sex, even if he was about to go in and watch women strip.

'Do yourself a favour, pal, and learn to use the top floor before the lift opens up at the bottom.' Harlan pointed his finger into the guy's forehead to hammer home his point.

The point was clear, think before you speak.

'Yeah. I'm... um. Erm... sorry.'

'Not to me, say sorry to her.'

Rihanna was standing in her underwear. She was shivering. But she was safe.

'I'm sorry. I didn't mean –'

'OK. Now piss off.' Harlan had heard enough. They quickly left and scurried up to the club.

Harlan turned his attention to Rihanna. In the rush to get her safe and get her out of there, what he did forget was to get her dressed. Harlan took off his hoodie and handed it to her.

'Here. Put this on.'

Rihanna looked up at him. She had no idea who he was, or why he had done what he did, or what it was he wanted. She just hoped he could be trusted. That he wasn't another wolf dressed up in sheep's clothing like Edward Broadbent.

'Thank you.'

He watched as she slipped it over her head and down over her chest. It dwarfed her. That was a good thing, it covered everything that needed covering. Harlan looked at her hands. They were shaking. A cocktail of fear, adrenaline and the cold. He wrapped his hands around hers, encapsulating them to try and make them warm. Harlan knew you lost most of your body heat through your extremities and he wanted to help. It was a non-imposing gesture. He had become her knight in shining armour. Her instincts said to trust him, whoever he was.

'Who... who are you?' she asked. Her teeth had started to chatter with the cold.

'That doesn't matter. Where's home?'

Rihanna started to give her address but before she could finish, she broke down. She dropped her head into Harlan's chest and started to sob.

'We need to get you home.' Harlan was in work mode. Emotionless. Decisive. Strong.

A taxi pulled over into the rank. Harlan watched as someone from the back seat leant forward to pay the driver and then the back doors opened and three men got out, all a little worse for wear. They were dressed smartly. White collar workers. Ready to end their night surrounded by buxom blondes and busty brunettes and spend accordingly.

The three men looked over at Harlan and a half-dressed girl in heels holding onto him. They thought about making a comment but Harlan's dead-eyed stare made them think twice. Harlan gently lifted her head from his chest, his thumb and forefinger supporting her chin. His t-shirt sodden from the tears. 'Let's get you in the cab.'

She nodded her head, faintly. She looked broken. A lost little girl.

. . .

He took her by the hand and walked over to the taxi. They had to stop on the pavement for a car to go past. The driver honked the horn. A mechanical wolf whistle aimed at the scantily dressed woman wearing nothing more than a hoodie. Harlan just wanted her out of there fast, he wasn't sure how much more he could take of these blatant acts of sexual harassment.

They got to the cab and Harlan opened the rear door, holding it open for Rihanna to get in first. He got in next to her and slammed it shut, harder than he had intended. The taxi driver was balding, with a thick short, stout neck. The driver tilted his rear-view mirror. It was a voyeuristic move. Designed to get a better view of her legs. Harlan saw him do it. 'The mirror was fine where it was.'

His tone was flat. Commanding. The driver took the hint that he had been busted and readjusted the mirror back to its original position. 'Where to?' he asked. Almost apologetically.

Rihanna gave the address. Her voice was frail and her head was down, avoiding eye contact. Aside from the guy dressed in black beside her, and her daddy, she no longer trusted men.

The taxi indicated and pulled out into the road. Harlan looked back at the Mercedes and made a mental note of the registration number. He had homework to do.

11

_____

The taxi pulled up outside her home. It was just after midnight and the house was in darkness. They hadn't spoken on the drive. He knew she would be a mix of emotions. Embarrassment. Fear. Regret. He didn't know how she had gotten into it but he knew it hadn't been through choice. Nor was it for the money. Harlan looked across at the house. It was spacious and newly built. The brickwork was still looking new and the driveway had three cars parked. She came from money, not ostentatious, but definitely middle-class money. Nor was it to fund a habit. He had looked at her arms, no pinpricks or track marks. Her face wasn't gaunt and her eyes hadn't dulled. She had a clear complexion and still looked young and vibrant.

There had to be a reason she was there, in her underwear, looking frightened and out of her depth. He needed to know more. Needed to know if the men in suits made her do it.

'Driver, I need you to give us a minute.'

The driver looked up at his rear-view, not quite getting it. 'Alone,' added Harlan.

The driver still wasn't sure what he meant. His quizzical look told Harlan he needed more clarification.

'Driver, step out of the cab. I need a minute.'

'I just... I just can't leave my –'

'You can, and you will. We just need a few minutes to talk. Don't make this difficult.'

The driver got it this time. The harshness of Harlan's tone ensured it. Harlan wasn't a bully, never had been or ever would be, but he did make sure he got what he needed. And right now, he needed to talk alone with the girl in heels wearing his hoodie.

The driver got out of his cab reluctantly and closed the door, feeling like a fish out of water. In his job, aside from stopping off at an all-night garage for a toilet break and an energy drink, or three, he got in his cab at the start of his shift and then didn't leave it for the next twelve hours. Which was where the paunch had come from. He took the packet of cigarettes from his tracksuit trouser pocket and pulled one out, lighting up and tilting his head back puffing the first plume of smoke up into the sky trying to ignore how many fares this was costing him.

Harlan turned to face Rihanna. Her eyes were red and puffy and her mascara had run. She had been through the wars, mentally, so Harlan knew he needed to go gently. To show empathy. Not always his strong point in the past but a skill he had learned over time. 'I need to ask you some questions. Are you OK with that?'

She nodded, still not lifting her head up to face him. She was swathed in shame.

'What's your name? And look at me, please.' It was said softly and with sincerity.

She went to speak, but paused, sniffled and rubbed her nose on the sleeve of his hoodie. She tried to take a deep breath but struggled, her chest was rising and falling fast.

'Take a second. There's no rush.'

'What... what about the driver, it's his, his –'

'Don't worry about him. It's just you and me. Talk to me.'

Rihanna knew this was her chance. To come clean, tell how some bad choices had ended up leaving her here, barely dressed and crying into a stranger's chest. She took a second to compose herself, to control her breathing. She didn't want to look at him, or out towards her home, her safe place, as either would make her cry, again. And she didn't want to cry, she wanted to find the resolve to be strong. She started from the beginning.

'I made a stupid decision a few months back. And I got caught.'

'What decision?'

Rihanna knew she had to go back a little further with the story.

'I had a good upbringing; my mum and dad work hard and have good jobs. I did well at school and got a decent enough job. But I felt, I don't know, bored? Different?'

That resonated with Harlan. He had felt different at her age. Lost. Looking for something to excite him. To give him an outlet. Harlan knew that some people were born rebellious, born with a special side to them, to exist outside the rules, to dance with the wolves. Rihanna wasn't one of them. This was down to being gullible, or being groomed. He sat there waiting to hear which one it was. Rihanna continued.

'I changed my circle of friends a couple of years ago. I just felt too safe, too tame. I started going out more. Clubbing. Getting drunk. I wasn't bad. Just different to how I was before.'

'And mum and dad were fine with that?'

'Not really – but I always let them know I was safe and it wasn't as if I came home really wasted, I was just tipsy and would spend Sundays in my room lazing. We are a quite outdoorsy family and Sundays are a family day but I retreated a bit. God, I feel so bad.'

'Don't. Guilt is a wasted emotion. Guilt doesn't change shit, only changing things does.'

Rihanna looked up at him, for the first time since they got in the taxi. She was too young to know he had guilt in his own eyes, a lifetime's worth, but she could tell that what he just said had some poignancy to it. She didn't know him, but she trusted him. She continued: 'One of my mates' brothers was a dealer. Only small time, but he was the go-to guy in our circle, and wider, if you wanted anything.'

'Anything? Coke, you mean?'

'Yes.'

Harlan knew coke had changed club culture. No longer a party drug reserved for those with deep wallets. It had become a drug for the everyman, and woman. It had cheapened considerably over the years making it affordable, and if you make drugs affordable, you sell more. Basic commerce. And the cost price had come down too, so now more people could afford to deal it, or at least be part of the chain. But the chain was dangerous. Closer to the source you were safe, but at the opposite end, you were out in the open, sitting ducks if your wits weren't about you. The police made their numbers by hitting the roadmen, those on street corners with a handful of £40 wraps in their pockets. Or in the door pocket of their car. The MC had a tight operation where dealing was concerned, the chain was controlled. He didn't think it would be the same for her.

'I made out with him a few times and started seeing him for a bit. Nothing serious. We weren't together or anything like that. Just seeing each other, I guess. Then one night he was sick, with food poisoning or something, but his trap phone was going crazy. People wanted their baggies. So, he asked me if I would do the runs. I didn't want to at –'

'Did he force you?'

Rihanna sensed the change in his voice. His eyes had narrowed. He'd become taut. Tense.

'No. No, he didn't. He was only asking and he knew it was a big ask. He said he would pay me. Like I said, we weren't a thing, but I wanted to help him. He was too sick to do it. So, I said yes.'

The taxi driver had lit up a second cigarette. He was bouncing from foot to foot, trying to keep warm, still trying to ignore the money he was losing with his cab parked up and occupied.

'He talked me through it. The different sizes and prices. And the best routes. How to stay off the main streets and to delete each message after each drop. He showed me what to text and who had to pay upfront and who got it on tick. It was a lot to take in but I felt, I don't know, excited, I guess.'

Harlan knew so many like her had fallen into this trap before. The buzz from driving around town, dropping off wraps and taking their cash. For some it was seductive, but for all, it was stupid. You were ripe for a pull. Searched and your cash seized. Charged with possession or worse, possession with intent to supply. That came with a prison sentence. And, for what? It didn't affect the one higher up the chain, he already had his money. He sold to you as a whole. A one-off transaction.

But the runners needed to make multiple drops, breaking the bigger piece down to the smaller, more manageable, cheaper pieces. And it was those many pieces, those many little bags of white weighed-out powder, that needed dropping off countless times a night. Harlan knew that in life, the more you do something you shouldn't, the more chance you have of getting found out. She continued: 'I went out and it went okay, a few mistakes but overall, it went well. I'm not going to lie; I was shitting myself the whole time but by the end everyone had been seen and I took a big wad of cash back to him. He gave me fifty-quid for doing it and that was it.'

'But it wasn't, was it?' he replied. Harlan knew how for some, dealing in coke was more addictive than actually taking it. And it was for one reason and one reason only, money.

'You're right. It wasn't. We weren't seeing each other after that, not that we were an item anyway, like I said, but I was a bit short of cash one week, my car had failed its MOT so I asked him if he needed me to drive. He said I could take a small round of my own. He would front me the coke and then once I had paid him back, I could keep the rest. Like a mug, I said yes and then before I knew it, I went and got myself a burner phone and went out that night delivering coke around the city. It went better than the first time, and I made enough to pay what I owed and had enough to reload again, so the next night I made some money.'

'How much?'

'A few hundred. I had doubled my wages.'

And there it was. The lure. That was the dragon so many dealers chased. For them that was the high. Harlan had seen and heard it a thousand times. Money was all too often someone's mistress and here was another victim to the incentive of earning easy cash, forgetting it was, in fact, criminal.

'I wasn't greedy. I didn't deal much. If anything, it was just the customers he didn't want, and I hardly got anyone new. I would drop my mates in and out of town and then in-between went and delivered. And my customers knew I only did it on weekends.'

Harlan had heard enough, he needed to know what had happened to put her here, with him. Needed to know why he had to rescue her, dragging her out by her arm in her underwear and sitting in the back of someone's taxi in the early hours of a Sunday morning.

'So, I take it that something happened. As most dealers I know don't end up stripping. Unless it is another side hustle but then judging by how nervous you looked, it didn't look that way.'

Rihanna dropped her head, again. The embarrassment had returned in earnest.

'I got stopped, a few weeks ago. The policeman stopped and searched me.'

'You got searched kerbside? Two officers. Male and female?'

Harlan knew the law, he had been on the wrong side of it all too often, spending time in the back of cars and in holding cells, but as of yet, not a prison cell. Living like he did, you needed to know the law if you were going to break it. Harlan knew that a female couldn't be searched by a male cop and he also knew it was rare for a bobby to be driving around alone.

'No. Just a male.'

Harlan pressed her for more. 'Was it a patrol car. A uniformed officer?'

'No. It was a private car. It did have lights in the grill though.'

Undercover, or CID, Harlan knew. 'So, what happened?' He could smell a rat already.

'He made me empty my pockets and I had quite a few baggies on me.'

'Did he charge you? Read you your rights?'

'Erm, kind of?'

'Kind of isn't an answer. Think. It's important.'

'He... erm, he told me I had too much to claim posses-sion and that I would be charged with P, something?'

'PWITS – possession with the intent to supply. Did he record what you had?'

'Record?'

'Record. Write it down. Any formal means to say what you had on you?'

'No? Don't think so?'

'What happened next?'

'I was told I was facing two and a half years. And to get a solicitor. And he took my number.'

On the prison front he was right. Harlan knew 18 months was a likely outcome, but there were other factors in play. Previous. Number of wraps. Mobile phone messages.

'Did he ask to see your mobile?'

'No. But he wanted my number saying he would call me to tell me the next steps.'

'OK. So, after that, what happened?'

'The following day he rang and told me to come to the station so I could be formally charged. But then he kind of changed?'

'Kind of changed? What do you mean?'

'He said he knew of a solicitor and that he could arrange for me to see him later that day.'

'And you did?'

'Yes – he seemed nicer on the phone and that he wanted to give me a chance to avoid prison. I arranged to meet them both for a coffee and when I got there it was just the policeman waiting for me, he said the solicitor was on his way.'

'What was the copper's name?' Harlan hoped to Christ that she had actually asked him.

'DS Sermon. No, wait. Sharman. Yes, DS Sharman.'

'You sure? 100% I need you to be right with this.'

'Yes. 100%.'

'OK. Good. Carry on.'

'Then this posh guy walked in. He was well-spoken and well-dressed. He was thin. Bit of a beak nose. I remember he had long, thin fingers. Bony. He was scary but was trying to come across as nice. To begin with.'

Harlan knew this was the moment. Where she was given her ultimatum. 'Go on.'

'They worked as a team. I was told I was definitely facing prison however I could try and fight it, but it would cost. A lot.'

'I take it you were given a proposal?'

'How did you know?'

'Let's just say I have been around. I'm right though, yeah?'

'Yes, you are. I was told I could try my luck in court but the solicitor would need £2k up front to retain him, but there was still a high risk of prison, or...'

'Or?'

'Or... I could do some dancing. Pole dancing, and then the charges would be dropped, but only when I had made enough money to pay off the bill'

'What bill?'

'They just called it the 'Cost of freedom.''

'You were basically bullied into it.'

'I had no choice. I mean, how do you tell your parents you have been arrested for selling drugs? It would break them. They are really good, decent people. Never been in trouble and nor has my brother. And my sister is a grade-A student. I couldn't tell them. I can't tell them.'

'Hence tonight.'

'Yes. I'm sorry...'

'You don't need to apologise to me, or to anyone. The clock doesn't go backwards, unfortunately. Instead, we need to get a grip of this situation and get you back in control of your own life.'

'Will you help me?'

'Haven't I already?'

'Yes. Thank you.'

'No need for thanks. So, the two in suits, they aren't the ones behind it. It's this Sharman fella, and the solicitor?'

'Yes. They seem to be behind it, the other two in the suits just seem to be running it. But they are real gangsters, I think. They checked me out, looking me up and down. I found them scary.'

Harlan had all the pieces now although the jigsaw had changed a little. The men in the suits with the Mercedes weren't the brains, merely the brawn. They still needed removing, but unless he took out the men at the top, the brawn would just be replaced.

'Did you get the solicitor's name?'

'Broadbent. Edward Broadbent.'

Harlan stored the names in his head, along with the Merc's registration.

'What did you leave at the sports bar? Clothes, bag?'

Rihanna hadn't even thought about that until now. She had left her clothes, purse, car keys and mobile. Her life, basically. 'Shit. What am I going to do?'

'Leave that to me. But I want something from you, in return.'

For the first time since he had got her safe, she felt

uneasy about him. Was this the moment he would try it on? Maybe grope her, or worse.

'What?' The fear in the reply was deafening.

Harlan took her hands, cupping his own around them, and sensing her fear, spoke with a real sense of kindness. He knew his physical appearance could be intimidating, so he lowered and softened his voice to change the perception.

'I want you to go inside. I want you to go and wake up your parents and then sit on the edge of their bed and tell them. Tell them everything. Start to finish. Face up to what you have done and let them know. Let them know you messed up, but that it won't happen again. Don't live with guilt. Kill it, dead.'

Not for the first time, her eyes welled and a single tear started to fall. But this time it was different. It was a different tear. There was a sparkle of soul shining through it.

'Why are you doing this, helping me, I mean?'

'Let's just say that if I had a daughter, I hope someone would look out for her if I couldn't.'

Rihanna went forward to hug him, but stopped. She was still too fragile to take any form of rejection. She opened the car door but as she went to step out she stopped.

'I don't even know your name.'

Harlan smiled, 'It may be best for you if you don't.'

She smiled. It was a sweet smile. 'Well, my name is Rihanna.'

He watched as she got out and walked over to her house and knocked on the door. He watched as a moment later, a light went on from a room upstairs, her parents. He waited until the door opened and watched as Rihanna stepped inside, throwing her arms around her dad. He knew she would break down, was breaking down, but that moment of shame would be what stopped her from going back down that road again. Shame is so often a catalyst for change and this was her chance to change. He watched as her dad looked over her shoulder and out into the street. Looking to see who may have brought his daughter home like that but then his paternal instincts took over. He shut the door, she was home and she was now safe.

12

The driver was just glad to be back behind the wheel. He was normally one to make small talk with his passengers but the guy in the back seat of his taxi didn't seem to be the sort, or in the mood. Instead, he turned up the volume on the radio just a smidge to drown out the silence. Harlan was mulling everything through. The status quo had changed, it wasn't quite as clear cut as he first thought. There were other players behind the scenes, but they weren't players, not in the sense that Harlan knew.

The MC had dealings with most of the major gangsters in the country, and had links with international criminals and cartels. This wasn't that. This was a bent copper and a crooked lawyer. Scumbags. Harlan knew the importance of having a policeman on the take, they provided intel and could make the smaller stuff disappear, but he didn't like them. Harlan was very staunch on his opinions, you were either inside the law, or outside of it. Law-abiding, or an outlaw. Living in between the two was dangerous for you, and dangerous for others. The gang were due at Guy's wine bar the following Friday which gave him a week to disband them. Piece by piece. One by one.

Carla had finished her dance. She was the highlight of the night. She oozed pure seduction and her pole dance was bordering on the pornographic. The floor by her feet was awash with crumpled cash. Carla was the star and her takings reflected that. She was in the toilet getting dressed when she heard a phone ringing. Instinct told her to check hers. Her hand rubbed up against her buttock, feeling for her mobile in her jean pocket. It wasn't hers.

Some of the other girls were still out in the bar. They would be flirting, sitting on laps, still in their underwear, or topless, maybe selling themselves, or maybe just selling the thought. But Carla was past that. She had been in the game for a while, starting out when it was a necessity, a single mum, struggling, but now it was just a job and she was good at it. Carla had danced for one of the men in suits in a seedy joint six months ago and that was where she had been propositioned. They had made her an offer. Lead dancer and with none of her takings sliced off the top. There was a catch, she was to train any girls that came her way and with no questions asked. She knew they weren't nice people, but so far, they had been nice to her. So far.

The phone stopped ringing. She slipped her jumper over her head and down over her sequinned bra. She used the back of her hand to lift her hair back out of her jumper and shook her head to unfurl the curls. The ringing started again. Whoever was on the other end needed answering, it could be a family emergency, which is why Carla rooted around the handbags and coats that were spread across the ladies bathroom in search of the ringing phone. She found the bag where the ringing was coming from, it was Rihanna's. The newbie. Carla hadn't seen her being dragged out of the bar by her wrist, but one of the other girls had told her, all surmising it had been her fella who had done the dragging. Carla felt bad opening up Rihanna's bag but she was also a mum, and maybe there was a problem at home and she wouldn't forgive herself if that was the case and she had ignored it. She rooted around and found it, sliding her false nail across the screen to answer the call.

'Hello. Rihanna's phone.'

Harlan didn't speak straight away.

'Hello?' Carla repeated.

'Are all her things still there?' Harlan spoke directly. Distrust and disgust in his voice.

'Who are you?'

'A family friend,' Harlan lied.

'Really?'

'Yes. Really. Now back to the original question, is her stuff still there?'

'Yes, but I'm not sure –'

'You don't need to be sure. But what I'm sure of is that she was there against her will.'

Silence.

'You're not disagreeing. Which confirms it.'

'Who are you?'

'I told you, family friend, but I have a question for you. Are you a decent person? Are you someone that knows there was a young girl there tonight, stood in her underwear and scared. Are you someone that will do the right thing and get me her stuff so I can return it?'

Carla prided herself on sorting the sinners from the saints. He seemed genuine and she had liked Rihanna, wishing she hadn't gotten into whatever mess it was that ended with her needing to learn how to strip.

'OK? But you're not a creep, are you? I can trust you?'

'No. And yes. In that order. Now I need to trust you. Grab her things and then tell me where to meet you. And keep this number to yourself.

'OK.'

'I'm trusting you here – don't make me regret it. Neither of us will want that.'

Harlan added just enough overtone to the sentence. Not too much to scare her, not too little to doubt him. Harlan was adept at playing the stick and the carrot.

The taxi driver had pulled back into the same rank as where he had found them and, being honest, was glad his passenger was getting out. He pressed a couple of buttons on his meter to ring up the bill, still trying not to think of what the last hour had cost him. '£34.60, mate.'

Harlan put his hand into his pocket and pulled a roll of used notes. The driver watched him in his rear-view mirror, hoping his passenger would round it up to a nice even forty. 'Thanks for earlier. I know you would have lost out on a couple of quid. But I appreciate it.'

Harlan leaned forward and put his arm through the gap in the Perspex bulkhead, handing the driver his fare. Harlan opened the door and got out. No more need for talking.

The cabbie watched Harlan walk across the road and down the street and then opened his hand and found he had just been paid a ton for his troubles. His opinion about his passenger changed.

Harlan looked around for trouble before getting on his bike. It was ingrained in him. Throwing drunks out of bars tended to lead to reprisals and if you weren't alert, they could be painful, or worse, permanent. He had lost a friend the same way. He hadn't been a club member but he was known and liked by the MC and was a fellow doorman. The story went he had evicted someone from a club for fighting and had been given the usual threats as to what was going to happen to him later, something he had heard a thousand times before. What he didn't know was that the person he had evicted for being a pain in the arse, was the cousin of a known face. The guy had returned a little later, with his cousin in tow, just when the doorman was going home and the last thing the doorman felt as he went to open the door on his Audi was the force of a steel baseball bat crashing into the back of his skull. He was dead before he hit the floor. It was a wakeup call to all the doormen across the city, hammering home the sad fact that in this job you need to always have one eye open. Always.

There was no-one that concerned him. Just a few punters leaving the sports bar on the way home to fantasise on the flesh they had just seen. That they had paid to see. Harlan put the key into the ignition and pressed the starter button, bringing the bike back into life. The sound of the growling exhaust made some heads turn his way. Harleys have that special sound, so sexy but equally, so menacing. The sound was synonymous with the outlaw biker. He kicked away the stand and pulled out into the road. He needed to ride. To relax.

Carla had a count up, just over five-hundred quid. It had been a good night. It was her son's birthday coming up and she had a big party planned. The cash would come in handy as she liked to spoil him. It was just them. Mum and son. Carla and Connor. They were inseparable.

The sports bar was still open but the strippers had finished and now it was just the girls seeing if there were any extras to be earned. Carla looked around, checking if she could get out with Rihanna's bag. She knew the men with the suits would be gunning for revenge on whoever it was that took Rihanna out of the club, and now she was on her way to meet him. She was feeling scared herself. She had heard the rumours; they weren't to be messed with and their violence had made them notorious.

The man-mountain, as he was known, was still sitting there, surrounded by cash. He was a giant of a man, his neck wider than the chest of most mere mortals. He had basketball-sized shoulders and forearms to rival that of Popeye. When you went over to get your cash, you said 'Thank you.' Carla had very little to do with him, he would smile at her whenever they were in close proximity. It was a sweet, nervous smile. A smile that despite his size, said that he lacked self-belief, especially around confident, sexy women.

Carla waited for the right moment, hoping it would come soon. She stood just outside the toilets, looking far from inconspicuous. The customers were drunk, loud and leery. It wouldn't be long before she was spotted and accosted. And then it came, the suits were behind the bar with the till drawer open, going through the takings. Their takings.

Carla put her head down, her own handbag over her left shoulder and Rihanna's sport bag in her right hand. The door wasn't too far, but there was a sea of seedy men to navigate. But she made it, there were a few stray hands grabbing at her as she got to the door but she was used to that. In this profession you are just seen as a piece of meat. It was a sad, but true fact.

Her car was parked in the next street. It was permit-parking but so far, she hadn't got a ticket. She was walking fast, power walking. Hard, fast strides. She didn't look back over her shoulder to see if she was being followed but prayed to God that she wasn't. Carla dug around for her keys, found them and pressed the fob to unlock the doors, all without actually removing them from her bag. She got in, passing both bags over onto the passenger seat and locked the doors from the button on the dashboard. She started the engine and turned on the headlights, illuminating what was in front of her, lighting up any would-be nasties. It took her a minute to relax. Nobody had followed her and the street was asleep. Carla took the scrap of paper from her jean pocket and reached over for her phone. She typed in the eleven digits, stopping to take a deep breath before hitting the call button.

Harlan was sitting in an all-night café. He had ordered and eaten a bacon sandwich and was on his second cup of tea. The café was quiet. There was someone sitting at the back, reading a paper, probably left there during the day. He was wearing a check shirt with a body-warmer over the top. Harlan guessed he was a trucker, refuelling himself before refuelling his truck. There was a young couple sitting a few tables in front of him. Nineteen, twenty, but no more. Munchies after a night out or two strangers on a very cheap date. He didn't know, or care. He had picked up his mug when his phone rang.

He looked at the number. He could trust her. He accepted the call.

'Hi, is this... Rihanna's friend?' Carla's voice was croaky. He sensed she felt out on a limb.

'Yes. Are you OK? Any problems getting it out?' Harlan appreciated the risk she had taken and wanted to make sure she was safe. If she wasn't, he would be back on his Harley before she had time to end the call. If Harlan liked you, or better, respected you, he kept you safe.

'No. But I'm not sure if I was seen.'

'OK, let's get you out of there.'

Harlan gave Carla the name of the café and listened as she clacked the name into her phone, finding the postcode before then entering it into her satnav.

'Says I'll be there in eight minutes.'

'OK, good. I'll order you a bacon sandwich.'

'No, I'm good, thanks,' laughing. Harlan laughed, too. High-end strippers don't tend to dine out in greasy spoons. 'Coffee, then?'

'That would be nice. Thank you.'

The men in suits had cashed up. It had been a good night. Except for the newbie. They needed to deal with that before their boss found out. They were the face of the operation, but not the owners, and they knew they were replaceable. Whoever it was that took the newbie out the door had made them look weak. He needed to be found. And fast.

By the time Carla arrived, the young couple had gone. It was just him and the trucker left. Harlan had no idea what she looked like but it was obvious it was her when she walked in. Her body was tight, it was clear she worked hard to keep it so. Her hair was loosely curled and buoyant. She had the failings of falseness but he had to admit, it suited her. He stood up and beckoned her over. Carla walked over and he gestured for her to sit down, nodding to the server to bring over the coffee he had ordered. To any passers-by looking in through the window it was like a scene from Beauty and the Beast. The biker, with flecks of grey in his beard, dressed in cheap black clothing with heavily tattooed arms sitting opposite a beautiful woman, tanned, toned and in figure hugging clothes. Opposite ends of the fashion world; but maybe both cut from the same cloth.

'Thanks for coming. Is that it?' Harlan asked, pointing down to the gym bag beside her.

'Yes. Is she okay?' The concern was genuine. Harlan knew true sincerity when he heard it.

'She will be. Do you know her well?'

'No. not really. I was just told to meet her and to show her the ropes.'

'Told?'

'Yes. Told.'

'Don't tell me, by Pinky and Perky in those cheap suits.'

Carla laughed, holding her hand over her mouth. Harlan liked that. It was cute.

'I'm right, aren't I?', he added.

'Yes. Every now and then I get a call to say to meet someone at the flat. Some take to it, some, like Rihanna, don't. It's not for everyone, trust me. You need a thick skin, you know.'

Harlan did know. Satan's Security had a lot of women that hung around the clubhouse and its members. Some were nothing more than groupies. There to be had by all. Others had married members, and they were off-limits to the other guys, known as 'Old Ladies' although the old part wasn't meant literally, more a figure of speech. It took a certain type of woman to be attracted to the lifestyle of an outlaw biker, and from a certain background. It wasn't for the faint hearted. Many couldn't hack it. The lifestyle too rowdy, too reckless. You were seen as the inferior sex. Yes, he knew full well what she meant.

'Are these women there against their will?'

'Yes. Kind of. It's like they are trapped. Or rather they have something over them. I don't pry, but I don't think they would tell me even if I asked. Instead, I just try and give them some advice, you know, look out for them. They are just kids, really.'

Harlan could tell she was a good person in a shitty profession. He was glad she was there to help the girls, those there not through choice. It wasn't sex slavery, but it wasn't too far off.

Carla's coffee arrived and she blew across the top, gently. Harlan didn't know if she was doing it seductively on purpose, or not, but it had worked. She was sexy, but she knew it, and Harlan knew women like that could be dangerous. Exciting, but dangerous.

Harlan ordered himself a third cup of tea. He wanted more intel on the suits, but also was in no real rush to leave her, after all, he never said he was a choir boy. Carla started to loosen up. She knew what was going on was wrong, but her own survival instincts had told her, if it isn't happening to me, then don't get involved. But she herself was someone's daughter, someone's little girl and these girls were the same. It was wrong. Stripping should be done through choice, or necessity, it should never be done against your will. She looked at Harlan. She could tell he wasn't family; he had a loner look about him. So, who was he?

'Are you going to go to the police?' she asked.

Harlan laughed. She knew as soon as she had said it that it was a stupid question.

'Sorry.'

'It's fine – but no, I won't be going to the police.'

'But you will make sure she is safe. That they won't hurt her.'

'Trust me, it won't be them doing the hurting.'

Carla knew she could trust him on that front, she could just feel it.

'Tell me about this flat,' he asked.

'They own a building in the asshole end of town. It's pretty much derelict. I'm not sure even squatters would doss there. It's damp, it's dirty and it's disgusting. There is one room though that they have put a pole in, that and a single light bulb, minus the shade. And an Alexa. It's where they send the newbies to learn the pole. It's a right dive. I hate going there.'

Harlan asked her how she got involved with them and she ended up giving him her life story. On how her boyfriend got her pregnant but then left her when she found out. On how she struggled trying to raise her baby on income support. On her decision to start stripping, putting her own body fears to one side so as to provide for her son and then ending up on how she met Pinky and Perky. Harlan hadn't gained much, really. He knew pretty much all this about the suits from Rihanna, but he now knew they had a flat and also that Rihanna was just one in a long line of girls doing this under duress. And if there was one thing Harlan hated, it was a bully. Be it singular or plural.

'I really do need to go.' She said, tapping on her screen to check the time.

'Yes, of course,' and as she stood up from her chair, so too did Harlan, as an act of respect and good manners. A criminal? Maybe. Chivalrous? Absolutely. His mum had done a good job.

'Do you have the address?' he asked.

Carla took a napkin and with the lipstick that she had in her bag, wrote it down. She turned it over, the words now facing the plastic tablecloth. Harlan held out his hand and she took it. It was a firm grip. She wasn't a wallflower. He liked that.

'Please keep her safe,' she said, before releasing her hand from his.

'She'll be fine – and thanks for bringing her stuff.'

Carla smiled. She had shiny white straight teeth. Harlan suspected veneers, or a trip to Turkey. Either way, her smile was strong, bright and confident. Like her.

He watched as she left. The trucker watched too; he hadn't expected that tonight.

He waited until she was out of sight before turning over the napkin to see what she had written. On it was the street name and house number, underneath she had written something else: *Call me again sometime. C xx*

13

The suits were up early. They had skipped the gym and instead had gone looking for intel. Low-level thieves and street dealers were called, asking if anyone new was in town. But no-one had heard anything. It was proving to be a bigger city than they thought. Whoever he was, he wasn't known, no-one of substance knew him, meaning he was a loner. He was a no-one. A family member, protective uncle, probably. He would be found and he wouldn't be a problem.

Harlan left his bed and started his routine. Stretched and twisted. Push-ups and sit-ups.

A routine he had done for years; so much so that it had become as natural to him as breathing did. It wasn't overly strenuous, but it was too much for the average man. Push-ups done with his fists balled, not open-palmed. Inverted sit-ups. Basic exercises but made harder. He didn't work out to look good, he did it to feel good. There was a difference. A big difference. He took a shower and stood at the mirror, checking his face from side to side, deliberating on whether to shave. Decided against it, the fur on his face could go another day. He put on a fresh pair of jeans, stained, but clean. He was naked aside from his jeans. Not even under-wear. Harlan removed a top from one of the cheap wire coat hangers inside the rickety wardrobe. One of the doors had dropped, meaning it didn't close fully, which annoyed him, not because it was faulty, but because it wasn't aesthetically pleasing to the eye. Harlan didn't particularly care what he looked like, but he did care that everything around him should look in order. He was a fan of symmetry. He glanced down at Rihanna's bag that was by the bed, needing to be returned. Since last night everything had changed. He had gone from taking on another man's problems to pulling a young woman out of the lion's den. But he had been in these positions before, where professional had turned personal. He needed to return her bag, he needed to do some digging, but first, he needed breakfast.

Lenny was carrying through a tray of bacon and eggs when Harlan entered the dining room. He nodded his head by means of acknowledgment. Harlan nodded in return. As always, he took a table that gave him the clearest view. It had become a bad habit but it had also once saved him. He wasn't prepared to change it. Lenny walked over with his notepad and pen already in hand.

'Morning, mate. Sleep well?' A generic question, prob-ably asked to every guest, every day.

'Morning. Yes, fine.'

'Good. Glad to hear it. What would you like? 'Again, asked without any real interest.

Harlan missed Carol, her warmth and cheeriness. He would call her later.

'Full English. With tea and juice. Ta.'

Lenny scribbled on his pad and left. Harlan watched him as he walked out of the room. He took his personal phone out of his pocket and checked for messages. Another habit. There weren't any. The two who had his number never used it. He stopped himself from reminiscing and instead took out his other phone. The little black Nokia. Cheap and untraceable. He flicked down through the contact list, it was a manual task, needing constant dabs with his thumb. It was old school. He got to who he was looking for. He was a brother, a fellow club member and the one who was tasked with finding shit out. Mighty Mouse was so-called due to his lack of height but he more than made up for it in ferocity and bravery, had scouts on pretty much every street corner in the club's hometown, providing the club with the intel on what was happening, and who was doing it. Mighty Mouse also had links in the places that mattered, one of which was the DVLA. A lot could be gained from a registration number. And Harlan had one of those; it belonged to a black Mercedes.

Lenny arrived with Harlan's food. Harlan knew he needed to cut back on his cholesterol level, it had more chance of killing him than his job. But he was a sucker for a Full English and the breakfast looked colourful and well-cooked. He sliced into the fried egg, the yoke flowing like yellow lava onto the pink bacon beside it and he took a large forkful of the fried food into his mouth, savouring the crunch in his mouth of the golden bread and crisp sausage. Throughout his breakfast he made a mental note of what needing doing today, and in what order. Harlan was a man of efficiency. He liked time to work for him; not the other way round. First order of the day was to speak to Mouse, task him with getting details on the Merc. That call would be done outside. Walls, as he knew only too well, have ears.

Then he would drop off Rihanna's bag. Her phone had been pinging well into the early hours and started again first thing but then stopped. Her battery must have died, he thought, but didn't want to rifle through her bag to check. That was her personal stuff. Not his place to pry.

Edward stepped out through the conservatory and into the garden. He beckoned his dog. It wasn't a pet, there wasn't any affection. It was there purely to protect him. The house had cameras everywhere, he had thugs on the payroll and a policeman in his pocket, but there was something soothing in having a 10st dog about the place. The dog trotted past his master and over to the far end of the garden to do his business. Edward shook his head in disgust but he knew that would be his gardener's problem to deal with, not his. Edward understood the food chain, what money enabled. It bought you subordinates; it bought you safety.

The dog walked back across the tended lawn, past his master and back to his place under the sprawling staircase. Edward felt calm. There was no storm. He had all the right people in all the right places. He took a cigar from the pocket of his cardigan, snipped off the end with his cutter and placed it between his lips and lit it. Success, and the trappings that came with it, felt good. He checked the time on his Rolex, a gift to himself, and started to make his calls.

Her mum knocked on her door. Rihanna wasn't asleep, she thought she would sleep for eternity but she had just catnapped. The knock was gentle. Kind. Rihanna answered the knock and her mum entered the room, a cup of tea in one hand, some toast on brown bread in the other. She placed them on the bedside table. Rihanna sat upright in her bed and her mum plumped the pillows behind her. She was fussing, her baby was in a bad place and she just wanted to make it better. Rihanna gave a weak smile, a cross between sorrow and shame.

'How are you feeling?' Her mum's voice was soft and sweet. Heartfelt.

'Ashamed.'

Her mum ran her finger down her daughter's cheek. Rihanna felt like crying but this time the well was dry. She was out of tears, instead, she was just numb. Numb and nervous. And that was never a good place. Rihanna had always been a confident girl, but now she was feeling first-hand the pains of anxiety. She placed her own hand upon her mums, holding it still on her cheek.

'How's Dad?' She asked. But she already knew the answer, that he was disappointed in her. She had let him down. And it hurt.

'He's... He is...'

'Mad?'

'No, not mad. Not really. But he can't understand why you got involved in all that. Nor can I.'

Rihanna knew there were some tough conversations to have. Last night her parents were just glad she was safe. She had touched upon the events that led her there, but it was more a glossary, the devil in the detail would come, it had to. The first step in her road to redemption. Her mum nestled herself down onto the bed with Rihanna moving across to accommodate her. She put her arm around her daughter and cradled her into her bosom, back in her mother's nest. She was safe. For now.

Harlan's plate was empty, aside from the swirling of the sauce created by his bread and butter. The mug and glass were empty, too. He had his agenda in his head and it was time to cross the first one off. He placed his knife and fork together, closing the meal. Lenny was busy wiping down tables and didn't see him leave. Harlan walked through the corridor and out through the reception area and into the street. There was someone across the road washing their windows so he walked a few metres down the road before making the call.

'Mouse. It's me.'

'What's up. You good, brother?'

Mouse had been a member for some time. He didn't hold a prestigious title, but he was respected and his commitment through the years had been faultless. Harlan liked him.

'I need a favour.'

'Sure thing. Club business?'

Harlan was now a nomad, he was no longer sitting around the table involved in the decisions the club took, but he was still a prominent player and his CV couldn't be questioned. If Harlan was needed, he was there. If he needed something, it was given.

'Not really. Not yet, anyway, but there may be some pickings, after.'

'Rich pickings?'

'Would I bring crumbs?'

They both laughed at that. The MC liked to have its fingers in any pie where pound notes were the main ingredients.

'What do you need?'

Harlan reeled off the registration number from memory.

'I need that put through the system. Name, address, the whole shebang.'

'Anything else?'

'Yes – once you find the owner, dig around. See what you

can find on them. I don't think it's a bogus plate, I actually feel the car is registered to the fella I need to chat to.'

'The kind of chat we like?'

'That very one.'

More laughter. A brother's bond often went deeper than blood.

'On it. Give me a day or so.'

'Cheers, Mouse.'

Harlan ended the call. Next up was Guy. It was just to check in. He sent a text.

I have some running around to do today. I'll meet you Monday. 11am. Later.

That was how he said goodbyes, a single word. An adjective. Later.

Rihanna took a shower but the sleaziness she felt all over her skin wouldn't wash off. She felt cheapened. Not violated, but not far off. She had left her car at the sports bar and she hoped it was still there. She kept thinking about the two men in their suits. She couldn't get the look they gave her out of her mind. She was just a shape to them, a contour. Who she was didn't matter, she was a piece of meat. Soapy water ran down her body and down the drain but it didn't take her shame with it. She turned the shower off. Stepped out and took a warm towel off the rail and wrapped it tightly around her. She wiped her feet on the bath mat and walked back across the landing into her room. It felt weird being incommunicado. She had left her phone in her gym bag along with her keys and make-up bag. She felt naked without her mobile and make up. She felt like a little girl. She wished she was a little girl.

Her mum and dad were milling around downstairs. The radio was on in the kitchen and Rihanna could hear the tip-tapping of the dog's paws on the laminate floor. Her dad had bought the dog for her younger sister, she loved animals and wanted to be a vet so she was gifted with a Spaniel puppy, who she named Benny and he was both fun-loving and full on. Rihanna walked down the stairs but without her normal gusto, and into the living room. She was dressed in an old flannel tracksuit and her hair, still wet, in a bun on top of her head.

Her dad was reading the paper when she entered, he was an amateur stock trader and liked to read up on the world of business looking for valuable clues. Rihanna stood nervously by the door, unsure whether to stand or sit. Her mum patted the palm of her hand onto the cushion next to her on the sofa, gesturing for her daughter to sit down beside her.

Harlan had made a note of the name of the street and had a vague idea on how to find it. He was wearing his cut as riding his bike without it felt wrong, unless a situation required him to do so. He rode through the back streets of Stonehouse. The ladies of the night who he had ridden past on his first night weren't on duty, it was before midday and they would be resting. He hoped they had stayed whole. It was a dangerous way to earn a living, more dangerous than his. He pulled out onto the main drag that ran through the city centre. It was linear, like an axis with an X and Y. At one end were the shops. Brand names sat within a newly built shopping mall commissioned by an architect with delusions of grandeur. At the other end was the city's nightlife. Pubs, clubs and casinos. Where babies were made and fortunes were lost. Every city has their own strip. Some are seedier than others, but every city has one. There were parts of the town that had bars, sprouted up in posher postcodes with more picturesque surroundings and away from the dank smell of the strip.

Plymouth's nightlife had suffered worse than others. In the 70's it was bursting with life, the Navy was at its strongest and Plymouth basked in the glory of a drunken sailor and his money. But over the years the size of the Navy's fleet had shrunk, so too had the number of sailors, so too had Plymouth's nightlife. Harlan had admiration for Guy, and Andy, both having set up elsewhere in the city. A fresh offering in a fresher part of Plymouth. It made sense and, up until the suits showed up, it had been successful. Harlan was getting bored of the traffic. He opened up the throttle, overtaking the row of cars in front of him and heads turned as he raced up through the drag with the sound of roaring venom spitting out of the back end of his bike.

'But why? Why Rihanna?' Her dad had stood up from his seat, his posture was one of bewilderment. He didn't raise his voice often, preferring reason over rage.

'I don't?... I really... I –'

'Not good, Rihanna. Not good enough by a long way.'

'Jim, please, let her speak,' her mum interjected, trying to diffuse the situation.

'OK. Speak. Why did you decide to deal drugs?'

Rihanna's parents had sent her younger sister to her nana's for a bit, on a ruse. They didn't want her knowing what had happened. She looked up to her older sister and was at that age where she was impressionable. Rihanna knew she had let everyone down, including her baby sister. But the question wasn't easy to answer. She had made a bad choice for a good reason, or so she thought at the time and then greed stepped in and the rest, well that was history. Bad history. Her mum was holding her hand but Jim shot a look at his wife and she let go. She loved her daughter very much, but her husband was right, this wasn't the time to wrap her in cotton wool. 'Hadn't we done enough for you?' Was this our fault?'

Rihanna hated her dad asking that. He said it in a way that sounded like he believed it.

She wanted to cry, but knew she couldn't. She had come down to face the music and needed to take it on the chin. 'No. Of course it wasn't. It was mine. My own stupid fault.'

Her dad went to speak but was interrupted by a guttural sound coming from outside.

It was getting louder. And closer. Jim walked across to the window and twizzled open the blind. He saw a guy, dressed in black, getting off his bike, and unclipping his helmet from under his chin.

'Who is it, Jim?' his wife asked, sounding a little unsure. It wasn't a neighbourhood that had loud bikes. She felt her stomach start to go over. Had they come to find their little girl?

Jim took his phone out of his pocket, ready to call the police if needed and watched as the biker started to walk towards the house.

'Jim?'

'Sssh. Rihanna, take your mum upstairs.'

Rihanna looked at her mum. She, too, believed they had found her. She wanted to get up and run away but she couldn't. She was frozen by the fear of the unknown, or rather, the soon-to-be known.

'Rihanna. NOW.'

Her dad's voice, raised by having to ask a second time, set her free. But her mum didn't want to leave, even though every fibre in her body was telling her to do so. They needed to be strong. They need to be a family. She gripped her daughter's hand tightly. Whatever it was that would happen next, they would face it together.

Harlan knocked on the door, unaware of the ensuing drama his arrival had caused. The dull thuds from his knock only added to their imaginations that were already in overdrive. 'Stay here,' Jim barked. He wasn't a confrontational man by any means but he was the man of the house and it was his job to protect his pack. He had already typed 999 into his phone and his thumb was at the ready if needed. Another set of dull thuds. Whoever it was outside wasn't leaving. Rihanna's dad knew he needed to do something. It was decision time. Invite or ignore. His body was screaming to ignore, to hide, but his head said something different. He left the front room and made for the front door, his thumb still resting on the call button.

He got to the door; each step he had taken having raised the what-ifs. But he had taken the decision to open the door and now he was there. A protective father trying to make everything ok again, like he did when she was a child. But back then monsters weren't real. He opened the door ever so slightly, keeping his hidden foot upright and against it. If the intruder wanted to barge in, Jim didn't want to make it easy for him.

'Good morning, is your daughter home?' Harlan's voice was unassuming. Non-invasive.

Jim was unsure whether to answer. Or how. In the early hours his daughter had arrived at his doorstep, dressed only in her underwear and a hoodie, shaken and scared. She had told her dad she had been arrested for selling drugs and then had been told to strip off and dance to stop her going to prison. And now there was a strange man standing at this door dressed like the Grim Reaper. Jim felt his mouth go dry. Harlan asked again, this time, with fewer words. 'Rihanna, she in?'

Jim's head nodded but his mouth wouldn't open. He was as frozen in fear now as his daughter had been in the front room. Jim was slight in frame and quiet by nature and no match in size or presence for the bearded biker stood at his door. He hoped it didn't turn violent.

'Mate, your daughter. Is she home? I haven't come here to cause a problem.'

Jim finally spoke. 'Yes... she is.'

'There, that wasn't so hard was it. I'm here to return her bag.'

Over Harlan's shoulder there was a neighbour taking a keen interest in the man at her neighbour's door, and the bike he had ridden in on. Both biker and bike stood out.

'Come in,' said Jim, without even realising he had said it. Harlan stepped over the threshold and into the hallway. He wiped his feet on the floor mat. The carpet was cream and plush. The pile was deep and he felt bad crushing it under the weight of his boots. But not that bad. He followed Jim through in the front room and saw Rihanna on the sofa, next to her mum. She looked washed out and weary. The last couple of weeks had taken its toll.

Jim walked over to the centre of the room, the log burner to the back of him, his wife and daughter to the front. A man trying to hold on to being the king of his castle. Harlan could sense the tension, the trepidation. He needed to break it. He was to help, not hinder.

'How are you feeling?' his question, directed to Rihanna.

'I'm ok. I guess,' she said, lacking the conviction to make it believable.

'No, you're not. How much do they know?' Harlan asked, referring to her mum and dad.

'Pretty much all of it, kind of.'

Harlan got the hint. She had skimmed the surface but to

move forwards, you need to go back, something Harlan had learned over the years. The hard way.

'Listen, you messed up. You danced with the devil and got burnt. You got stopped and searched by the Old Bill and maybe you should have got a bit of time. But what you didn't deserve was to get stopped by a bent copper, and then bullied into having to sell your clothes for some scumbag criminals. That's where I draw the line. That shit stops, now.'

Rihanna felt her mum squeeze her hand, not knowing who this man was standing in her house except that he was a knight in not-so shiny armour. Harlan read the room for the second time. In one short speech he had addressed her mistake, told her off but also drawn a line under it.

'So, what happens now?' Rihanna asked.

'Nothing. That's what happens. You go back to being a daughter, not a dealer. You go and find a nice young man and take your clothes off for him, no-one else. If not, it will be me kicking your ass.'

The well she had built up since the early hours, since she confessed to her sins, since she had stood naked in the shower and since her mum sat on her bed and held her like a baby, broke.

Jim started to pace, 'I just want to get my hand on them and wring their bloody necks.'

'And they will break yours. This isn't your life. Keep it that way.'

'But a policeman, I mean, Holy Christ, what is the world coming to?'

'The world has always been like it; it's just you don't get to see it.'

'So, what can I do? That's my little girl.'

'And that is why you are too close. I will deal with this. There is one thing you can do for me.'

'Anything. Name it.'

'Continue being a good guy. A good dad. Be the head of your family.'

'But what are you going to do?'

'What I do best.'

Harlan let his sentence linger. He knew not saying much, said a lot.

Rihanna stood up and went to give him a hug, but he baulked. Emotional affection scared him. Instead, he turned to her dad and held out his hand. Jim gripped it and shook it. It was a firm shake. Firmer than Harlan had expected. Her dad did have some balls; good for him.

Harlan said his goodbyes and left. He took his helmet from off the handlebars and clipped it back up under his chin. He got on the bike, flicking the button to start the powerful 1200cc engine and roared out of the street, with the nosey neighbour still looking, although trying her very best to hide. It wasn't working.

They all went over to the window, standing next to each other, shoulder to shoulder, and subconsciously in rank order. Jim, his wife and his daughter. They watched as he rode off and out of sight. In the space of a few minutes, a man stood in their front room, in his dirty boots, had gone from a scruffy unkempt menacing biker to their very own guardian angel. Jim turned and kissed his wife on her cheek. He wasn't sure why. It just felt right.

14

Guy was in his office when he heard the sound of Harlan's bike. He had already been there for two hours. He would have gone in yesterday but after reading Harlan's text he decided to take a personal day and spent most of Sunday on his sofa. He had started in the toilets, changing the rolls, emptying the bins and mopping. It was the worst job in the cleaning schedule which is why he started in there first, to get it out of the way whilst he still had the vigour to do so. He had employed a cleaning firm but when he started having his profits taken away, he needed to cut costs, until there was nothing left to cut. Guy had wiped down the bar and loaded and unloaded the dishwasher twice. The stocktake was done and the new order had been emailed to the supplier. His forehead was starting to glisten and his armpits felt wet.

Harlan arrived carrying two cups, bought from the coffee shop next door. It was a welcome gesture and Guy took off the plastic lid and started to blow on his.

'Did the bar stay busy all night?' Harlan asked. He was all about the business.

'Yeah, it was a good night. We did well.'

'Talk to me in numbers. What did you turnover?'

'A little over two bags.'

Harlan laughed at Guy's friendly dig at his street slang.

'Two bags. Not bad.'

'Nope. Four monkeys!'

'OK, enough,' Harlan said, still smiling. He then did the math in his head, working out the margin on last night. 'Not bad, fifteen hundred in your sky.'

'Sky?

'Your pocket.

Guy nodded, not understanding the correlation between the two.

'So, I went to the sports bar last night.'

'Did you?'

'Yes. Quite the operation, commercially. It's our turn to host this weekend, isn't it?'

'Yes. They will show up later this week, just to flex their muscles.'

'Good, I fancy a dick-measuring contest.'

Guy sensed that Harlan wasn't fazed by them, if anything, he was looking forward to it. He had never met anyone like him, a true outlaw biker. He had seen the 70's films and read about the myth and mystique of these people, heavy drinkers, living off the grid and generally a menace to society. But the man standing in front of him was different. He was scary as hell, yes, but he was sharp, too. He understood Guy's business better than he did, and had already increased profits and introduced new pricing. And that was without the upcoming day trade that was about to start. There was just one thing, the elephant in the room.

'Are we letting them set up? If so, last night's profit doesn't end up being actual profit.'

'*We* won't be doing anything. My rodeo, remember?'

It was asked as a question but with the answer already known. Harlan needed to reaffirm their position. They weren't friends. He was here to reclaim Guy's business and give it back to him. He didn't need a friend. Didn't want them. Guy needed to get to grips with the deal.

'I told you; I made it very clear, whilst I'm here it's my bar, it's my business. That's it.'

Not for the first time Guy saw Harlan's eyes darken, the change was frightening and they were on the same side so he sure didn't envy being on the opposite end.

'Yes, sorry, I know. I just don't know what happens next?'

'You don't need to. That's why I'm here, to win the war'

'And how do we win the war?'

'By having better intel, and a bigger army.'

The coldness in Harlan's voice sent a chill down Guy's spine.

DS Sharman was sitting at his desk when he felt his phone vibrate in his pocket. The office was busy with other detectives sitting at their desks. Desk phones were ringing and the copier was busily churning out paper. Mark Sharman pulled out his phone and read the screen: **Need some digging done on someone.**

It was rare the suits messaged him. It was a triangulated relationship, Edward, the suits, and him. Each with a role to play, each with a stake in the enterprise and each needing the other two. But he didn't want to hear from them unless it was crucial, either to the business, or their freedom. Mark held his phone under his desk and typed back two words: What's up? Blunt and to the point.

He watched as the message turned to 'read' and the little bubble of dots. They were replying. He looked up from his phone and around the office for prying eyes. Nothing.

The reply came: **Bearded fella. Some sort of biker. Heard anything?**

Mark felt his blood start to boil, what sort of lame message was that, could be anyone, and what did they need to know for? He typed back: **Meet me. Usual place. 3.30**

He hit send, waited for the whoosh then locked his phone and put it back in his pocket. He sat up straight and shifted some papers around on his desk to look busy. No harm, no foul.

Carla's phone showed four missed calls. The first two were a minute apart. The second set of two, the same. She knew the number only too well. It was her bosses. Carla had thought she had got away with it. She had waited for an opportunity to slip away and then when it came, she had taken it. She had delivered Rihanna's bag without being seen or stopped and had got home safely. But now her phone was saying the opposite. They must know, mustn't they?

Carla knew they weren't shy with their fists, on men *or* women. It was a dictatorship and they dictated it. But it wasn't a job, you couldn't just quit. They decided if you could leave. They knew where she lived, what car she drove, what school her son went to. They made it their business to know. It now wasn't looking like a good idea taking Rihanna's bag back after all. She checked the time. A little after two. An hour until Connor finished school, she felt sick to her stomach. Carla grabbed her keys from the coffee table and made for the door.

Harlan needed to find out more about the city's underworld, were the suits connected to anyone with any currency, any kudos? He didn't think they were, just a couple of chancers on someone's payroll, someone who didn't want to get his hands dirty. He knew that was Edward Broadbent QC, but was he also someone's puppet or did he just have a criminal mind and the money to make it happen? He didn't know the answer to that one yet, but he would. The one that he needed more intel on was the copper. Was he in other people's pockets, too? Did he tip dealers off when a raid was planned? Did he sell info on surveillance operations? Harlan knew he must have a connection to the vice squad, either he worked in it, or had done. He didn't know enough about the city to answer those questions himself, but he knew some people who could.

Carla parked her car as close as she could to the school, stopping just short of the yellow lines. She released her hands from the steering wheel and felt the pain in her fingers from how tightly she had been holding it. She kept balling her hands into fists and releasing them, trying to free up the cramps. It was still forty minutes until the bell rang but she would wait. Watch, and wait.

DS Sharman picked up his pass from his desk and made for the door, leaving his desk, his day job, behind him. He walked down the stairs quickly, his hand on the stainless-steel handrail, steadying him as he went. He passed a couple of uniforms on the stairs, heads nodded, nothing more needed than that. He leant forward lightly, allowing his card to become parallel to the reader on the door and he waited for it to click to let him out. He walked, not fast enough to arouse intrigue, not slow enough to waste the seconds. He walked over to his unmarked car and unlocked the doors before he got to it. He knew they would already be there, not in the exact location, but around. Close. Circling. Checking.

It had once been a pub; a three-story building that had belonged to the brewery but had been sold off when the recession hit and then repossessed when the recession got worse. It had been sold at auction for less than a third of its original value and now the windows had bars on the outside and the wooden doors with the brass handles had been replaced with steel. A camera hung above the doors with its little red light flicking angrily at anyone standing outside. There was no signage outside, no markings of identity, nothing except for the choppers that were parked up in a row outside. Harlan had spotted the building, and the bikes, when he first rode into the city. He knew that there was an MC here, it was only a small club, a standalone, just one charter, but they had a good reputation and the word was they were a stand-up crew and could be trusted. Harlan killed his engine. took off his helmet and hung it over the handlebars. He looked around for prying eyes but aside from the drunk sitting in the doorway of the abandoned building opposite, happy in his own little world and singing to himself, there was no one else around. He walked around to the door and pressed on the buzzer. A few seconds passed before he heard the crackling over the intercom and then heard a gruff voice, barely audible, speak through it.

'Who is it?' The voice was challenging. Distrusting.

Harlan didn't take offence. Security was paramount if what you did could get you some jail time.

It was the same at his club, distrust first, trust later, but much later. Harlan turned around so his back was facing the camera. Or more importantly, his clubs' colours were. He knew that was his passport to getting inside. Satan's Security had no beef with this club, no bad blood and the smaller clubs liked to support the bigger ones, as there may be a possibility of a patch-over at a later date. The big boys would often send a senior member to scout out a smaller club if a patch-over was on the cards and Harlan knew that's what would be on their minds when he turned to show his colours and he knew that was what would make the steel door open. A few seconds later he heard footsteps. Someone walking down the stairs. He could tell from the noise the steps weren't carpeted. He waited as the door was unlocked, hearing the sound of a steel brace, or an iron bar, being lifted from across the door, the final piece of adversity for someone trying to get in.

The guy on the other end of the door was shorter, wider and scruffier than Harlan. His hair was long, but straggly and his beard was unkempt. A true 70's biker throwback. He held out his hand, and there was a swallow tattooed on the web of skin between his thumb and forefinger. Harlan shook it, both men gripping hard, a real man's handshake.

'Come in, brother,' said the biker, smiling at his fellow comrade.

'Thanks.' Harlan accepted the invite and followed him. He was right about the stairs.

They stopped on the second floor. It was an expansive area with once white walls now stained and showing signs of yellow. There was a pool table but the baize was torn and the dartboard had as many holes around it as it did on it. The members who were there all stood and held out their hands and one of them went around the makeshift bar to crack him open a beer.

'Cheers,' said Harlan, chinking his bottle to the brother stood to the left of him

'So, what can we do you for?'

It was a friendly question, if a brother from another club

was in town, and there wasn't any beef with him or his club, respect was shown and help offered. This is what created the bond between outlaw bikers, what made them wear the 1% patch, you offered loyalty and wanted it back. Nothing more, nothing less.

'I need the lowdown on a bent cop.'

'Plenty of them around here, mate,' said the fella who had got him the bottle of beer.

'What's his name?' asked another. He was tall, very tall. 6 '4, Harlan guessed and his patch said 'VICE PRESIDENT', so held rank here if the actual president wasn't here. He held out a hand introducing himself as Dolby. He had a handlebar moustache and short shaved hair at the sides but long at the back. Harlan wanted to ask him if he had cut it himself but didn't know him well enough to take the mick. Dolby was a mean-looking sight. Harlan knew that would have been one of the reasons he was trialled as senior member and that he must have come good to have kept the rank. In the life of an outlaw, you weren't proven until you were proven. It was a tried and tested technique at each and every level, from a prospect to a president. You needed to first earn your patch, then keep it.

'DS Sharman, heard of him?'

The name was clearly a cause for contempt among the group. A few grunts were made and one spat on the floor. It was clear DS Sharman was a wrong un', on both sides of the fence.

'Yeah, we know him. Snidey little bastard,' said Dolby, taking his fags from his pocket and offering one to Harlan, who shook his head but thanked him for the offer.

'What's the crack with him?'

'He is a shithouse, that's the crack with him,' Dolby said, taking in a long drag of his cigarette. Harlan waited for him to blow the smoke back out of his lungs before he pressed him for more. 'In what way? I take it he isn't in your pocket?'

Every club knew the importance of having a policeman on the payroll but you needed to do your homework first, a bent copper could be just as harmful as a straight one.

'No chance, wouldn't trust him alone in an empty room. Told you, snidey little bastard.'

'In what way? Too full of his own importance?' Harlan asked.

'A bit – but more he fits up the girls, the working girls I mean. He also likes to sample them, if you get my drift.' Harlan did. He thought back to Rihanna, and then to Carla.

'Anything else?'

'Yes, he isn't shy about planting shit. The word is he got his promotion by fitting up a fella called Pinkie, he was a dealer, fairly big, but never caught, always careful, know what I mean?'

Harlan nodded his head in agreement, wanting Dolby to continue.

'Then all of a sudden, his gaff got raided, and lo and behold, half a brick was there, behind the air vent, and some scales and bags. Now we know Pinkie, and he never kept gear at his house, in fact he would change his trap houses on the regular, but there it was, half a brick and bags, in his house. Proper fit-up. Pinkie got an 8-stretch for that.'

Harlan was getting the true measure of DS Sharman, and Dolby was right, he was a shit-house. 'Who is he on the take for? Any ideas?'

'Not sure – we won't touch him and he knows that. He stays away from us and touch wood, hasn't caused our own girls any bother but the prossies, they are rich pickings for him.'

'Married? Kids?'

'Nah, nothing. No one would miss him if he disappeared if you get my drift?'

Harlan did, and his mind was already thinking of DS Sharman's exit strategy.

'I may need a favour,'

'Anything you need, just say, brother.'

Harlan chinked his bottle together with Dolby for the second time. 'I will have that fag after all.'

Carla was first in line when the school gates opened and was the closet mum to the classroom when the bell rang signalling the end of the day. Connor was one of the first out and he ran over to see his mum, the knees on his grey trousers caked with mud. Carla knelt down to hug her son as he arrived, his own arms wide open ready for the embrace, his packed lunch box in one hand and his school bag in the other. Carla flung her arms around him, hugging him tighter than normal, and for longer. He was safe in her arms and she wasn't planning on letting him out of her arms anytime soon.

They walked back to the car, hand-in-hand with Carla constantly checking over her shoulder and back again. She clicked him safely into the seat and then got in the car herself, hitting the button on the dashboard to secure the doors, the same as she had done in the early hours of Sunday morning. A decision she now regretted. She was glad, of course, that she had helped return Rihanna's bag, but the question was now, at what cost?

15

DS Sharman drove past the Mercedes, then signalled right at the end of the street. He took the next right and then right again, putting himself back where he started, driving back down towards the Mercedes. A safety precaution, flush out any rats. The one with the buzzcut flicked the gear-stick into 'Drive' and pulled out behind him. They went over the first crossroads, and then the second, before pulling into a side street and parking up at the far end. DS Sharman killed his engine, got out of his car and walked over to the Merc, opening the rear passenger door and slipped into the back seat. He pulled his phone and cigarettes from his pocket and turned off the first, and lit up one of the second.

'So, what's the panic,' he asked, his face masqueraded by smoke.

'We had a bit of an issue the other night,' Buzzcut said.

'Define issue?' replied Mark.

'A fella came in. Stood out.'

'Stood out, how?' Mark's voice getting irate at the staccato sentences.

'He wasn't dressed right, didn't look right, wasn't there for the pussy.'

'What was he there for?'

'Think he was family for the newbie, he just kind of, kind of took her.'

'What do you mean, kind of took her? You're not making sense.'

'We mean, he kind of took her,' said the tall one, an attitude to his tone.

Mark felt his spare hand grip the seat. He wanted to lose his shit on these simpletons but the odds were two-to-one, plus there was Edward to consider; he swore by these two thugs.

'Talk me through it. What actually happened...'

Harlan finished his second beer. He had played a few games of pool and one of the brothers had gone out and got some food. Fried chicken and chips, his paid for by the MC. It would have been easy to stay there for the rest of the day. Get hammered and maybe sample some of the women the club had on speed dial, but he was no longer that sort of outlaw, fast living and loose women was then, this was now. Dolby gave him a nod, meaning he wanted a word out of earshot. Harlan followed him out and up to the top floor. The room was dark and dusty, mostly empty except for some cardboard boxes on the floor and some old bike parts knocking about on rusty steel racking. Dolby lit another cigarette. He was a chain smoker.

'This Sharman fella, he needs sorting. I know some guys who could rough him up, keep you and us out of it. Could make it look like a mugging, but with some extras. Sound appealing?'

It did, and Harlan smirked at the thought, but he didn't

want a simple beat-down for the cop. He needed him hurt, but not physically, not right away, at least. He had a better plan for him.

'We squared up, but he didn't fancy it,' said the tall suit in the passenger seat.

'In the bar?' said DS Sharman.

'Yeah. I walked over to him and asked him what he was doing, why he wasn't paying for a dance, or throwing money at the girls. I asked him if he was a fag.'

'And he just stood there?'

'Yeah, pretty much. I then told him to spend, or sling his hook.'

'So, what happened with the newbie?' asked Sharman.

It was Buzzcut's turn to take over and tell the story.

'The newbie was shit, like total shit. Nice body, I'll give her that but didn't have a clue how to use it.' The suit sitting next to him laughed in agreement.

'What happened?' said Sharman, keen to speed things up.

'It was her turn to dance. But she just stood there, shaking like a shitting dog.'

'Then what happened?'

'Then the fella with the beard came and grabbed her. He just took her by the wrist and made for the door.'

'What the –, didn't the bouncers stop them?'

'Clearly not,' said the suited passenger. 'If they had, we wouldn't be sat here, would we?'

Mark felt his temper start to rise once again; their lack of respect towards him was starting to really test his patience.

'And they both left, him and the girl, together? No trace?'

'Vanished. We think the head dancer may know where the newbie lives, but as for the bearded fella, no one seems to know him, don't think he is a local face, if he was, we would know by now. That means he must be family, so if we find her, we find him.'

'OK. I get it. I'll ask around my end, see if anyone knows him and I'll dig into the family, see if anyone has any previous, see if he shows up that way.'

Mark Sharman leaned forward, between the seats and held out his fist, both men bumped it with theirs. Mark preferred that to a handshake, these weren't his friends, so no point pretending otherwise. Mark got out of the Mercedes and walked back to his car, turning his phone on in the process.

Harlan said his goodbyes, handshakes and bear hugs, the mark of an outlaw, the mark of a man. He pulled the steel door shut and over to his bike. The drunk was still there, still in a world of his own, still singing, and didn't flinch when he started his bike. Harlan envied him. If only his own life was so carefree. Harlan pulled out into the traffic, the wind had picked up and he could feel his beard blowing in the breeze. He had arranged to meet Guy at his house to go over the figures for the lunchtime trade. He was at a red light when he felt his phone vibrate against his leg. He pulled over when he could and checked who had called. It was Mouse.

Harlan pressed redial and waited for it to connect. It was answered on the third ring.

'I have some intel on the Mercedes. I'll have more in a bit, but this should get you started.

'Go on,' said Harlan.

'Seems like the fella the car is registered to, is a bit of a snake.'

'Meaning?

'He used to knock about with a dealer, Pink, something, and this Pink was under heavy observation. The Old Bill knew he was becoming a real player and wanted him nicked, stat.'

'Carry on.'

'They had kicked the door in of his trap houses, but each time, nothing, just a couple of crack heads in there, but no dope, well, not enough to nick him anyway.'

'What has that got to do with the Merc owner?'

'My intel tells me, and it's being double-checked, that the fella you are asking about used to run with this Pink character, and was also under observation. Guaranteed to get tugged when they had Pink, but guess what?'

'I'm not the guessing type, you know that. Spit it out.'

'Well, this Pink character did get busted, and at his house.'

Harlan knew this. Dolby has already told him, but not about the link to the suits. 'Go on.'

'His mate never got a tug. Nothing. Nada. He was literally just forgotten about. Now, I'm not sure if he is a grass, but something doesn't sit right. This Pink wasn't a doughnut, no way he would have gear in his own place, not a chance, but his door goes in and they find a parcel and all the packets. Seems well fishy to me. I reckon the guy you are after either planted it, or knew it was going to be planted.'

The line went quiet. Instead of Harlan's voice, Mouse could only hear the faint sound of traffic. Harlan was known in the MC as a thinker, he wasn't one to rush into words. Harlan knew the loose lips had sunk ships and had no interest in his own vessel suffering the same fate. It was becoming quite a tangled web, each person intrinsically linked to the others. Harlan needed more intel,

'Mouse, dig deeper, see which of the two it is.'

'Sure thing. Speak soon, brother,' said Mouse.

Harlan ended the call, put his phone back in his pocket and re-joined the traffic.

It had been a success. Much better than he'd thought. Harlan had been right. The till report was showing sales of just under £400, three hundred of that would be pure profit. He had run the place by himself so there were no wages to pay, just in case it had been a flop, but he was happy to say that Harlan had called it right. He put two bottles on as specials, a red and a rosé, the dearer one coming with complimentary olives. There was still the problem of wrestling his bar back from the heavies, but in terms of business, Harlan had already been a godsend, and so far, it hadn't cost him a penny, that was, until he checked the time on his watch and then the deal they had in place showed itself, literally. But he didn't mind, not really. Not deep down. He knew handing over a watch was a small price to pay to keep both his business and his sanity.

Guy had phoned Andy, the co-owner of the sports bar just to see how it had gone at the weekend. Andy had told Guy about Harlan and the girl. Guy didn't know whether he should bring it up with Harlan when he arrived. Harlan wasn't one for talking freely, he knew that. He also knew that Harlan only answered the questions he wanted to, and even then, the answers weren't exactly detailed. His microwave pinged, his lasagne was ready and it was at that exact point he heard Harlan at his intercom.

Edward had finished for the day. The day job was over. The one where the law respected him. Now it was time for his other job. The one where the law would detest him. Two sides of the same cloth, a thought that always made him smile, if only they knew. It had been a busy day on the markets, both the UK and US had closed down, the FTSE and Dow Jones, both feeling the hit from the Federal Reserve's statement earlier in the day. Edward wasn't concerned, what he traded was free from economic bullshit, and what he traded was away from the financial regulators, in fact, it was as far away from any sort of authority as possible. Edward typed in his details. Username and encrypted password. He had put a lot of thought into both. He was into his account and looking at his trading platform. He didn't really trade, he only purchased. With other people's money. His balance was not modest, far from it, Bitcoin had done him proud, but he wasn't seven figures happy. Close, but not there, yet. He took out the burner phone from the drawer and entered the eleven digits and let it ring.

The suits were at an Indian restaurant when the phone rang. They looked at each other when they saw who it was. Had the copper gone back and told tales? They didn't trust Mark. How could they? He was a cop. They didn't want to lose this gig. And for two reasons. It was lucrative, and it carried little jail time. If they did get nicked and sent away, they would get a few years at the most, whereas previous things they had been involved with carried double-digit sentences. Big difference. That would be if you discounted the violence, of course. If that was added, they would be back up there, and that's a lot of porridge.

The suits had grown up together, not related, but as good as. They had rolled with an older gang when still in short trousers, not yet in senior school but already stealing from shops and nicking bikes. By the time they were teenagers, they had moved into dealing weed and selling knock-off fags. By their twenties, they had carved out a bit of reputation and would sell their fists for the right price, a debt recovered here or a kicking handing out there. Buzzcut was the brasher of the two. More gung-ho. The taller one, a bit more strategic, but only just. They had parted ways for a while but had come back together and had gotten stronger, believing two bullies were definitely better than one.

'Answer it. Better see what he wants.'

Buzzcut picked up the phone and accepted the call. 'Boss.'

'Good evening. I hope you are well?' The voice on the other end was professional.

Courteous and charming.

'Fine, thanks. And you?'

'I'm well. Another busy day. Nose to the grindstone, I'm afraid.'

Buzzcut didn't know what to say, so instead just gave a little laugh. It was a token gesture.

'But that isn't the reason for the call. I have been thinking to myself.'

Buzzcut listened, believing his boss hadn't finished his sentence.

'I feel we need more venues. We should be doing three nights a week. Twelve a month, fifteen on a five week. And that needs 6-8 clubs. I would like you to go out canvassing.'

Buzzcut felt this was risky, and his lack of response said as much.

'And of course, if we increase the nights, we increase the turnover, and if we increase it by say, an extra ten thou a week, you'll get an extra thousand yourself. To share, obviously.'

Money, as Edward knew, was a huge motivator, and the sound of the extra slice of the pie would soon change the employees' thoughts. And he was right.

'Yeah, extra nights sound good, boss. No-one ever gets bored looking at tits, right?'

'Quite.'

Buzzcut knew that his boss didn't like crass talk and so quickly tried to get the conversation back to business, something his boss did like talking about.

'We're on it.'

'Good – and remember, check on the owners, we don't want to tread on toes on those who could cause us a problem, if you get my meaning?'

'Yes, got it. There are a few that are ripe for the picking, I reckon.'

'Good. My mother often told me there was no time like the present.'

Buzzcut took the hint. He said his goodbyes, then they paid the bill and left the restaurant.

Harlan could see the satisfaction on Guy's face. He had listened and it had worked. It had been a success and Harlan was impressed that Guy had done it all himself, it showed commitment and desire. Both of which were admirable traits. He may not be able to fight his way out of a paper bag, but Guy had proved to Harlan that his business meant the world to him and that he was able to grind it out and do whatever was needed to make it work. The only fly in the ointment was the scumbags stealing his money, and that's why he was there. It was time to earn his dough.

Guy poured himself a glass of red. The flavour said Merlot, the bottle said Australian. Harlan didn't know much about wine, except that he didn't like it. He declined an offer for a beer and took a tea instead. The apartment was modern. Everything was shiny. But it lacked depth, lacked a story. Nothing like the Satan's Security clubhouse, where every leather chair was ripped, bits of masking tape holding in the foam. Wood panelled walls with photo frames containing history. Faces of members from the past to the present, the caged to the dead. Anyone who was anyone in the club's history was somewhere on the wall. The clubhouse was where you could switch off, get wasted, get high or get laid, or all three. Guy's apartment was shiny and sterile. Harlan's clubhouse was dingy and sordid. Horses for courses.

'I spoke to Andy today; he told me what went down on Saturday. With that girl.'

Harlan knew he was referring to Rihanna, but waited to see if there was more to come.

'Andy said you just took her out of there. Saved her, basically.'

Harlan's face was expressionless. His poker face, impeccable.

'Reckon that could backfire? I mean I can't imagine it would have gone down well.'

Harlan sipped his tea and then spoke; it was time to drip feed his plan.

'You need to be aware that it could get a little loud for a bit, busting heads isn't a silent affair. Chances are, there will be kickback, noses will be put out of joint. Which is ironic, really, as it won't be long before they will be permanently out of joint.'

'This could get serious, couldn't it?'

'This isn't Netflix, you do know that, don't you?'

Guy nodded, but his nod worried Harlan. 'I'm serious. There is a good chance, a good chance, that the claret we spill will be as dark as that wine you're drinking.'

Harlan let the sentence sink in, slowly. He watched the colour in Guy's face drain away.

'I am getting that.'

'It's cliched, but I can't make you an omelette without breaking some eggs.'

'Define break?'

'Obliterate.'

That one word said it all for Guy. Sat on his sofa sipping tea was someone you didn't want to meet in a dark alley. Harlan was an enigma. He was rough and rugged. And ruthless.

'Can I ask you a question?' Guy asked.

'Try me.'

'Have you ever come across someone you can't sort?'

'I'm here, aren't I?'

Guy had been told this man was the best in the business, and so far, he believed it. Guy topped up his glass, trying his best to get his head around the surreal situation he had found himself. He had set up a wine bar to give himself a better life and right now, there was a biker in his house telling him the chances were that blood was soon to be shed.

'Is she okay?' asked Guy.

'Who?' replied Harlan.

'The girl you saved, on Saturday.'

'I didn't save her. Her parents will do that.'

Guy saw, for the first time, a softer side to the guy who was dressed in black, sitting on his sofa sipping sweet tea.

16

L enny was at the reception desk and on the phone when Harlan opened the front door. Harlan was tired and hungry. Never a good combination for him. He stuck his head into the dining room. It was empty and the lights were off. The kitchen was closed. He walked back through the landing and up the stairs to his room. His Nokia needed charging and his body needed resting. It had been a productive day. Mouse had already been back with intel on the suits and the MC had the lowdown on the cop. What he didn't expect though was somehow the two were linked. Not that it mattered, not really, but just reaffirmed the difference between a gangster and a grass. And that bent cops are the sludge between the two.

He took off his t-shirt and gave it a sniff, it wouldn't go again. He threw it into the corner of his room, the dirty washing pile. He sat on the edge of his bed and pulled off his boots. His feet absorbed the feeling of being free, even if they were still stuck inside sweaty socks. He went to the bathroom and turned on the shower, and took a shit whilst it heated up. By the time he had finished the room was awash with steam and the mirror was unable to reveal his reflection.

He stepped out of the steam and grabbed a towel. Drops of water coming off the base of his beard and hitting the tiled floor in heavy thuds. He felt like an early night, to get some much-needed shut-eye. He had a heavy weekend coming up, his already trained senses going up a gear, as was so often the case when the stakes were raised. Harlan had been lucky, luckier than most. Being an outlaw always carries the threat of incarceration, and being a nightclub bouncer, that too came with a possibility of prison each and every weekend.

He had always been able to punch with power, even as a young kid, knockouts were common, but what had made him even more prolific over the years was that he had acquired precision. He knew exactly where to hit, and then what happened next was just a formality.

He only had a towel wrapped around his waist when there was a knock at his door. Harlan wasn't expecting guests but he *had* been asking questions. Only at the MC though and there couldn't be a rat in there, could there? Harlan took the brass knuckles from the drawer in the bedside cabinet and went over to the door, pressing his eye up to the peephole, looking through, ready to explode in a ball of fury if there was anyone who fancied their chances. Harlan relaxed, the person on the opposite side of the wood was Lenny. He opened the door and saw Lenny standing there holding a plate. On it were two fried eggs on two slices of toast.

'I saw you check the dining room, presumed you must be hungry.'

'Yeah, I was. I am. Cheers, you didn't have to.'

'I know but I was feeling peckish myself and it didn't

take anything to double up the frying pan. If you fancy a beer, I'm going to be watching the football in a bit?'

'Yeah, maybe.'

'Anyway, enjoy,' and he handed Harlan the plate, noticing the knuckle dusters but trying to make out he hadn't.

'Thanks.'

Harlan closed the door and walked over and sat on the edge of his bed. The eggs were slightly overdone but beggars can't be choosers, he told himself.

Carla finished the story. It was about a caterpillar that went for tea. It was her son's favourite; he could pretty much recite it fully himself but there was something magical when his mum read it. She tucked him in and kissed him on his forehead. She left the hallway light on as he was afraid of the dark. She loved his innocence, his little fears, and funny ways. Carla wanted him to stay five years old forever. She went downstairs and into the kitchen. A bottle of wine was open on the worktop. She had bought it on the way home to settle her nerves. The four missed calls had turned into six and the white wine had taken the edge off. She checked the door; it was locked and the chain was across but she knew that before she got there. She knew that because she checked it half an hour before. And an hour before that.

Carla had grown up tough, her childhood required it. Her dad had split when she was eleven. The relationship had been abusive, her mum would use her mouth, her dad, his fists. Money had always been tight but had gotten considerably tighter when he left. Carla understood the importance of a strong work ethic from a young age and always understood the power of sex appeal. She was an attractive teen and the older lads all wanted a piece of her. She would entice them with false promises and would often not have to pay for her fags or bottles of cheap booze, the lads only too keen to hand them over if they thought they would be getting their leg over. Carla wasn't easy, far from it, and a virgin until she was sixteen, unheard of in her circle of friends who were already at it like rabbits and swapping partners quicker than phone numbers. But she understood commerce, and that being sexy had a value, a monetary value and her body soon became her business.

Carla was still attractive but she now had lines to her face. The sort of lines that come from stress and worry, and right now she was experiencing both. She poured another glass when her phone started to buzz. It was set to vibrate and she watched as it shimmied across the white worktop. She knew she should answer, they would keep calling, or worse. But she couldn't. And then she did.

'Hello?' her voice, shallow. The tone, sheepish.

'Well, you've been hard to get hold of. Anyone would think you're avoiding us.'

The taller of the two had her on speakerphone. She heard his partner cursing someone. They were clearly in the car. Were they coming to see her? She didn't know.

'Anything you want to tell me?' he asked. She knew it was an order, not a request.

'Such as?' Carla replied, trying to bat the question back, stalling for time.

'Um, let me see,' he paused for effect and then continued, changing from mockery to menacing in a heartbeat, 'Why the hell did you take the new girl's things with you?'

Carla didn't know what to say. Or do. She ended the call and ignored it when it rang again.

. . .

The plate was empty, aside from the collection of crumbs from the toast. It had filled a gap. He had put on a fresh pair of jeans and was looking for a clean t-shirt when his phone rang. He knew the number. She had rung once before. Harlan answered the call.

He didn't get a chance to say hello. The person on the other end was already talking.

'I'm so sorry to call. I just...I don't... I'm scared they are going to come here.'

The panic in her voice was evident. She was shaken and Harlan knew who by.

'What did they say?' he asked. His voice was controlled, it was commanding. Work mode.

'They said, um... They said... why did I take her stuff? What if they come for Connor?'

'Text me your address. I'm on my way.'

Carla went to speak but the line was already dead. Before she even had a chance to realise, her fingers were already busy typing.

Harlan put on a clean t-shirt and grabbed his leather cut from the chair, and his keys and both mobiles from the desk. Lenny was sitting in the front room; he was sprawled out on the sofa and was resting a can of beer on his stomach when Harlan entered the room.

'Going to have to take a rain check on the footie, next time though, yeah?'

'Yeah, sure thing. Off anywhere nice?'

'Just a bit of business,' replied Harlan.

'Is that what they call it now,' Lenny said, believing he was off to get a bit of action with a lady.

'Something like that. And thanks again for the eggs.'

Lenny went to reply but got side-tracked by the shot on

goal and the oohs from the crowd and the next thing he heard was the sound of his front door closing.

Harlan was a skilled rider, both at pace or when swerving and was using both attributes now. The streets were fairly busy, Ubers and black cabs ferrying punters back and forth to different pubs. He wasn't concerned about being pulled by the police. His bike wasn't officially registered to him and he had no qualms in roaring off should a blue light appear behind him. He hadn't liked the sound of her voice. Women shouldn't sound scared; no man had a right to do that. Maybe shout, or even curse, but never frighten, that just showed weakness as a man, and made you a bully, and Harlan hated bullies.

It was a nice little cul-de-sac. The houses were neatly arranged and neatly kept. And not cheap. She had obviously done well. Harlan had no problem with how she provided for her son. Some people strip down cars for a living, she stripped off her clothes. No difference, really. You do what you need to do to put bread on the table. It was as basic as that. He pulled up and parked on the street even though there was a space next to her car on the drive. That would be too presumptuous. Too personal. He knocked on the door, his helmet off and in his hand, he was trying to downplay his arrival into the street but his roaring Harley hardly had him down as being the local pizza boy.

Carla opened the door and it was clear she had been crying. The door had only just closed when she threw her arms around him. She just needed to be held, to feel safe, just as she had done for her son a few hours earlier. Carla finally unpeeled herself from him and he followed her past the living room and out into the kitchen. It reminded him of the one in Guy's apartment. All shiny with stainless steel appliances. Minimalistic and modern. On Guy's fridge was his to-do list, on hers was a painting of a green dinosaur held up with magnets. She offered him a glass of wine but he declined.

'Beer?'

'No. I'm riding. I'll take a tea though.'

Carla took the expensive-looking kettle from its stand and filled it up from the fancy tap. She put it back down and set it to boil and then checked her phone for messages. There weren't any, but that didn't mean they weren't coming, quite the opposite, it just meant they weren't announcing it. Harlan could see she was all over the place, and decided not to probe her on what had happened until she started to relax.

'Sugar?'

'Two and a bit, please.'

'Christ, surprised you have any teeth left.'

'A spoonful of sugar helps the medicine go down; someone once told me.'

'Would that someone be Mary Poppins?'

Harlan laughed. Carla followed. The tension had been broken.

They moved to the front room and Carla sat on her sofa, putting her feet up under her. Harlan took the opposite chair. It was one of those fancy Italian jobs, all frills and no comfort. He never understood the appeal to go all art-deco where sitting your ass was concerned. He caught looking down at his boots, wishing they weren't planted heavily on her carpet but that was her problem, not his. They were his problem, not his boots.

Carla told him again what had happened. She was a little clearer this time, and a little less upset. She apologised for calling him but didn't know who else to call.

'It's fine. More than fine, it was me that asked you to get her stuff, after all.'

'I owed it to her; you just gave me the balls to do it.'

'Owed it to her? How?'

'She came to me to learn to dance. I should have just told her to run. To stay well clear.'

'But they would have found her, and maybe the second time around they would have been more forceful. If you are trying to blame yourself, don't. This is their doing, not yours.'

Carla gave a small smile. He was trying to make her feel better, and it was working. He liked her smile; it broke through the confident bravado she was so used to wearing and made her look soft and sweet. He knew the false lashes and brows were just a front. It was her mask, and he wanted to see what was underneath it.

They made small talk, nothing heavy, killing time really with Harlan getting up every now and then to walk over to the window and peer out through the blinds. In his front pockets were the brass knuckle dusters, one in each. Ready to slip on and punch straight through bone and out the other side. He could take on two against one, he had done many, many times before but he didn't want to just fight them if they turned up tonight, at her house, he wanted to destroy them, he wanted to batter them until even their own mothers wouldn't recognise them.

It was getting late. It was closing in on midnight.

'I'm going to get another wine; you sure I can't get you a beer?'

'I'm riding, remember.'

'You don't have to ride tonight. You can stay here.'

Harlan wasn't sure how to take the invite. Carla gave him a smile, a cross between shy and sultry. He stood and walked over to her, she looked at him. The confidence was back, but not too much. He took the wine glass out of her hand and put it on top of the radiator, checking first it wasn't on. He put his hand around her waist and pulled her in towards him. It was a fast, sweeping action, both decisive and dominant. She put her hands inside his leather cut and onto his chest, liking what she felt. Harlan slid both his hands down towards her ribs, then she felt his fingers widen as he gripped and lifted off her feet. She wrapped her legs around his buttocks as he walked her backwards towards the wall. The kissing was frantic, the breathing heavy. He was in control of her and she loved it, loved the submissiveness of it all. He pawed at her top, exposing her breast and she felt the nuzzling of his beard as he ran his tongue over her nipple. The sex was dirty. It was hard and fast. He was barely undressed and nor was she. The second time was softer. The lust replaced with lovemaking. Her body arched, twisted and turned, her muscles tensing and releasing. Her breath, hot and panting, her voice muted but moaning. The second time was slower, and deeper. And in bed. The first time she climaxed from behind, the second time, on top. Each time was different, each time was perfect.

Harlan looked over at her. She was asleep. And she was safe. The duvet had fallen down from her, her breasts were on show. He gently leaned over and pulled it back up. He got dressed and carried his boots with him and walked down the stairs. He picked up his vest from the floor and left. He didn't want her son to wake up and find a strange man in his mum's bed beside her. He knew she wouldn't want that either. It was the right thing to do.

17

Except for the early morning delivery trucks, the roads were empty. He cruised, there was no need for speed. He had left her sleeping and he knew they wouldn't dare turn up in the day, they weren't complete novices. He would check in on her later and if there were any strange comings and goings in her street, he felt sure he could rely on the local MC to do a drive-by and provide some security. He liked Dolby, he seemed a good VP. The strength of a club came from its management, if the top tier was tight then the club would be a solid unit, if not, it was nothing more than a house of cards and local gangs would smell blood from a mile off. He felt bad sleeping with Carla, it wasn't his intention but he didn't make the first move, his conscience was clear. She wouldn't have expected him to stay, she knew what last night was. She was scared and he had become her saviour. Tarzan to her Jane. It had happened before, many times. It would happen again.

The B&B was in darkness, except for the emergency lights. It would have been a local council decision to have them fitted, or the fire service. Or both. He needed to get some more sleep. He had purposely slept lightly, not wanting to fully switch off, half for her protection, the other for her self-preservation. Her son didn't need to see him. In a month's time, he would be just a memory anyway, best to start that process now.

He was in need of a shower but didn't want to wake the other guests. That wouldn't be fair on Lenny, having to deal with disgruntled punters over breakfast. Lenny had been good to him; the use of the garage, the washing machine, last night's supper. If you did right by Harlan, he did right by you. The way it should be. He stripped down to just his jeans and slid under the covers. Within seconds he was asleep.

DS Sharman was up and about early. He knew a lot of his snitches would be about. Meeting in secret to score, getting their first fix set up. Being a detective required having ears on the ground. It was a two-way street, you got your intel, and they got a pass. The difference was how you played yourself, a good cop didn't bully their snitches for intel, but the bad ones got off on the power, and this made them both unpredictable and unprofessional. DS Sharman fell into the latter category. The people in his pocket hated him.

So far, it had been a waste of time. Nobody he paid to tell him, had anything to tell. No-one had seen anyone fitting Harlan's description. The suits had said he looked like a biker, dirty, scruffy looking, 'Needing a fashion transplant' was what Buzzcut had said. The members of the local MC were known to them, they had scored off them before and they were hardly non-descript looking, but the snitches were sure whoever it was, wasn't anyone from the club, although they all agreed he did fit the bill of a greasy biker.

DS Mark Sharman got back in his car and sparked up. It

wasn't a total disaster, his intel had confirmed what the suits had told him, that whoever he was, he wasn't a threat. It was like they said, probably just a family member trying to do a good deed. The sucking on the cigarette soothed the stress. It was difficult, being on both sides of the law, but the hard-on he got from being a criminal more than made up for the treachery.

The wine bar was busy when Harlan arrived. Most tables were taken and the bar itself had customers standing around talking and drinking. He walked in and over towards Guy, who was busy corking a bottle for two women who looked like they liked to do lunch. Harlan didn't want to interrupt him so he went through to the office and sat down, resting his feet on the desk. Guy came through a few minutes later, his face smiling from the busyness of his bar. He looked energised, and invigorated, money may not make the world go round, but it sure does make you smile.

'Looks good out there' Harlan said, his feet still up on the desk.

'Very. If this continues until we close, we will beat yesterday.'

Harlan found it funny the way Guy kept referring to himself as a 'we.' It was him, a sole trader. His circus. There were no monkeys. 'Any news on your end?' Guy asked.

'Nothing that needs to wipe that smile from your face.'

The comment put Guy's mind at rest. He didn't want his bubble burst, just yet.

'You hanging around to the end?'

'Might do. Not sure.'

Guy went to speak, but heard his name being called from the bar.

'You best go, your audience awaits.'

'Yes, boss,' replied Guy, it was a tongue-in-cheek comment, but they both knew there was an element of truth to it.

She had checked her phone so much that she had annoyed herself. So far, though, her phone had only received calls from friends, the suits had left her alone. She didn't think she was totally out of the woods, but maybe they had got the information they needed elsewhere. The thought made her feel bad, she didn't wish Rihanna any harm, but the reality was it was a dog-eat-dog world and she focused on number one. Connor was sitting at the table, drawing. He loved to draw, and with each finished picture he would run over to his mum to show her. Carla loved those magical moments. Taking her clothes off at night was her profession, but being a mum, that was her passion.

She wanted to call him. But she wasn't sure what to say, thanks? But what was she thanking him for? Coming over? Staying there? Or sleeping with her? Maybe it was all three.

She knew it had been meaningless, hot as hell, but meaningless. She liked him, he had a strong set of values, she could see that, but she also knew he came with a price, and that price was too high to pay, being a mum. She knew he wasn't a good guy, and as exciting as that was, she needed a decent, honest man if they were going to be allowed into her son's life. One that came without drama.

Harlan helped Guy take in the tables and chairs from outside. The afternoon had stayed busy and Guy was right, he beat yesterday's takings by a clear fifty. He was tired, though, the last few days he had run the afternoon shifts alone but it was clear now it worked and he could afford to put his staff on the afternoon rota. The owner of the coffee shop was happy, too. Most of Guy's punters, after leaving him, went next door and got a coffee to go.

Harlan was alone outside, waiting for Guy to shut the place down when he spotted a Mercedes pulling in to the complex. He clocked the registration when it first pulled in, it was his friends in the suits. Maybe they were novices, after all. He watched as they sat and waited, but couldn't tell if they were on a call or just talking amongst themselves. He knew they weren't the brains, only the brawn, that they operated on instructions, not initiative.

Guy came out, his iPad in one hand, his keys in the other.

'Go back in.'

'What?'

'Go back in. Now.'

Guy wasn't sure what was happening but Harlan's voice made it clear that whatever it was, was serious. He pushed his back against the door, keeping his eyes forward for as long as he could, before he was back inside the bar and the door closed up in front of him.

They got out. A split-second gap between each door closing. Harlan watched as they stood by the powerful car, and smoothed down their suit jackets. They were all about the appearance. Harlan was all about the result. They had no business being in his arena.

They walked over, side by side, a swagger in each step but there was a big difference, it wasn't going to be who they thought it would be when they got there. The one with the buzzcut spotted him first, stood there with his arms crossed high up on his powerful chest.

'Well, well, fancy seeing you here.' Buzzcut said.

They had spent two days trying to find him and there he

was, standing in front of them, it was like all their birthdays had come at once.

'Likewise, but it appears you are a little lost?'

'Really? And why is that, exactly?'

'Because you seem to be here, a place that, trust me, you really don't want to be.'

'You don't know how this works, do you?'

'No. But I'm all ears.' His arms were still crossed.

'Where's the other fella, the owner. He knows the crack.'

'This is where we have a problem then, fellas. I'm the new owner, and whatever used to happen here, doesn't anymore.'

'Is that right?'

'We can discuss it in detail if you want, but you may want to take off your jackets, I hear blood stains.' The delivery was cold. Emotionless. His arms were still crossed. His stare, steely.

'We're up for that,' said the taller of the two, and opened the three buttons on his jacket and flicked one side of it back, revealing a handle protruding out of his black leather belt.

Harlan's disgust for them went stratospheric, you didn't bring weapons to a fistfight. He dropped his arms, and went into a 45° stance, ready to launch from his back foot. It was on.

And then it wasn't. The owner of the coffee shop came out, totally oblivious to what was taking place. She looked over and smiled, it was courteous to acknowledge someone else's customers. Harlan and the suits returned false smiles. She started to sweep outside her establishment. She wasn't going anywhere any time soon. The taller of the two let his jacket fall back to its natural position; the handle, now hidden. It had become a stalemate. Harlan against the suits.

Two eyes versus four. But odds like that never fazed him. Being honest, he preferred it.

'I think this needs to continue.' Buzzcut said.

'Like you won't believe.' replied Harlan.

The testosterone was there for all to see. All except for the owner next door, still sweeping outside her shop.

'We will be back at the weekend, ready for business.'

'Over my dead body.'

'You said it,'

'Yes, but you pair of muppets couldn't do it. But I'll give you a tip, for free, you'll need more than that Swiss army knife down your trollies to do it.'

Buzzcut took a step forward and spat down near Harlan's feet. Harlan laughed at the petulance, knowing they would soon be spitting blood, not saliva.

He watched as they sauntered back to the Merc, laughing to himself at their attempt to intimidate. If that was the best they could do, then they needed to go back to gangster school.

They drove out of the car park slowly, tyres barely turning. The taller one, sitting in the passenger seat, had wound down his window and put his fingers to his lips as they drove past and Harlan shook his head in disbelief at the teenage attempt to leave a threat.

Guy opened the door looking flustered.

'What was that? I mean I didn't catch it all, but that looked, well, intense?'

'They just popped in to say hello.'

'What, with a bloody knife?'

'Maybe they had stopped to peel an apple on the way?'

'Looked like they were ready to peel you!'

'They would need a bigger peeler.'

They both laughed, Harlan, heartily, Guy, nervously.

The lady next door had gone back inside, but reappeared, this time with two polystyrene cups in her hands. 'These are for you. Thought you chaps might need it, seeing as you have had a busy day.'

Harlan thanked her for her generosity, knowing she had absolutely no idea just how close she had been to witnessing a knife fight.

'I am so glad you have opened during the day. So nice to see.'

Guy knew there was an element of selfishness in her statement, but he didn't mind. If she did good trade on the back of his then everybody won. The way business should be. Guy knew Harlan would be sipping his coffee out of courtesy, not choice. Harlan was a tea drinker, with two sugars, minimum. A flat white wasn't his thing. They stayed and made chit-chat for a few minutes before saying their goodbyes and leaving. Guy into his financed car, Harlan onto his Harley.

Harlan stopped off at The Trafalgar. It was pretty barren. Two people were playing darts, both sporting beer bellies and the table next to them was festooned with empty glasses along with a couple of fresh ones, partially drunk. The barmaid with the cute smile wasn't working, replaced by a smaller, less pretty version. Harlan took a window seat. He could watch the world go by, if he wanted to, but he didn't. He wanted to check in with a few people. He pressed his thumb down through the contact list, finding Mouse's name once again. He dialled the number and waited for an answer. It wasn't forthcoming. He knew he would call back; a brother never ignores a brother. Next, was Carla. He dialled.

.   .   .

Carla was putting the hoover round when she felt her phone vibrate against her ass. As before, she felt her stomach go over, fearing the worst. She pulled the phone out of her back pocket and felt a huge sigh of relief when she saw who it was calling.

'Hey.' She tried to hide the excitement in her voice. But failed.

'Just thought I would check in. No calls from Pinky and Perky?'

'Ha, no, nothing today. Thank God.'

He liked the sound of her laugh. He didn't think she laughed much, not deep down.

'I was going to call you today, just to, you know, say thanks.'

'I think you showed me your thanks.'

She laughed again.

'But seriously, you don't need to thank me. You went out on a limb for me, I'm just sorry it backfired. But you don't need to worry, I'll soon be sorting it.'

Carla could tell he meant it, she just didn't know what sorting it meant, and didn't want to.

'If you are free later, you can pop over if you want? I can cook, if you're hungry.'

Harlan thanked her, but he didn't do dinner. Dinner could lead to dating. Dating could lead to a relationship. And relationships could lead to being hurt. Why would he want that again?

18

Harlan stayed until closing. Only because he couldn't think of any other place better to be. The pub picked up in numbers, but only just. He wasted some time throwing some darts at the board, playing by himself, and having some food. Burger and chips, picking out the salad that sat inside the bap. He had two bottles of beer and a coke, full fat. He wanted to be on familiar territory, a pub, a place where he felt at home. Harlan became a bouncer through the club. Satan's Security had some protection rackets going on back in the day and he would often man a new venue for the first weeks to let any troublemakers know that things were going to change, and fast. Then when he pulled away from the day-to-day of the MC as a nomad, he went freelance, taking on the worst of the worst.

The MC supported his play, a deal was struck, he wouldn't touch the pubs already under their control, but anything else was fair game. The first pub was just out of town, the takings weren't big enough for the MC to stick its claws into it and the local, licensed security firms wouldn't touch it, the violence was too much. Harlan took it on, for his standard fee, a grand a week, in cash. It took a few weeks to turn it around. Bones were broken: not his. Teeth got smashed, not his, and some big egos got busted. By the end, the troublemakers stopped coming and the spenders started. By the time he left he had two good guys working the door and any female leaving would be escorted to her taxi, and with the door held open. He knew the key to a successful bar was when the women felt safe. Women might like a bad boy, but they like feeling safe, more. The last decade had seen him all across the country, taking on what others wouldn't, or couldn't. A violent bar became somewhere he felt safe, ironic really. The barmaid had rung the bell and was starting to collect glasses, it was time to go.

It was chilly outside. He zipped up his hoodie under his chin. It was rare he wore gloves; his fingers didn't feel as nimble as they needed to be when constrained in leather. He got on his bike and fired it up. Those first few seconds of his bike idling underneath him never ceased to make him smile. The Harley was his pride and joy, everything else was just chicken feed. He had a collection of expensive watches, more for collateral than kudos, and he had a good cash reserve, but the bike, that was what it was all about. It was his life, not a lifestyle.

He took a drive through the city. He hit the dual-carriageway hard, opening up the throttle and letting loose, the tacho reading well over a ton. He also took in the back streets, the dirty end. Cars parked up and people running over to a wound-down window to score. Women in short skirts waiting to get picked up. Harlan knew that no matter how affluent a city appeared, each and every one had an underbelly of crime, grime and depravity.

By the time he got back to his room the day had ended and the new one had just begun. His cheeks were cold and he needed to stretch out his fingers. He knew the time didn't stand still, those seconds never stalled and that pretty soon it would be the weekend. It would either be their weekend, or his. But he knew where he would put his money.

'I hear we are expanding?' said DS Sharman.

'Yes. I feel the time is sufficiently right to speculate.'

'So to accumulate, right?'

'Exactly, dear friend.'

The casino was busy. Oriental girls in sequinned dresses with never-ending legs were walking around with expensive drinks on solid silver trays. Their eyes selling a dream, for a price.

Edward liked to hide out in the open at times. And it wasn't out of the realm for a high-flying lawyer to be out spending his salary on chips. DS Sharman knew he didn't fit in, as much as he tried. His blazers never seemed to fit properly and expensive clothes still looked cheap on him. He was an out of shape, out of place cop, and felt like it. Edward looked the opposite, oozing upper-class and speaking with a silver spoon. The casino was a members-only affair, it wasn't part of a chain and the working class weren't welcome. The membership spanned doctors, doctorates, millionaires and masons. A who's who of the city. Edward pushed his chips onto his favourite numbers, he was feeling lucky. He always felt lucky.

The croupier closed the bets, smiling elegantly and knowing just as many eyes were on her as they were the wheel. The dice disappeared from view, caught in it the vortex of the spin before starting to slow, bouncing between the numbers, the sound of it clacking against the stainless steel. The wheel finally stopped. The ball was in 17, Bond's favourite number, and the reason Edward liked to choose it.

Edward had won. Mark hadn't; the wheel acting as a metaphor of the differences between them.

Edward took his chips and gestured for another drink. They walked to the window, Edward leading, Mark following, another metaphor in play, and when he was sure he couldn't be heard, Edward spoke.

'The process is proven. It's now time to increase the profits.'

'Do you not think we should be happy with what we have already? Why risk it?'

'Because fortune favours the brave, dear fellow.'

'But aren't we being greedy? I mean, we have a good thing going.'

'Have you not seen Wall Street? As Gordon Gekko once famously said, 'Greed is good.''

Mark could see the excitement in Edward's eyes. As much as he didn't want to admit it, it was contagious. He remembered why he got involved in the first place, and that was to be able to be in places like this, being served by sexy women in skin-tight dresses surrounded by money. His attitude changed.

'You're right. It's time to expand our little enterprise.'

Edward didn't like the use of the word we, there was no we, there was only him. He ignored it, hiding his displeasure at being grouped into some sort of consortium, his face not showing the offence he took from it. This had been his idea. Edward Broadbent. Q.C.

The sound of his phone ringing woke him. He reached across the bed and over to the bedside table. The Nokia was there, on charge and his attempt to grab it with his eyes still half-closed only served to knock it on the floor, still ringing.

By the time he leaned out of his bed to scoop it up it had

stopped. The screen said it had been Mouse. It was 2am but time didn't hold much weight with bikers. Late nights and later starts were the norm, 9-5er's they were not. Harlan pressed redial. Mouse answered.

'Did I wake you, H?'

'Yes. But it's fine. What you got for me?'

'That fella we were speaking about, the dude with the Merc.'

'You mean the whole reason why I called you?'

'Yeah. Anyway, I found out he didn't plant it, but he did know it was going down. Word is there was a copper involved. Bent. And this fella had something going on with him. That was why he didn't get nicked. Not even a pinch. His mate got a ten, Merc man, nada.'

The link that was already between the gang, just got tighter, Harlan could see the jigsaw was pretty much complete. A cop gone bent. A scumbag turned grass. A lawyer gone rogue. Each needed the other two to make it work. A triangle. Three points of execution. Not a perfect triangle, more of a scalene. Each with a different angle. Literally.

'Thanks, Mouse. Top work.'

'Anything else you need, brother?'

'Not right now, but be on standby.'

'Always.'

And that was what being a biker was all about. The brotherhood. Being there for each other. No matter what. In the land of an outlaw, if one person was cut, you all bled. A trouble shared was a problem halved, or in the eyes of a MC, a problem dealt with. Most members of the club had menial jobs, a few hundred a week, at best. Just enough to pay their rent, feed themselves and pay their dues. But it didn't matter if you were skint. The beers were bought wholesale, or better still, stolen and sold to them by a local fence, and were then sold at the clubhouse for just a few pennies of profit on top, just enough to cover the clubs' overheads. Weed was shared and anything harder wasn't allowed in the clubhouse anyway.

If someone hit a tough time, the other members would scrape together what they could and you only needed to pay it back when you could. For all its misdemeanours, Satan's Security protected the community and helped out the old and the needy. Kids were encouraged to knock on the door of the clubhouse on Halloween night where shit loads of sweets were handed out with the members dressed up as ghosts and the Grim Reaper, and the clubhouse dressed with fake cobwebs and dripping in pretend blood. It was the same at Easter, the local hospital and children's hospice found itself with a full entourage of bikers walking in handing out chocolate eggs and colouring books. The club was a criminal enterprise, that was a given, but it also had a heart, and that was often forgotten.

Harlan put his phone back on charge and went back to sleep. The next few days would be interesting, but it was foolish to fight on an empty fuel tank. Fatigue was a dangerous thing, from misreading a situation to misjudging a junction. Tiredness kills, as the signs on the motorway said, and they were right.

Edward opened his safe and placed inside his winnings. It was a few thousand. Closer to five than three. But he knew that cash, in the paper sense, was no longer king. It was becoming more of a hindrance. But his crypto account, that was his golden egg. That was his passport to a life spent on board the yachts of Monaco and the sandy beaches of the Caribbean. He had been busy creating the companies needed to live as a tax exile, not a tax avoider. The second carried a prison sentence. He needed to be seen as a success, someone who had made his money through skill and cunning, not through criminality. His knowledge of the law made understanding the complexities of moving cash through umbrella companies easier and what he didn't know, his other lawyer friends did. Everyone was there to be used. Manipulation was an art from, and Edward had his easel at the ready.

The guard dog started to bark. Edward went into his phone and onto the app. He brought up the cameras into a single screen. Eight cameras. Eight segments. He studied each one. Looking for movements. Looking for someone to lighten up in bright white. An intruder wanting to get what he had. That was why the dog was there. To serve and protect. Four legs of fury and the power to break bone with its bite. Edward kept scanning the screen. What had made the dog bark? And then it came into view. A fox. He laughed out loud.

'Sssh, Zeus. Back to bed.'

The dog went back to its bed under the stairs feeling pleased with himself for alerting his master to the sound outside. He wanted a biscuit for his troubles but didn't get one.

Harlan ordered toast for breakfast. No eggs. And an orange juice. The toast came and looked lost. He asked Lenny for some eggs, after all. He had put a wash on, so was in no rush to leave the breakfast table, not until it had finished. It was busy. Different guests. Mostly men. In town for a conference, Harlan guessed. Not high enough up the greasy ladder to be in expensive hotels, though. Lenny was looking flustered. Up until now he had looked composed, but up until now the place hadn't been busy. Harlan stood up and followed Lenny out of the dining room and through to the kitchen. 'Let me help,' he said, as Lenny was trying hard to stop the fried eggs from sticking.

'You sure? Mate, that would be amazing.'

'No worries. Those two plates there, done?' replied Harlan, pointing to plates of fried food on the metal worktop.

'Yes. Table 7.'

Harlan's face said it all. He had no idea where table 7 was.

'Far end of the room. Two tall chaps. Shit haircuts.'

Harlan laughed as he picked up the plates. Nothing like speaking your mind.

He carried them through and delivered them to table 7. 'Enjoy,' he said, but not particularly caring either way. They looked up at him, nodded and then carried on talking shop. Harlan walked away, thanking his lucky stars he had chosen the life of an outlaw. And that Lenny was right; they did have shit haircuts.

He stayed helping until the end of service, and then loaded the dishwasher whilst Lenny wiped down the tables and replaced the cutlery. Harlan was squeezing out the teabags with his fingers when Lenny walked into the kitchen.

'Sugar?' he asked.

'A sweetener, ta. Cupboard above your head.'

Harlan reached above him and took out the sweetener and popped one little pill into the tea. Harlan found himself often liking the owners of where he rested his weary head, which reminded him he was still yet to call Carol. His opinion of Lenny had changed since his arrival. He worked hard, kept himself to himself and ran a tight ship. Not bad seeing as Harlan could tell his heart wasn't really in it.

'Busy out there, today. That's good, no?'

'It is good, it's also needed. Been tough since we reopened. Real tough, actually.'

Harlan knew B&B's often struggled, what with the budget hotels having moved in on their trade over the last few years and with dedicated car parks and better buying power, they now rivalled the little overnight stays in terms of price. 'How bad is it?' Harlan asked.

'Two months behind on the mortgage, soon to be three.'

Lenny's parents had gone on holiday, but it was more of a sabbatical. His dad had suffered a minor stroke and they had all decided he needed some time away. His mum and dad worked hard, and had built up a good reputation, but the building was getting old and the repairs, more expensive. Lenny told him he was running it minus a wage, but the food was free, so too the beer. Harlan liked people who would cut their cloth when needed, and would dig in when faced with tough times. It's what gave you character. Lenny's youthful looks were hidden by his shaggy beard and lank hair. He looked like a student who wouldn't accept he had to dress like an adult, his t-shirts had pictures of album covers on them and were all at least one size too big. They finished the rest of their tea in silence before Lenny started cleaning down the kitchen and Harlan removed his clothes from the washing machine.

Rihanna was still off work. Her mum believed she was depressed. She wanted to call the family doctor but Rihanna had said no. She just wanted to sleep. Forever.

She woke up a few hours later. The sunlight had ignored her curtains and shone through, and she checked her phone. There was a number she didn't recognise. She tapped on the message: **I hope you're okay, hun. Stay safe, please. C xx**

Rihanna liked Carla; she had been nice to her. She wanted to text back but didn't.

The wine bar was busy for the third day in a row. Beth, the new waitress on duty was busy delivering a fresh bowl of olives to a table and Guy was pouring a glass of Portuguese red for the same customer. But Guy had that feeling in his stomach, a feeling he had gotten accustomed to. It was anxiety. He knew he had hired help. He knew the biker had balls the size of basketballs but what he didn't know was just how bad things might get before it got better. And what he also didn't know was what would happen when Harlan left. He had watched in awe yesterday when Harlan hadn't flinched when he saw the knife. Guy could never do that, in fact it had kept him awake all night. Maybe it was just better to let the gang continue. They could take his cash, just not his life.

'Careful, you're spilling it everywhere.'

Guy's mind had been too engrossed in the what-ifs to notice the glass was overflowing and red wine was dripping onto the floor, 'Shit.'

19

The drunk wasn't there. He was probably propped up in another doorway, or sat in another pub. Harlan parked his bike in the same spot. Which was right at the end of the row of the bikes already parked up. The Harleys were an eclectic mix of old and new, customed and chopped. Some were 70's Sportsters and 90's Fat Boys. Custom paint jobs and factory fitted upgrades. Owning a Harley gave the rider a plethora of possibilities, and just as many prices. But a true biker didn't care. Their bike was their baby. It was a maternal affair. A biker may appear to be broke to the outside world but to them, their bike was priceless. He went through the same rigmarole of pressing the buzzer and turning around to reveal his patch. He waited, again, for the heavy footsteps to come down the wooden stairs, unlock the door and remove the iron brace. The clubhouse was emptier than last time. Only three members were there. But the one person he needed to see? He was there, as arranged.

Dolby was behind the bar, stocking up the fridge with bottles of American beer. The empty cardboard boxes waiting to be collapsed were on the bar top. Harlan shook hands with the other two and talked club runs and bike parts whilst he waited for Dolby to finish. The president of the club was still away, on a bit of business, but Dolby had spoken to him and had signed off on Harlan's plan.

Dolby came around the bar with two bottles of beer, taking the lid off the first and handing it over to Harlan. After the chink, and the small talk, Harlan followed Dolby up to the top floor.

'The Pres is on board. And we can have someone do it.'

'No. I don't want that. I don't want someone else possibly getting pulled in for this. Plus, I'm not local. I will be in, out and away. Pretty sure my old dear told me never to shit on your own doorstep.'

'Your mum was wise.'

'Yeah, she had a side-line writing fortune cookies, too.'

Dolby laughed at Harlan's joke and then lit up a cigarette. The first of many, Harlan knew.

'You sure, though. There is a chance this could go wrong. And some big bird if it does.'

Harlan knew the risk. It wasn't small. But he held the copper in high contempt and his demise needed to be in line with his despicable acts. 'Yeah. I'll do it.'

The plan was firmed up. Money needed to change hands, but not immediately.

A biker's bond was in their handshake, and Dolby held his out. Harlan shook it. The deal was done. The afternoon was spent shooting some pool, on the torn table and telling stories. Some true, some tall. Harlan liked the MC. If his own club wanted a presence in Plymouth, they could do a lot worse than patching over this lot. He checked the time; he needed to leave. Not that he had anywhere to be but common sense said it was time to go back to his room, have a shower, chill out for a bit before bed. But then a few more members walked it, no doubt coming over straight from work, by-passing their family for a few beers. Instead of going home, he took another bottle from the fridge, threw a fiver down on the counter and decided it wouldn't hurt to stay a bit longer.

It had been a good night. The first two venues they visited had buckled under the pressure. The boss would be impressed. He wanted more and they had delivered. The first one, owned by two sisters, was easy to convince to sign-up to being a strip joint. The sales pitch was short, but not sweet. 'This is happening, or we will take away everything you have.'

The two sisters were no match for the men in suits. The suits didn't have to play good cop, bad cop, they were just bad, to the core. The bar was fairly busy when they entered. It started off as a cocktail bar, set up to attract fellow females, somewhere they called their own. It was successful but the laws of attraction say if you have a lot of women, you need to add some men into your mix. They decided to then offer shots. Just shots. From there came the name change, Cocktails and Shots, literally doing what it said on the tin. The new business plan and branding made it a popular place to go, with colourful cocktails and powerful shots proving the perfect pit stop before you moved on to a night-club. It had a 1am licence but generally trade died off around midnight as the punters were boozed up and ready to rave.

The older sister was serving behind the bar when they approached. They told her they had come to make her an offer for the business and they had, just not the kind of offer she had in mind. They told her to bring the drinks over to the table they would be sitting at, so they could have five minutes to discuss their deal. She went to get her sister, who was in the office on the computer clearing down invoices. They were punctual payers. Together, they went over to see the two strangers who apparently wanted to buy their business.

The sisters came carrying a tray of complimentary shots, doubting they were porn star martini men. The small talk and smiles the suits gave lasted less than two minutes before the conversation turned sour and the smiles, menacing. By the time the suits left, the women were visibly shaking. They were told they would be back next week to go through the set up ready to open that weekend. They watched the two men walk out and sat there, frozen to their seats, and unable to speak.

The second venue had been a harder sell. It was run by a Turk, who for some reason had a mainly Romanian clientele. It served Eastern European beers and white label spirits. It was a large venue with an enclosed, rear garden. The Turk was short and powerful looking. Barrel chested with a perfectly sculpted stubble. He was game, too, and didn't buy into their intimidation. They left, apologising for trying it on and he watched them cross the road and get into their car. He felt good about himself, he hadn't backed down and they had caved first. That gloating feeling lasted all night, all the way until he felt the bat come across the back of his legs and the pain of being kicked repeatedly in his ribs. The plan was presented to him again, and this time he agreed. Especially when they mentioned his sister's children. What these owners didn't know was that the men in suits always did their homework, helped by having the answers they needed given to them by a certain corrupt detective.

· · ·

A few more members had arrived, and some girls. Dolby had put the word out that a brother from Satan's Security was in town and they needed to show some respect for a member of a national club, one that paved the way for doing criminal things, correctly.

It turned into a raucous affair. Two women were on the pool table and had taken off their tops, their breasts bouncing to the sound of the rock music that was on in the background. The floor was awash with cigarette butts and the smell of cannabis was enough to get you high without the need to smoke it. There were no more than twenty people but they were partying like there were two hundred. If there was one thing a biker knew, it was how to party. The fridge that Dolby had stocked was looking empty so the bottles of spirits were getting a good going through instead. Bourbon and gin first being poured with a mixer, then neat and then, straight from the bottle. None of the women were Old Ladies, meaning they could be enjoyed by anyone, and most of them had been, but they all liked the look of the new biker. From their alluring glances to fondling their own bodies erotically, they were doing anything they could to personally entice him but Harlan wasn't interested. Biker groupies weren't his thing. They had been, of course. As a young man with a fiery temper and good looks, the offers came thick and fast and he took up each one. But over the years loose sex had lost its appeal, not that he was now a monk, Carla was testament to that, but he now knew that sex could come with feelings; the worst being a feeling of loss.

Harlan woke up, his head feeling heavy. He had fallen asleep in one of the chairs. The girls had gone, all bar one and she was asleep on the pool table, dressed only in her pants. Dolby was asleep on another chair, a cigarette hanging from his mouth. Which was apt. Harlan stood up and tried to stretch out the aches and pains from sleeping, sitting upright. It was still dark outside but he wasn't sure of the time. His Nokia had died, as had his personal mobile. He often wouldn't charge that one for a few days. No need, it never rang, he never received a message to reply to, so the battery never had any real work to do. Harlan put a twenty-pound note on the bar, to cover his expenses, and left the room as quietly as a man with a hangover could.

He stepped outside into the early morning. The air was crisp, which helped. He thought about riding back, it was only a few miles and he doubted there would be much of a police presence but he also knew, from experience, that bikers with patches on their back riding around in the early hours would often get a stop and search. He didn't know any taxi numbers but there was a phone box across the street. London red. He was sure there would be business cards of taxi companies in there, next to the cards of escorts and massage parlours. He pulled open the cast iron door, admiring its antiquated beauty, a trip back down to old Britain, and stepped inside. His thought process was correct, in-between a card for Luxury Thai Massage and The Naughty Schoolgirls there was a business card for a cab company. He took out a pound coin and dialled. It seemed no sooner did he speak, the pips started and his call ended. He took out a two-pound coin, hoping for double the talk time and redialled. He spoke quickly to the voice on the other end, giving his whereabouts based on rough land-marks he could see and the operator, through a blend of detection and guesswork, told him to wait there and someone would be with him in around six minutes.

Her timing seemed about right. He waited in the phone box and pretty soon a Toyota Hybrid pulled up. The driver looked as boring as his car. Harlan got in and gave the address of his B&B, and the driver told him to buckle up, before pulling away, slowly. He wasn't sure if he nodded off or not on the drive, if he had it would have been through the lack of conversation or the lack of speed that the driver was showing. Harlan didn't drive cars much, but when he did, he liked to rag them. He didn't believe they had the same beauty as a bike. Fake wood and faux leather were there just to bump the price, not the passion. The cab had a green tree hanging from the rear-view mirror, and Harlan thought it was there to offset the driver's breath, which was ripe, to say the least. The fare came to less than a tenner, but Harlan rounded it up and got out, glad to get away from the halitosis. The air had warmed slightly and the upcoming daylight was starting to become apparent. He stepped inside the B&B, past the garish wallpaper and up to room number 3.

They had swapped their suits for baggy jogging bottoms and tight t-shirts. The gym was busy, full of dedicated lifters and carb beaters. It was an old-school place; free lifting weights being preferred to fancy machinery. All the walls were mirrored, giving everyone the opportunity to pose at once. Buzzcut was working his triceps. The taller one doing dumbbell curls. The gym had become the place for the dedicated criminal, the way ice cream bars were used as criminal fronts. They weren't the biggest two guys in there, but they weren't the smallest. They tended to workout most mornings and take a high protein shake to go when they had finished. Before working for Edward (to anyone who asked, they said 'with' Edward), they were game for most things; ram raids, carjacking, debt collection and for one of them, drug dealing. They were known in the gym but the general feeling was that they were arrogant and there was a common feeling, although not proven, that one of them may have the ear of a copper. It was only a rumour but their passion for using violence was most definitely not.

Harlan made himself a cup of tea. His mouth was dry and he needed something sweet, and fizzy but the tea would have to do. It had been a good night; the unexpected ones always were. But that was yesterday, this was today, and there was work to do. Both his phones were showing full batteries. It was a 3:1 ratio between the two mobiles, the smartphone, his only connection to the grid, would last three days, the working one, the little black Nokia, the one that made him his bread, lasting just one. He didn't fancy breakfast. This was just as well because Lenny had finished serving, so if he wanted anything, he would need to call in a favour, or make it himself. The first one he wouldn't do, the second one he didn't want to do. He took a quick shower and shaved, but only his neck. He didn't mind fur on his face but when it got too long on his neck it made him itch. With the minimum of grooming done, washed hair, a clean neck, brushed teeth and fresh set of threads, he was good to go. He took both his phones, one in each pocket, his keys and his cut.

DS Mark Sharman had a look through the ANPR system, he didn't know what he was looking for exactly. A biker, maybe? His snitches had told him that whoever it was, he wasn't a local outlaw, that was for sure, but they could be wrong on the biker part. That was the thing with having a couple of crackheads on your payroll, their brains were mostly mush. He was looking at the screen when another detective came in, carrying a coffee and a savoury snack.

Elevenses. Mark was feeling peckish himself. He had tried slimming down, he wasn't going to get to 3rd base with the casino girls with a gut, and if he did, it would be expensive. His coat was behind him, draped across his chair. He swiped it off and started to head out the door before swiftly turning back around and over to the desk to log out of the camera system. You couldn't trust a room full of coppers when your back was turned, and he should know. He leaned forward to activate his key card and soon found himself in his car and driving across town to his favourite burger van.

Harlan arrived first. It was a scrap piece of land, apt as it was opposite a metal merchant. The concrete was bitty, and broken, and Harlan needed to weave in and around the pot holes. But he couldn't fault the location. He knew that no matter how off the grid you may be with your phones, someone, somehow could be listening in. He knew of a few brothers in Australia who were using an encrypted app, believing it to be totally safe and anonymous, with messages disappearing before your eyes ten seconds after being read, was actually an app created by the feds. The messages were stored, saved and used as evidence and the brothers got 15yrs for conspiracy. The other concern was the clubhouse itself, not the members, they seemed well picked by the counsel, but he knew the clubhouse could be under surveillance. It had been known.

He hadn't witnessed anyone check for listening devices when he was there, which concerned him. But then again, he hadn't been sitting at the table talking business and taking votes, which was where the checks for bugs would be done. Even so, he was too well-versed to make a schoolboy error, especially when the stakes were this high, so it was better to chat outside, close up and whispered, with background noise serving as a further deterrent to anyone trying to eavesdrop. Even better if you could be looking out to sea, your backs to the world. He also knew the local MC knew it, too, hence the meeting place. His respect for their club grew on each meeting and Dolby impressed him. He was of a high standing and seemed to have earned it, no mean feat but he still took a consult with the club's president before acting. Dolby knew his place and his worth, admirable attributes for a VP. They were definitely worth considering as a possible patch-over if his club wanted a west country charter. A few minutes later he heard the low grumbling sound of an exhaust.

He knew that sound anywhere and he smiled to himself as he looked out over to the couple of trawler boats that were out there. Dolby had brought the club's Sgt at Arms, who Harlan was yet to meet. Harlan wouldn't turn to face them, too risky, so the handshake would wait, but it would come, you always shook the hand of another brother, providing there were no outstanding beefs. They all stood in a row, a straight-line running horizontal against the choppy sea out in front. Three men. Two different patches. But brothers in arms. All three mobile phones were turned off, each one showing the others it was the case. Brothers, yes, idiots, no. Dolby laid out the mechanics of what was going to happen. Who Harlan had to meet, where and when. He asked him again if he wanted the club to do it, which was why he had brought his Sgt at Arms, as this was a job for a prospect or even a newly patched in member. Harlan said no, but thanked him for the offer. Dolby then explained the cost; fifteen bags. It wasn't small change and it was on Harlan. The bill was his to pay, and his alone. But Harlan had a plan for that.

Harlan watched as Dolby and his Sgt roared out of the wasteland. The clunking of machinery hitting metal had played its part as had the beeping sirens as lorries reversed ready to unload. It had been a good location to conduct a bit of business. He had tasked Dolby with one favour, so far, and he had come through. He had a plan for the policeman, and pain for the suits, that just left him with the lawyer. He needed to know more. A lot more.

20

Mikey was busy grilling his bacon. The smell alone was worth the drive over, Mark Sharman thought. There were a few guys standing to the far right of the van, each holding a bap. One of the three had egg yolk running down his chin but hadn't noticed. He heard the sound of banal banter. Tales of tight reversing and worst ever traffic jams. True trucker talk.

He exchanged pleasantries with Mikey, nothing of real importance. Mikey wasn't one of his grasses. Mark still had a niggling doubt about the man with the beard. It was just a feeling. Nothing too deep, though, maybe just his policeman's head coming through. He had just bitten into his bap when his phone rang. It was the thugs in suits.

'What?' Mark said, his mouth full of bacon rind.

'What's with the attitude?' replied the one with the buzzcut.

'I'm busy,' Mark said, lying.

'Just to let you know we have a couple of clubs working for us.'

Mark hated them referring to it as 'us'. This was his and

Edward's gig, they were just hired as muscle. But more importantly, and what they hadn't yet worked out, was they were to be the fall guys if it all went south. It was them doing the intimidation. The threats. The violence. If it came on top it would be them doing the bird, not him.

'How many?' Mark asked.

'Two, so far, probably double that by tonight. I can smell the extra readies already.'

Mark heard his partner laugh at that comment in the background.

'If the gaffer wants more nights on each week, we are going to need more girls.'

'I'm sure you think they fall out of the sky like snowflakes.'

'Ha, no, but that's your end of the pie. Your problem.'

Mark felt the heat in his cheeks. Pink to crimson red. He knew one of them had been helpful in the past, but that was then, this is now, and now their arrogance was starting to grate. 'I'll fulfil my end – you don't need to concern yourself with that.'

It had become a pissing contest between him and Buzzcut.

'Just saying, I don't want punters sitting there with nothing to gawk at.'

'And I don't want the girls I get you getting taken away again. Capeesh?'

'That wasn't our fault. I told you that.'

'Well, it sure as hell wasn't mine. You guys run security. If you can't do it. Maybe we need to look elsewhere for someone who can.'

Mark had emphasised the word, 'we'. He wanted them to understand the pecking order. He wasn't their bitch; it was the other way round.

Buzzcut wanted to rise to the bait, his temper was

starting to boil but then reality set in. They were there at the boss's choosing and if Mark did have his ear they could be out. It was too good a gig to lose, so he begrudgingly piped down and bit his tongue.

'Is that it? Like I said, I'm busy.'

'Yeah. That's it. We have a bit of business ourselves to take care of anyway.'

The call ended and Mark went back to being busy; biting into his bacon roll.

Guy was getting ready. It was a nice day. It would have been better if it was the height of summer, as that would have made the sea sparkle. Everything just looks better when the sun is shining. But it was dry with no wind, so sitting outside was still an option. And that's what Guy was doing, setting up the stylish metal tables and chairs, which he'd bought online at an auction. A top London eatery had foreclosed and all of its possessions were being sold to help pay the debts so Guy had paid only a fraction of the price of what they were worth. Beth hadn't arrived yet. Guy wasn't worried, she was punctual and polite, a good find. The men liked her, too, she was eye candy which always helped your bottom line. The tables were set and he had put paper doilies on each one ready for his customers to receive their drinks. He liked to think he did the small touches well.

Beth got out of a taxi and hurried over and started to apologise for being late. She tried to explain that her car wouldn't start and that she had called a cab but he hadn't arrived and that –

Guy interrupted her and told her to calm down, that it was fine, she was early, just not as early as she normally was. He poured her a coke and added a slice of lime. Guy felt good. Today was going to be another good day, he could feel it in his bones. What he couldn't feel, or didn't see, was the Mercedes pull into the courtyard car park. What he didn't see or didn't expect, was the one with the buzzcut to get out of the parked car, (the engine still running) and walk over to his bar. And what he didn't expect, but what he did *hear*, was the sound of glass breaking as one of the metal tables was picked up and hurled straight through it. Beth screamed in panic and instinctively squatted to the floor and scurried under a table fearing the worst. Guy ducked down, too, hidden out of sight behind the bar. The next sound was the sound of tyres screeching and by the time he had got back up he only just saw the back end of the Mercedes disappearing at speed out of the courtyard archway. Guy's immediate concern was for Beth, she still had her hands over her ears and had hidden under the table closest to her.

'Are you OK? Guy asked, his voice sounding shaken.

'Um... I think so. What was that?' Beth replied, getting up slowly from under the table while trying to hide her modesty with the skirt she was wearing. Guy sensed her embarrassment had overtaken the awkwardness she was experiencing in getting out and up so he drew back his open hand of help and instead turned around. Beth was finally up, dusting down her skirt and walking over to join Guy who was standing looking at his once intact window. It was now smashed and shards of glass surrounded his feet. It was at this point that the lady from the coffee shop next door appeared in view.

'Oh my, whatever has happened? Is everyone OK? Who in their right mind would do this?'

Guy knew exactly who had done it...

Harlan hadn't heard the three calls Guy had made to him. His phone was in his pocket and he was on his Harley, the sound of its powerful engine drowning out any chance of hearing a small phone ring. It didn't matter too much as, unbeknown to Guy, Harlan was on his way over to see him. By the time Harlan arrived the window fitter was busy fitting a piece of plywood inside the frame and Guy had already gone onto his social media sites and informed everyone via a status that unfortunately the wine bar would be closed today due to unforeseen circumstances. It didn't take Harlan long to figure out what had happened, in fact he hadn't even got off his bike before he knew the bar had been visited by Pinky and Perky, in their wannabe gangster suits. They had made a mistake; this was now his window. They had upped the ante but he knew they didn't have the where-withal to deal with what was coming next. He had wanted to deal with them last of all, their ending being slow, and torturous. But now they had elevated themselves to being in pole position, meaning their end was nigh. Harlan walked over, carrying his helmet in his hand. Guy and Beth were busy sweeping up the glass, the plastic dustbin from the office was outside and Guy was emptying the dustpan when Harlan got to him.

'I take it you've had visitors?'

'What makes you say that, Sherlock,' said Guy, the stress evident.

'When? Was this last night?'

'No, about half an hour ago, just before we opened.'

'Really?' asked Harlan. He watched as Beth nodded her head, corroborating what Guy had just said. She was a dainty thing and Harlan was glad they hadn't got their mucky paws on her and had gotten her to strip. She reminded him of Rihanna.

'Yes, really. Bold as brass. I was just pouring Beth a drink and the bloody window went through. Was this about yesterday?'

'Yesterday?' Beth asked.

Guy ignored her and continued. 'It has started, hasn't it? This war you talked about.'

'Yes,' Harlan replied.

Guy took out his wallet and went to pay the fitter but Harlan beat him to it. He gave the fitter a ton and declined a receipt. The fitter said he was hoping to be back tomorrow to fit the replacement glass. Guy knew it would be a big bill and was unsure whether to claim on his insurance or not. The lady from next door appeared again with some drinks, and three Belgian buns. She was sweet, Harlan thought. Nosey, but sweet. He still hadn't phoned Carol.

After a couple minutes of idle chit chat, she went back next door and then Guy thanked Beth for coming to work, saying that she could go home now but that unfortunately he couldn't pay her. He tried then giving her a single tenner from out of his wallet to pay towards a taxi. Harlan stepped in again, not happy she wasn't going to be paid, and pulled out his roll of notes, flicking through until he found a fifty and gave it to her. She tried to refuse but Harlan insisted it wasn't her fault the wine bar had to shut and told her to take it. She smiled and thanked him as Guy looked on, embarrassed.

Beth rang a taxi and waited outside and Guy followed Harlan inside the bar. His nerves were still shaken and he poured himself a large pinot to try and compose himself. Guy offered Harlan a beer, but Harlan declined, he was too riled to drink.

'So, run this past me again. There you were, setting up and next minute you see them walk up and put the window through?'

'Not, not exactly. I didn't actually see them.'

'I'm in no mood for riddles here, what do you mean?'

'Hey, I'm not exactly jumping for joy myself,' Guy fired back.

'Just answer the damn question.' Harlan's patience was thinning. He wanted the full story.

Guy's new found confidence fell instantly through the crack of his ass and he started again, as detailed as he could and minus the swag the second time.

'I was already here, setting up. I had got all the tables out and ready. Beth was a little late and came in all flustered, rambling on about her car breaking down, or not starting, I don't know. I told her not to worry, she wasn't late, and I went behind the bar and that's when I heard it!'

'It?'

'The window. It made one hell of a bang. We both just hit the deck. I honestly thought someone had blasted a gun at us.'

Harlan had no time for the dramatics. 'And then what?'

'Nothing, really. No-one came in, no shouting. Nothing, It went dead quiet, eerie really, but then I heard the sound of tyres screeching and an engine revving, I got up and managed to just see the back end of their Mercedes as they sped away.'

'It was definitely them?'

'I didn't see them, but yeah, it was definitely their car.'

Harlan went quiet. Thinking. And then said, 'I will take that beer, after all.'

The goading from DS Sharman needed an outlet, and the one with buzzcut felt there was no better place than the window at the wine bar. The guy with the beard had tried to play the tough guy, tried saying they weren't welcome at his venue now that he was in charge, but he had just flexed his muscles and there was plenty more where that came from should the guy with the beard fancy playing hardball. The taller one had tried to tell him it was a bad idea, to calm down, that it was the middle of the day, and there was a whole list of reasons to wait. But Buzzcut had no intentions of waiting, he wanted to make a statement, to lay out his intentions. Whoever this new guy was, he needed to be shown a lesson. To let him know who was in charge. They drove back in silence. There was nothing to say. It was done. Time to move on.

DS Sharman was looking at charge sheets. His log-in details for vice still worked and he was at his desk looking for possibilities. Looking for an angle. As much as he didn't want to admit it, they were right. He did need more girls. But it wasn't as easy as that, he needed an in, he was threatening someone with prison, even if there was no real chance the CPS would be sending them there. From there, he needed to ascertain if they were manipulable. Could he get inside their heads and use the threat of jail time, and shame, to make them take off their clothes as their way out. His success had been good so far, no reason for it to stop now. All he needed was the girls. He kept scanning through, looking. Looking and hoping. His cup of coffee had gone cold but he had finished his sausage sandwich. He knew it was time to cut down on bread but bread made everything taste better. The diet could wait until tomorrow.

Harlan pulled up outside the B&B. He put his bike up onto the stand and walked in and down through the hallway in search of Lenny. He eventually found him out the back, in the garden, he was flushing a bucket of dirty bleach down the drain.

Harlan got straight to the point. 'I need a favour later, if you don't mind?'

'Sure, what's up?'

'I need to borrow your car for an hour. I need to pick something up.'

'Ha, the perils of owning a bike, no boot space!' laughed Lenny.

'Yeah, something like that.'

'But yeah, sure, no problem. What time?'

'It won't be until late. That okay?'

'No worries. The key is hanging up in the locker on the wall in the kitchen. It's the red Renault 5 outside, fully wrapped. Wide rims. Totally rad ride. A classic, too.'

Harlan was already bored but stood and listened as he really did need to borrow Lenny's car. Lenny finally stopped talking about all the modifications he had made and Harlan took that as a good time to leave and get up to his room. He had some thinking to do and some calls to make. The smashing of the window had brought everything forward. He sat on his bed and sent a text to Mouse: **Edward Broadbent QC – Plymouth lawyer – find me everything you can. Yesterday.**

He closed his eyes and took in a much needed forty winks.

21

The key was exactly where Lenny had said it would be. In the small, metal locker on the wall, in the kitchen. Harlan lifted the key over the hook and placed it into his pocket. He walked down through the corridor, past the garish wallpaper and stepped out into the street. Lenny's Renault was a few cars down and on the opposite side. It was dark and the street lamps were on. They were evenly spaced and the furthest one from view was flickering. He put the key into the lock, turned it and opened the door. He put the key into the ignition and then was immediately deafened by the sound of the stereo. It was an Oasis album, a live recording in a large stadium but it sounded like they were playing right there, in the back seat of the car. Harlan fumbled around trying to turn it down, it was an old pop-off type stereo and it took a second to silence the band.

He started up the engine, it was louder than he had hoped, as he hadn't noticed the big bore exhaust sticking out crudely from under the rear bumper. Lenny was right, it was a cult classic and it was quick. Harlan was having to keep reading the tachometer to check he wasn't speeding, normally it wouldn't bother him, his Harley was registered to someone else's, someone fictitious, but this was in Lenny's name and he didn't want one of those nasty white letters that came with three points. Harlan hated the traffic police. Despised them. Didn't see the point of them. They were nothing more than uniformed bullies who were power mad and self-important, revelling in both, like pigs in shit.

When an MC went on a run, they were often fair game for the traffic police to act like assholes and they were stopped, searched and their names put through the system. Not all traffic cops were bad, just ninety-nine per cent, maybe the traffic police should have their own 1% patch, too, showing the ratio between the dickheads and the decent. Harlan kept checking, each limit upheld, never broken. Mouse had provided him with the address the car was registered to. It might be a ruse, but the name was correct so there was a good chance the address was kosher, too.

The street was just up on the right. 600yds. 300yds. 150yds. He indicated and pulled into the street. A row of townhouses. Nice cars on each driveway. Not too nice. No Bentleys or Porsches but there were plenty of Teslas on charge. It was white-collar estate. Middle management. Expensive mortgages and delusions of grandeur. Harlan knew whichever of the suits lived here, it would be rented. Gangsters didn't tend to get a fixed-rate mortgage or life insurance. This would be a cash deal with the landlord, with the taxman none the wiser or it would belong to their boss, a 'keep your friends close and enemies' closer type of affair. He slowed to a crawl. Slower than he wanted. Too slow, really, but he needed to keep the stainless-steel exhaust as quiet as he could. He trickled down the street, the tyres barely turning. The townhouses were in darkness. The white collars not wanting to burn the midnight oil. But one light was on. Middle floor. And on the driveway was a Mercedes. Tonight's recce was done.

Harlan was struggling with the bite of the clutch and the gearstick was stiff going into gear. But finally, the car was in reverse and he snaked the car back into the same space he had found it. He was about to get out and lock the car when his mobile rang. It was Mouse.

'Good time to talk?' Mouse asked.

'Course. What you got?'

'Not much, really, but that solicitor fella is a big deal in the law. Good rep, by all accounts. A straight, but I'm taking it you think he isn't? Likes a gamble, though. His name is listed as a member of a couple of gentlemen's clubs down there. That may be a way in?'

'Maybe. A wife? Kids? Gay?

'No wife or kids. Could be gay but I don't know.'

'No criminality at all?'

'Like I said, seems a straight, I'm digging around but drawing blanks.'

'OK, but keep going, yeah?'

'Course.'

'Thanks. You good? How's the club?'

'Yeah, I'm okay. Binned my bird the other week. Too clingy.'

'You'll be on Tinder, filtered photos and all that, trying to look half-way human!'

Mouse chuckled at the joke, 'Things were heavy for a bit, recently, on the club front, but the feds have moved on. For now, at least.'

The police were a constant thorn to the club. Random searches based on bogus tip-offs, and members were constantly under one investigation or another. But that was just par for the course for being a member in an outlaw motorcycle club.

'Anything I can help with?' asked Harlan. His loyalty to the club never switching off.

'Think it's fine. It was just a shake-down, really, but I'll see if Pres needs you.'

'Get him to bell me, personally. On here.'

'Got it.'

'And keep digging.'

'Will do. Speak soon, brother.'

The call ended and he pushed his phone back down deep inside his pocket. He got out of the car. Locked the door. Looked both ways, up and down the street. Looking for eyes. There weren't any. He crossed the road and walked back into the building, back down the hallway and put the key back on the hook.

Harlan was in the bathroom. He was barefoot and had taken his t-shirt off. His mouth had started to foam from the toothpaste when his phone rang again. The phone was set to silent but Harlan could see the Nokia shuffling on the spot on the bathroom worktop. He took the towel from the radiator and dabbed his mouth with it. The caller was Mouse, again.

'This is interesting.'

'What is?

'There is a photo online. I needed to dig to find it, but I did. You know that copper I was talking to you about, the one who had a snake working for him?'

'Yeah.'

'He is in this photo. Him and Edward Broadbent, arms around each other. At some sort of party.'

'Really. That's interesting,' replied Harlan. He knew they were connected; it was a chain. He knew the suits worked for the bent cop, that much had been proven as told by Mouse on an earlier call and confirmed by Dolby at his clubhouse. But what he didn't know, until now, was that the copper worked for the lawyer. Edward Broadbent QC, was definitely the boss.

Harlan woke to a text on his phone. It was from Dolby. One sentence long. Twelve words.

All set up. Meet same place. Black 1 series. Big black fella.

Harlan replied: 11. The eleventh letter in the alphabet is K, short for OK. He knew Dolby would understand the code. He got up and got onto the floor, his fists clenched and pressed into the carpet, his legs supported only by his toes. Harlan pushed out his reps. He found press-ups were the best for his biceps, pushing himself until they were burning. Next the sit-ups. His core crunched until it begged him to stop. He took a shower, barely in there long enough to get wet. The day would be long and eventful and he needed to get started. Lenny was preparing breakfast in the kitchen. There were sausages sizzling in the pan and the toaster had just spat out its contents. Lenny had shaved and his hair was being kept out of his eyes by a headband.

'Morning, you want anything?' Lenny asked.

'I would but I have some errands to run.'

'Need my motor?'

'No. I'm good. Cheers anyway.'

Lenny was too busy to see the intent in Harlan's eyes. Harlan's muscles were still taut from the earlier workout and his mind was fixated on tearing the gang apart, literally. Harlan hated bullies, always had, always would, but he also hated a copper that abused the luxury he had of being bent by the underworld and hated smarmy lawyers who thought their shit didn't stink. This OG had all three. He knew their demise would come soon. Knowing how these girls were being obtained, how concerned Carla was for the safety of her son and then with the window going through at Guy's, he didn't feel like waiting.

The gig with Guy was different, it wasn't a backstreet boozer with punch ups breaking out every night or a club with a dealer problem. He hadn't been asked to man the door. What he had been asked, or rather, begged, was to return Guy's business back to him and that's exactly what he was going to do. Harlan had on his cut, the two skulled bouncers minding the gates of hell in full view.

Normally when meeting someone like this, he would be more incognito, but Dolby would have let the fella know he was a biker so that's what he would be expecting. He also knew wearing his colours would command respect. His club was known all across the country, the media made sure of that. In general, the outlaw biker world was made up of lots of small, independent clubs with only a dozen or so members but there were a few clubs who had a national presence with charters across the country. Satan's Security was one of the few. The club had prestige and wielded considerable power, both in the size of its army and the willingness of its soldiers, and if they spoke, other clubs listened. Harlan had helped make the club what it was today, a monolith in the world of motorcycle clubs.

Harlan rode back over the tormented tarmac, swerving around the craters that had appeared in the asphalt, and parked up. The same two trawlers were out there. They looked so serene, like two lilypads on a still lake. He knew the reality would be different. They would be working hard hauling nets and decanting ice, hoping to get fully laden and back double lively to sell their wares to the fishmongers. It was a hard life, but it didn't come with the possibility of prison. The same couldn't be said of *his* life.

The black 1 series came into view, the driver not as nimble, and Harlan watched as the car's suspension dipped and raised time after time due to the potholes. The car pulled up and stopped. Harlan turned his back, went back to facing the sea, hoping the driver would get the memo. He did.

He got out but left the engine running, he also knew it was good to have as much background noise around you as possible when talking shop. He was as Dolby described, a big black man. His hands were like a baseball pitcher's mitt and his head sat squarely on his shoulders like he was minus a neck. Harlan was broad and barrel chested but this guy was built like the whole barrel. He was a good three inches taller, a foot wider and three stone heavier. They pulled out their phones and after holding down some buttons, the handsets were turned off. The driver of the 1 series seemed to know the score and didn't need prompting. So far, so good.

'Did you bring it with you?' Harlan asked.

The driver of the BMW nodded.

'Half, yeah.'

Another nod.

Harlan knew it would be enough for what he had in mind.

'I brought everything I was asked to bring. It's all there, in the rucksack.

'Good.'

'You know the deal, right?' said the driver. His tone wasn't threatening, but not far off. Dolby had said he was decent enough. Harlan knew the guy would have to treat the local biker boys with some respect if he wanted to conduct some trade on their patch but he didn't know Harlan from Adam and he was flexing his muscles. Harlan was too long in the tooth to be impressed by the driver's own inflated view of himself and decided to let it be known.

'Yes, I know the deal. Do you know why? Because I set it

up. You're here because I want you here. That's how this works, big boy. You are just bringing me what I want. Now take the air out of your chest and turn your ego down before you start properly pissing me off.'

Both men were still facing forward, yet to directly look at each other, which was just as well, Harlan thought, as if not, Billy big bollocks would be in the drink by now. The guy did as he was asked, and lowered his bravado. His size meant he was used to coming across as intimidating but something told him that Harlan could play the game, and furthermore, looked like he was used to winning.

'So, shall we start again?' Harlan asked.

Another nod.

'And I told Dolby the crack, that you'll be squared away in a few days. In full. You good with that? If not then speak now as once I take the bag, that's the deal. Fifteen large. Paid in a few days from now. In used notes. We cool with that?'

'Yeah, I'm cool with that.'

'Good. Bag in the boot?'

Another nod.

They walked over to the car, the engine sat purring and the big, black fella popped open the boot of his hatchback. He put his hand and it came out holding a black rucksack, perfect for putting on your back when riding a bike. 'Everything you asked for is in there.'

'Everything? Including the burner?'

'Everything.'

Harlan manoeuvred the rucksack onto his back, one arm at a time, and then shuffled to get it to sit square. 'Pleasure doing business with you,' he said, not offering his hand.

The driver got back into his car, the seat sinking under his weight, made a three-point turn and then drove back down the road, a little more carefully this time.

Harlan knew the risk that was on his back. He was

already feeling bad for Lenny for storing it up in his room, but as his mum once told him, what you don't know can't hurt you. Harlan fired up his Harley, his colours now covered by the rucksack and walked the bike back far enough to turn the handlebars into a full lock, ready to drive out and in-between the large holes that looked like they had been created by meteors.

The window fitter had finished. The new pane of glass was in and the bar was back open for business. Guy was still feeling bad about yesterday, about telling Beth that she wasn't going to get paid and he couldn't face her, which was why he had swapped her shift today for another member of staff. Guy didn't like confrontation, or feeling embarrassed. He lived his life avoiding both but being a bar owner and employer meant there were times when he couldn't, but it wouldn't be for the lack of trying. It was getting close to the weekend, his turn to become a strip joint. His turn to have both his bar and profits taken from him. Guy hoped that it was only the window that would be broken by the time this ended, and not himself.

Harlan was having trouble getting intel on the man with the card machine. Guy had described him as something out of a Marvel movie and Harlan had seen him with his own eyes that night at the sports bar and the description was fitting. He was built like a walking wardrobe and ran the card machine side of the business. He seemed to be a small part, a bit player. Like an extra in a television show. But he was involved in the scam and that was good enough for Harlan. That put him on his to-do list, which wasn't a nice place to be. The issue was, he appeared mythical. Dolby didn't know who he was, meaning he didn't know where he hung out and Harlan didn't have enough on him to task Mouse on finding his whereabouts. There was only one person who might know.

Harlan rode back across the city like a choirboy, there was no need to risk a stop and search by riding recklessly. There was a space directly outside the B&B and Harlan pulled in and rested his bike onto its stand. There was something sexy in how a Harley leaned to its side.

Harlan purposely bypassed Lenny, not wanting to stop for a quick chat. Being a criminal himself, people on his periphery could often get accused of being an associate and he didn't want any heat from this landing on Lenny. He opened the door to room number 3. He shut the door behind him, and listened for any sound of movement, anyone walking across the landing to one of the two communal bathrooms. It was silent. Harlan knelt down on the floor and lifted up the valance sheet and pushed the rucksack under the bed frame as far as his arm would let him. He dropped the sheet back down, gave it a ruffle, and then sat down on the edge of his bed and took out his phone. It was a long shot and the person may not answer, but it was his only play. It rang and rang.

And then stopped. A voicemail kicked in but he declined the request to leave a message

There was nothing more to do but sit and wait for a bit before trying again, so he decided to make a cup of tea. He was just about to start tearing open the third sachet of sugar ready to shake into his mug when the phone rang. He didn't notice that he was smiling when he saw who it was calling, until he caught sight of himself in the mirror above the table.

'Thanks for returning my call,' Harlan said. There was a gentleness to his voice.

'I'm so sorry I missed it. I was getting my nails done, you know how it is!'

No, I can't say that I do!' and found himself looking down at his less-than-perfect fingernails as he said it. Carla gave a little giggle. Harlan liked her laugh and liked her laughing.

'Ha, true! Maybe I should take you for a manicure one day!'

It was then Harlan's turn to laugh and then after, turn a little more serious.

'Listen, I may need a favour.'

Harlan listened hard, trying to sense any hesitance or fear but she came back to him instantly.

'Sure, what is it?'

Her confidence was back. Harlan could tell. He knew it was just a wraparound cape, allowing her to appear nonchalant in the face of adversity, but even so, it suited her and it was nice to hear it back in her voice. 'The big fella with the card machine. What do you know?'

Carla began to speak but Harlan interrupted. 'Don't tell me over the phone, fancy a tea?'

22

They met at the same place. It wasn't her sort of establishment, but it was his. The café was busier than it had been the first time they met. But only just. The lunchtime trade was over and now it was just the stragglers left with nowhere else to be and a couple of mums killing time before the schools kicked out. Harlan had taken a table at the far end, nobody able to come and go without him seeing. It was the basics that kept him whole. He watched her walk in. She was looking smoking hot. Her hair was in a ponytail and her jeans gripped her ass better than he ever could. She spotted him and gave a little wave before walking over. Harlan had taken the opportunity to order them a pot of tea. He went to stand to pull out her chair but she was too quick and soon they were sitting opposite each other with Harlan starting to pour the drinks.

'How have you been?' Harlan asked.

'Been better, if I'm being honest but just keeping my head down and doing my thing.'

'Had any bother?'

'No. Not really, a few more calls from them but I just kept ignoring them and they stopped.'

'Good – you don't owe those scumbags anything. Dance for yourself, for you and your son, not to line their cheap ass pockets.'

Carla could see him tense up. She thought his mug would shatter if he gripped it any harder. She could see he had something deep behind his eyes. She wasn't sure if it was rage, or regret. Or both. Carla took a small sip of her tea to allow him to simmer. Harlan wasn't sure if she had seen the change in him, his red mist. He hoped she hadn't. He spoke again, but more passively this time, not wanting her to feel put on the spot or pressured.

'I just want your body to be yours, not theirs.'

Carla smiled. She liked being around him. He made her feel safe.

'Not yours then?' She said with a sultry stare. But it was said in jest, just harmless flirting but she did notice Harlan stare right back into her beautiful eyes.

'Can you run me past the cretin with the card machine one more time?' changing the subject, although a certain part of his anatomy not wanting to.

Carla told him what she knew. He was unusually big but then had further enhanced his frame with steroids. A true juice head, and had moved into dealing them. He had a good thing going, right up until the day he didn't. His car got stopped one night, he was seen talking on his mobile phone and the next thing he knew there were blue lights appearing behind him. The check on his details revealed some previous, petty stuff, handling stolen goods mainly, and that's what prompted the uniforms to perform a search. And that was what got him in front of a certain DS Mark Sharman. The detective had told him he had a personal distaste for steroid junkies, believing them to be nothing more than fake muscles and hot air. He turned the screw in the interview room. Telling him he would do some time for this. DS Sharman had him on the ropes. He was just a boy in man's clothing, extra-large man's clothing, granted, but he was ripe for the picking and that's when Sharman told him there might be a way out...

'Where do I find him, this freak of nature?' asked Harlan.

'He has a little lock-up. It's just a single garage. He does 1-2-1 training in there.'

'Doesn't he use an actual gym?'

'The bust scared him, I think. He went to ground, I hadn't seen him for months and then one day he was sitting there in the club, surrounded by piles of cash. I tried to speak to him but they shooed me away. I mean you would be daft to mess with him. He is huge. Like, scary huge so there is never any aggro with that side of things. But it's all such a shame'

'What do you mean?'

'The whole thing. People are roped in, against their will. No-one is there through choice, not even me, not really. They are bullies and it needs to stop. Stripping should be someone's own choice. Not someone else's.'

Harlan knew that she was talking to herself, not him. He knew it all needed to stop.

'I need one more thing.'

Carla raised her eyebrows, the favours he needed kept coming, but she knew he was there to help, although what she didn't know was why.

Finding the garage was harder than he thought. The city was covered in small clusters of back street garages and little lock-ups but he eventually found it. Carla was right, it was just a household garage, just like the one where he had left his van. And that reminded him, he still hadn't phoned Carol to see how she was.

There were two cars outside. One German, One Japanese. An M5 and an Impreza. A classic choice of car for today's gym freak. Harlan pulled back a bit. Not too far out of sight that it was obvious. He wanted to see who was in there. Harlan didn't have to wait long. The garage door started to come up, sticking a bit at first but then loosening, the person pulling it up coming into view in stages. It was who Harlan was waiting for. The walking, talking, card-machine-carrying rock ape. Harlan held back and watched. There were two cars. That meant two people. Minimum. A few seconds later someone else came into view. He was dressed in baggy shorts and wearing gym shoes. He was minus a top and a large tattoo covered the right side of his chest. Harlan was too far away to make out what it was, possibly a tiger. Possibly not. He watched as they bumped fists and waited as the man minus his shirt got into his car and fired up the engine, popping the throttle a few times for dramatic effect. The Impreza pulled away and Harlan turned his face from view, making out he was checking something on his bike. The driver didn't pay any attention, he was too busy texting on his phone.

Harlan walked over to the garage; the door was still up. The guy he was after was on the bench, on his back, and pushing up a barbell. The bar was arcing under the weight. He was in the zone, taking in short breaths, eyes fixated on the prize. The first thing he saw was a pair of hands coming down fast onto the steel bar. The first thing he felt was the bar pressing down into his throat. His eyes started to bulge but Harlan kept the pressure on a little longer. He needed his message to sink in. Harlan finally released his grip and watched as he struggled to move the bar away from his throat and onto his chest. The mountain of muscle was gulping for air and then started to cough. Harlan stood over him, his face contorted, his eyes coal black.

'You need to start talking. Whilst you still can.'

Card machine guy was rubbing his throat.

'Ready? I suggest you are.'

He tried to speak, but could only murmur a very faint whisper. 'Yes.'

'Good answer. A little birdy tells me you are friends with a certain bent copper. That true?'

It was still painful to speak with any sort of volume.

'No... we're not –'

'You need to think before you speak, or try to speak. Trust me, it's in your own interest.'

'Not friends. Not at all. I'm telling you the –'

'In my experience, most people who start by saying they are telling the truth, aren't.'

'I am... I really am.'

'OK. You have sixty seconds to convince me. Use that time wisely, my friend.'

Harlan towered over and listened, wanting to see if what Carla had told him was hearsay or if in fact what she had said was true, that like the girls, he had been groomed. Through bouts of broken breath and spluttering coughs, he told his tale. That his car had been stopped. He had been given a producer, which turned into a search and his stash was seized. He told him of the interview he had with DS Sharman and that he was telling him there was no way he was getting off with it, that he personally would convince the CPS to pursue the case and that he wanted him off the streets for a long time. He told Harlan of how later that evening his phone had rung and that it was the copper, telling him that actually he could maybe help him, that he had a lawyer who specialised in these sorts of charges and that if he wanted, he could set up a meet. He told Harlan that he met the lawyer the following day,. He had been picked up by the two men in the suits and driven down to the docks. Shortly after that, a car had arrived, or was it a 4X4, or an SUV, he couldn't remember, but anyway, the lawyer got into the car *he* was in and told him he could get the case dropped. To do so, he would have to do some work for Edward, a quid pro quo type of arrangement. If he didn't, the copper would press on with the charges and Edward wouldn't help him.

The whole story took longer than sixty seconds, but Harlan knew he had been telling the truth so he let him off. Harlan also knew the big fella was scared. He had seen it so many times before, big men with small balls. He tended to feel bad for them, but only if they deserved it. Harlan had often witnessed someone in a club digging out the big guy in a group, wanting to start a fight to look hard in front of his own motley crew. And it was often the case that the biggest one in the group didn't want to fight, or worse, couldn't. That didn't matter to a bully, the big guy stood out and he was getting it. Which was where Harlan would step in. If someone was looking to make a name for themselves then Harlan was more than ready to take a dance in the car park with them. Sometimes, the big fellas *were* the bullies, but he was going with his tried and trusted gut on this one and loosened up a little bit.

'What's your number,' Harlan asked.

'What number?'

'Your national insurance number.'

'Erm... I, um... I –'

'Your mobile number, dickhead.'

Card machine guy reeled off the eleven digits slowly, still coughing.

'This is what is going to happen tomorrow. Listen carefully and pay attention.'

He listened carefully and paid attention.

'Do that and everything ends. Don't do it, I'll make the copper look like an angel. And I've got a feeling you don't want to see me again, do you?'

The mountain of muscle shook his head, and then when he found his voice, added, 'No.'

'Then do the right thing'

He got a second nod.

Harlan's phone rang as he left the card machine guy where he found him; on the bench and on his back. It was Dolby and he was bang on time.

'I've got it.'

The line went dead.

It was all coming together. Except for the lawyer. He still needed more intel on him. Harlan knew he ran the show but apart from that, little else. That would change but right now, he had something else to acquire, something regarding a certain copper. Harlan rocked the bike off its stand and made his way over to see Dolby.

Harlan didn't need to show his colours. He pressed the buzzer and looked up at the camera and over the crackle of the speaker was told someone was on their way down. A prospect pulled open the door. Greasy hair and fluff on his chin, trying hard to fit the mould. Harlan had been him once, but that was a long time ago and had been around the block. Twice.

Dolby was up on the third floor and on the phone. Harlan stood back, not wanting to eavesdrop, not his business. It took a few minutes for Dolby to close the call and then he pulled out a fresh packet of cigarettes from his shirt pocket. Dolby had worn a shirt every time Harlan had met him. Black. Or dark blue. And always with the sleeves rolled up around his forearms. He was older than Harlan, probably around five years, Harlan thought, no more. Harlan declined the cigarette. He had quit smoking a few years before although a good party could sway him to spark up. Dolby reached into his jean pocket and his hand reappeared with a piece of paper folded up into a little tiny square. Harlan took it and put it straight into his own pocket, not stopping to read it. He didn't need to; he already knew what it was.

'All good earlier?' Dolby asked, referring to the rendezvous Harlan had down by the metal merchants.

'Yeah, so, so. He needed his wings clipped but apart from that, the deal got done.'

Dolby gave a little chuckle, 'Kids, huh, driving around thinking they're the shit.'

'Something like that,' Harlan replied.

'You got the few days from him you need?'

'Yeah.'

'And you're good with that? We would have given you the credit ourselves but we are a little tapped right now.'

'I wouldn't expect you to. I do need that favour though.'

'It's all ready to go – prank me when you're ready and it will happen straight away.'

'I appreciate it.'

'We aim to please, brother.'

DS Sharman had cleared down his emails. His desk was tidy and he had carried his cup over to the sink and swilled it around with hot water from the urn, the closet he would come to actually ever washing it. He was done for the day. Once was a time when he was first in and last out, but that all changed. If he was honest the job now had just become a burden, he had bigger fish to fry, but there was the pension to consider, it seemed silly throwing that way. He got into his car and pulled out of the station; glad it was over. But his day wasn't actually over, he still had to find some girls. Edwards wanted more venues working and the suits had been tasked with finding them and so far, they had come up trumps. It was his end that was letting the side down. His mind was still thinking of who he could round up when he pulled up to a stop at a red light and that was why, when it was his turn to go, he didn't notice a bike pull out behind him. Harlan dropped back. He had two cars between him and his prey. That would be enough, even if the copper knew his face, which he didn't, he was too far back to be noticed.

DS Sharman pulled onto his driveway, it declined slightly, down towards the garage door so he alongside pressing the button for the handbrake he always left it in gear. He got his briefcase from the back seat and let himself in, wiping his feet on the mat. He lived alone so there was never a cup of coffee waiting or a hot bath, so he did what he did every night after work which was to get a can of beer from the fridge and a packet of cheese and onion crisps from the cupboard and went into the living room and slumped down onto the sofa.

There was nothing to watch and he begrudgingly decided to stick the cricket on, even though he had no real idea of how the game was played. There were some menus on the coffee table and he leaned forward and looked through them, deciding it would be Greek for dinner. A couple of Lamb Koftas. But then he decided against it and played it safe and dialled his favourite Chinese instead.

. . .

The address he had been given was correct. He didn't think it wouldn't have been but it would be unwise not to check. Harlan checked his watch. A little after 6pm. He needed to get back. He put his bike into first and indicated to join the traffic, after now knowing exactly which house it was that the bent copper called home. The plan was set out to unfold them systematically. They had created a three-point axis. Each one accountable for their own end but each relying on the other two. A closed circuit. Harlan's plan would remove each point individually. Lessening its strength each time. 3, to 2, to 1. And then, nothing. It would no longer exist. When he was first told about the operation he had been impressed, but not anymore. The way they went about getting their girls had put pay to that and the gang itself, when you stripped it back, was made up of grasses, not gangsters.

Harlan turned the key into the lock of room number 3. He went back onto his knees and lifted back up the valance sheet. The bag was proving difficult to reach, his finger could touch it but not quite clasp around it. He cursed out loud before standing up and moving the bed frame up across a few inches so he could get to the bag. He then moved the bed back where he found it, lining up the legs onto the deep indents in the carpet. He liked being precise, or was it a touch of OCD. He didn't know. Or care There was time to eat, if he was quick. He locked the room and walked downstairs with the rucksack slung over one shoulder. Lenny was in the living room watching a movie, something sci-fi by the look of it. There was an empty pizza box down by the side of the sofa, he had already eaten, which meant a homemade dinner was off the menu.

The last of the chicken on the bone was in his mouth. The man behind the counter had asked if he wanted any seasoning or sauce on his wings but Harlan had declined. The chicken was okay, but he'd eaten better. But it was high in protein and edible. He shook the bag containing the sweet potato fries and took a large handful but they were too salty and he left them on the table. Harlan guzzled down the last of his coke before belching out loud and then apologising for it. Harlan checked his phone. He needed to leave. He had killed enough time. He had places to be.

The Chinese had finally arrived. The chicken fried rice was cold but he was too hungry to care and too lazy to heat it up. His fingers were covered in a sticky, orange sauce when his phone rang. It was from an unknown number. He wiped his mouth with the back of his hand and answered it. 'Hello?' he said, displaying his annoyance.

'I think I might have something for you?'

'What? Who is this?'

'Been told you are looking for some birds to dance?'

DS Sharman felt his blood pressure start to rise again, those suits and their bloody big mouths. But then he stopped and composed himself, he did need more strippers and up until now the cupboard was bare. 'OK, go on.'

Mark listened as the man on the other end of the end told him about two young girls he knew. Russian, early twenties and had done a lot of escort work. He explained that they had a brother who was facing a few years for a sexual assault but they swore blind he hadn't done it and that he was being fitted up. They had been told he was certain to go down. The man on the other end of the phone told Mark the girls were desperate to get their brother's charges dropped, and would do anything.

'Anything?'

'Honestly, anything. I'm getting a blowie just for trying

to help. Imagine what they will do for someone who actually can!'

The person on the other end of the phone couldn't see the smile on Mark's face, or the orange stain on his chin. 'Where are these birds?'

'They are with me, at the Hen and Chicken, but they are leaving soon, some escort work in London for a few days, so if you want them, I suggest you come down now and have a chat.'

'Keep them there, I'm on my way.'

'I'll do my best but don't be long.'

'And they're fit?', Mark asked.

'Top drawer, mate. Top, top drawer.'

Mark stood up, grabbed his coat and headed for the door before turning back around and picking up the last spare rib that was left inside the foil container. In his haste, he hadn't stopped to ask who had passed the caller his number or who in the hell the caller actually was. He didn't care as right now he had two Russian escorts to add to their portfolio and that was why, for the second time that day, he didn't spot a man on a bike, lurking in the wings.

23

Harlan watched as the car containing the bent cop turned right at the end of the road and disappeared behind a row of houses. He reckoned Mark would be gone for an hour, maybe two, if the girls were good. He wouldn't be that long, not even close. The Harley was parked far enough away so as not to arouse suspicion. To anyone looking out of their window, it was just someone visiting one of their neighbours who had come on a motorcycle. Nothing out of the ordinary there. It was also dark, which helped. Harlan put the hood up on his jumper. It was a cold night and that's what hoods were for. Again, nothing out of the ordinary there. The rucksack was draped over his left shoulder, one handle being held by his left hand, it looked casual. A man with a bag walking with his hood up at night to keep warm. Normal. The only difference was what was inside the bag. That wasn't normal. Not normal at all.

The house the policeman lived in was detached, which helped. It had a descending driveway to the garage door and the garage was built on to the side of the house. There was probably a connecting door inside the house to the garage, possibly in the kitchen, or a utility room. The garden was laid to lawn with a small flower bed at the end closest to the pavement, but the flowers had died off and Harlan couldn't see the cop having green fingers. Greedy fingers, that was more like it. There was a full-length gate on the opposite side of the house. There would be a path behind it that would run the length of the house and open up into the garden. That would be his way in.

Mark was excited to meet the two Russians. He had already pictured them in his mind. They would have long legs and probably both would be brunettes. He hoped there would be a little bit of flesh on show, an appetiser. After all, the caller said they needed his help, the least they could be was welcoming. He had missed a call from the suits, but they could wait. It wasn't as if he had an update. That was about to change, he could feel it in his water. He knew the pub well; it was a seedy little joint and had a reputation a few years back for a lot of stolen gear being passed through it. If you wanted something cheap and stolen, the Hen and Chicken was the place to find it. The pub was up on his left, just past the kebab house. The car park was empty aside for a couple of cars and a transit van. None of them new, or even close. Pubs were a postcard for the community they served. A pub in an affluent area would have cars still shiny, and plenty of tread still left on the tyres in their car park. A council pub would have cars with dodgy MOT's and blown bulbs in theirs. The Hen and Chicken was the latter. He parked up, got out and headed for the door, the thud of his car door locking as he walked across the car park, the music from inside getting louder with each foot step.

·   ·   ·

Harlan walked past the house, not even looking at it, just head slightly down and facing forward. Medium-paced, a man wanting to get home and get warm. Nothing out of the ordinary. He got to the end of the street, and followed it around to the left. At the end of the road, another left. And then left again, he walked past his bike, He was back to where he started. The beginning. In front of him a straight line of detached houses. Nice house for nice people. Except for one. One of the neighbours was a scumbag. And that was why he was here, to be his judge, jury and more importantly, his executioner.

It was obvious who he was there to meet. There were only a handful of people in the pub. Two stood around the fruit machine, one playing, one watching. Three men at the bar, chatting. Each with a full pint. All probably wishing they could have a smoke, like the good old days. The pool table still had a few balls dotted around on it but the young lads who had been playing were now sitting in one of the leather booths, each with their head down staring into their phones. He wasn't there to see any of them. The people he had come to see were sitting at a table. Four chairs and three were occupied. One left. For him. Mark had been right; they were both brunettes. Long, luscious hair running down their backs. Their faces had angular sharp prominent features. That European look of lust. The man on the phone was sitting wearing a puffed-out jacket and a baseball cap. He looked as he sounded, a chav. A nobody wanting to be a somebody. Mark got to the table, wanting to get past the pleasantries and down to business, or flirting, whichever came first. The man in the cap stood up when he got there.

'You the cop?'

Mark shook his head and glared at him, the stare saying, *shut the fuck up.*

The man in the cap realised he had made a rookie mistake and sat back down.

'Drinks? Mark asked, his eyes directly on the two Russians, already attracted to both.

'A vodka and coke, please,' said one of the girls, introducing herself as Dominika.

The woman to his side said to make it two, giving a wide smile, her lips a vibrant red.

'Just a lager,' said the reprimanded, baseball cap-wearing rookie.

Harlan gave one last look for anyone in bedroom windows, pulling curtains or turning blinds. Or someone putting the bins out. The opportunity was there and he took hard, fast strides to the full-length gate, his hood still up, his head still down. He put his hand on the handle, it was a standard garden gate latch, a bar lifting up and falling down into a hook. No means of deterrent. He turned the handle, the bar turning 90 ˚ and he pulled it open and slipped inside, pulling it closed behind him. The path was cobbled, autumn leaves on the floor. There were three bins up against the wall, each one a different colour, he wasn't sure why Sharman didn't keep them in the garage. He kept himself close to the house, walking along the length and then turning to walk along the width. A window, chest height, and dual panes. That would be the view from the front room. It was shut, and staying shut. Harlan went back around to the side and to the back door. He would have preferred an open window but the door would have to do. He put his hand on the handle, it wouldn't move, it was locked. Course it was, a copper lived here. He pulled out his set of picks from his pocket. He wasn't skilled at picking locks but he wasn't a total novice, either. The problem would be if the copper had left a key in the lock, but he hadn't, the pick went in and he started to feel for the mechanism. He found it within a few seconds and was able to push the lever down. He then added the second pick, it was shaped like a hook. He jiggled it around, working blind but working with a mechanical mind and then the handle turned and he was in.

The kitchen was bland, the décor nondescript. Minus a woman's touch; ironic seeing how often Sharman went looking for them. Harlan listened for an alarm. Nothing. He checked all four corners of the kitchen for motion sensors. Nothing. The copper wasn't security conscious. Probably too arrogant, believing in his own hype, a wannabe baddie in good guys' clothing. Harlan checked his boots for mud. The path outside was dry and his boots were clean. The kitchen floor was tiled and he strode across and out into the hallway. There were a few photos in frames, one of which was the owner of the house as a young PC. His first photo after passing out. Back when he wanted to do some good, back when he wanted to serve his community. Back before he started to then steal from it. Harlan went into the living room. There was a wide-screen television on the wall and a sofa with a footstool. There was a short-legged coffee table, magazines and some empty foil containers. Harlan had a look around but nowhere stood out. That only left upstairs.

The conversation started off awkwardly. Fits and starts, nobody relaxed. Guards were up. The next round of drinks started to loosen lips and Mark started to flirt with the girls, believing to himself that having some power would make them overlook his paunch and double chin. He looked like what he was, a sleazy little man. Mark moved the conversation onto their brother, wanting to know what nick he had been in, what the charge was, when he was up in court. He wasn't doing this because he cared, he was doing this to snare them, to make them believe he could help, when really, all he wanted was for them to help him.

They moved to one of the booths, it was more comfortable and slightly more discreet.

Mark had carefully positioned himself in the middle of the two girls and had given a twenty-pound note to the man with the cap to go and get another round of drinks, like he was his personal errand boy. The conversation had moved away from their brother and Mark was making innuendos at every opportunity. The two Russians were laughing, flicking their hair and an occasional suggestive suck on the straw. DS Sharman was in his element but with absolutely no idea he was being played.

There were three bedrooms. The master, then one slightly smaller and then the box room. The master bedroom had fitted wardrobes and the bed wasn't made. There would be a cleaner, Harlan knew. Someone to pick up his mess, somebody else he believed was beneath him. In the corner was a wash basket, it was full. A blue shirt sleeve hanging out of it.

The walls were bare. Painted white. Walls without warmth. No photos in frames or canvas prints. Same for the bedside cabinet. Just a lamp. And a book. A Michael Connelly novel. The book splayed open and face down, no respect for the spine but why would there be, he didn't respect anything. The middle-sized room was empty except for a bed. Curtains still drawn. Probably had been for a while. The box room had a Peloton but Harlan knew it had been an impulse buy, ridden a handful of times, at best.

There were some boxes on the floor. Inside were old insurance policies, manuals, remote controls minus the backs and batteries. Harlen knew that the boxes hadn't been sorted since he moved in. It would have been too boring a task. Instead, the copper would have just put them in the little room, and like the Peloton, it would have been a case of out of sight, out of mind. Harlan left the room and walked across the landing in search of another option.

He passed a plant in a large pot in the corner, an eggplant if memory served him correctly, he remembered his mum having one back in the day. Next, the bathroom. He went inside. Three standalone ceramic pieces. Toilet. Sink. Bath. There was also a separate shower cubicle and he noticed the glass screen was dirty. The whole room was white. White tiles. White towels. Colourless. Faceless. Harlan knelt down and inspected the bath panel. It was plastic. Fixed at each corner by a screw under a plastic cap. The caps were white, too. Harlan opened the bag and took out the small screwdriver, brought especially for tonight. He removed the four screws, careful to keep them together in a tight cluster. The panel was hooked under the rim of the bath so he had to pull it free with his fingertips, the panel bowing in the middle before finally coming free. He stood it lengthwise against the white towel rail. Under the bath it was full of cobwebs and he saw a spider run out across him and out of sight, the disturbance to his makeshift home spooking him. There wasn't much there. The pump for the shower and the guts of the bath. Copper and plastic pipes. Water and waste.

Harlan took out the surgical gloves from the pocket of his hoodie and pulled out the contents of the rucksack. Inside were three smaller bags. Each one clear. In the first one, a set of digital scales. Going to two decimal places. He knew the scales would look better kept in the bag. More authentic. The next one contained a lot of smaller bags. A lot. Two inches by two inches. Transparent. Most of them were empty, purposely. A few had remnants of white power. Like they had already been used, again, purposely. It was the touch that he asked for. The next bag had a mobile phone. Small and cheap. A Nokia, like his. Harlan turned it on and waited for it to do its thing. He then kept pressing his thumb down until he came across the icon he wanted, an envelope. He pressed to enter into the mailbox and saw the messages were there. Some sent. Some received. Not much to read. Just a few words. Which was what he wanted. Simple key words that spoke volumes: **Tenner a point. 2 keys. £200 a henry. Meet at the docks. Best top in town.**

To the ones in the know, these random words would confirm it was an operation. Harlan took the mobile phone from inside the clear bag and pushed it under the bath, behind the pipes, then added the two other bags, making sure one corner from one bag stood out. The last item in the rucksack was what had cost him fifteen grand. He took it out and held it in his hand. It was weighty, five-hundred grams, give or take. It was wrapped up tightly in masking tape. The size of the parcel would be the coup de grâce. No way anyone could say personal use with half a brick of blow in your house. DS Mark Sharman liked to play with fire, and now he was about to know what it felt like to get burnt.

Mark had his hand on Dominika's thigh, believing he had every right. She needed him, it was the least she could do. He had drunk too much to drive legally, but what did it matter? He was the law and he fancied his chances of getting her into bed tonight, and if he was lucky, her friend, too. The man in the baseball cap was getting restless, wanting to wrap up this little charade and get paid. 'So, what's the crack then? You want these girls to dance, or what?'

DS Sharman wanted more than them to dance, but yes, he needed to remember he was there on business. Edward wanted more venues but what use were venues if there were no girls there to get their kit off. He brought his seedy little brain back round to the matter at hand.

'Yeah. I do. And I want them this weekend. Both nights.'

'That could be a problem, I'm dropping them to London, remember?'

Mark's mind went back to the phone call, yes, he had been told that but there was no way he was prepared for these two beauties to slip through his grubby fingers. 'Cancel London.'

'I don't think we can – it's a good earner. And they need the dough.'

'They will earn more working for me. And that's without the extras,' squeezing Dominika's leg as he accentuated the last word.

The man with the baseball cap and puffed out jacket leaned forward, making sure both girls could see him speak. 'What do you think? Want to dance? Sounds like a regular earner?'

Dominika spoke. 'And you will help us. Our brother?' Broken English.

'You will get my full attention.' Another squeeze of her bare thigh and a little higher up.

'OK. That's agreed then. You've got yourself a couple of Russian lap dancers.'

Mark couldn't contain the smile that came over his face, completely unaware that his chin was still orange.

. . .

Harlan pressed the panel back into place. It clicked up under the rim of the bath and he put the screws back into the holes, securing the panel back against the hidden wooden uprights. He pressed down with his thumb on the white plastic tops that covered the screws. The panel looked exactly how he had found it. Harlan walked back down the stairs, checking each door was back to where it was before he entered. He needed to be precise, which wasn't a problem. Precision was his middle name. Harlan closed the back door behind him and fiddled with his picks until the door was locked and the handle wouldn't turn. The next part was the problem. He couldn't control who could be on the other side. A teenage son or daughter walking home. Someone unable to sleep and going outside for a smoke. A late-night dog walker.

Harlan put his ear up against the gate, listening for footsteps. For voices. For a car coming into the street. For anything. It was quiet. So far, so good. It was time to chance it. He turned the handle slowly, the bar lifting and he pulled back the gate and took a step outside. His hood was up and pulled forward as far as it would go. His chin pushed down into his chest; his beard hidden behind the fabric. There was one light on across the road, the house not directly opposite, but only one down to the left. It would be a bedroom light, or maybe a study but it was behind the curtains. Harlan took another step forward, directly in view now should someone be looking. There wasn't. He closed the gate, dropping the flat bar back into its holder. He walked up alongside the lawn and turned right and started walking hard back towards his bike. The first part in the demise of their triangle was done.

. . .

DS Sharman watched as the girl to his left struggled to get past him. She was wedged in between his legs and the table. She had to turn her body slightly, her butt brushing against the table with the bent cop not showing any desire to make it any easier. Mark watched them leave, checking them both out from behind. His dirty mind working overtime. He sat there for a few minutes, content he had found some girls and looking forward to his wet dream later. He picked up his glass and emptied the last mouthful of whisky into his mouth before getting up and leaving, a little unsteady on his feet.

He opened his car and got in, taking a second to get his breath. He reached into his pocket and pulled out his phone. He typed in his passcode, the first time getting it wrong and typed out a message: **Two absolute belters signed up. Bring it onn.** His blurred eyes not spotting the typo.

The man in the cap dropped the two girls back to their flat. He thanked them and pulled out two fifty-pound notes from his wallet. He gave them one each. Not bad for a couple of hours of work; a bulls-eye and some free drinks just for wearing short skirts and telling a few lies. They got out of the car and he watched them walk across the road and went into the complex. Mark had watched them for his own sexual gratification, the guy with the cap watched them for their own safety. He found himself chuckling out loud. The cop and the chav, one was supposed to come with morals, the other one, wasn't, the funny thing being the copper didn't have any, whereas, he did. 'Never judge a book by a cover' sprang to mind. He sent a text to Dolby: **All done.** He turned up. What a douchebag.

He felt good. His work was done. He had helped the MC

and made himself £100 in the process and had been sat with a couple of sorts. Not a bad night, all round.

Harlan was back on his bike, his hood still up. He looked around for any sign of life. Nothing except for a cat hiding under a car and watching his every move, not knowing if he was a friend or foe. He reached for his phone and sent a text: **Make the call.**

He fired up his bike, and the cat shot out and ran away down the street. He felt bad.

He was sat alone in his studio flat playing FIFA on his Xbox when his mobile pinged beside him. He jabbed the screen with his finger. He had received his order: **Make the call.**

The man who had nearly choked him had promised that if he did this, that it would be over. He would be free, no more sitting in strip joints taking people's money and pretending to be something he wasn't. He was raised the right way; to have manners; to respect one's elders. He was taught the difference between right from wrong and to be polite and kind. His mum was a single parent but she worked hard and he never went without. He had made a mistake. He had let her down. But now he had been given a chance to be who he used to be. To be someone that would make his mum proud. He dialled the number:

'Police, please. I would like to report a crime…'

24

———

Harlan was back in his room. Pacing. Wanting tomorrow to come. There were three components to the OG, and he had just removed a third of the triangle. He would have preferred pain over the police, but as his mum had once told him, some people need a taste of their own medicine. Harlan knew the bust would be swift; a police force doesn't like it when one of their own goes rogue and would need to be seen to act quickly. The police, like most people, hated bad PR, and the last thing they would want was to be sitting on their asses after being told one of their detectives was peddling drugs. Harlan hadn't made the call himself, that would be too much, a line he wasn't prepared to cross. Outlaws don't rat, no matter who the enemy. Instead, he had set it up, planting the coke, the bags and the burner and had then given the guy with the card machine the chance to free himself from the clutches of the bent cop, and in turn, free everyone else that DS Sharman had locked down with his underground tactics. Harlan had just been the catalyst. He knew now Rihanna would be safe. The policeman wouldn't be coming for her. He also knew what happens to bent coppers in prison. Harlan would have beaten him once; prisoners would beat him constantly. And mercilessly. Harlan found himself smiling at that.

He awoke early. No more than a few hours' sleep. Their house of cards needed to be destroyed in stages, but fast, allowing the gang no time to regroup, no time to recover. The next part he was looking forward to. Some people are born to hate confrontation, Harlan was born to enjoy it, or maybe, had just become accustomed to it. Being a bouncer came with altercation, it was in the job spec. It was a sad truth that if you fuel an asshole with alcohol, he just becomes an even bigger one. Another sad truth was the desire for someone to try and make a name for themselves wanting to fight a bouncer, but often forgetting they were up against a formidable force and someone trained in street warfare.

Harlan pulled back his curtains. It was still dark and the street lamp was still flickering. Most of the cars were still parked there from last night. Bodies still covered by thick duvets and their dreams still real. The urge to work out hadn't arrived, the lure of the kettle had. Lenny had been round and refilled the glass jar with sachets of sugar and little pots of milk and had replaced his towels and emptied the bin. Harlan tore open three sachets, the third one a little too gung-ho as the sugar spilt all over him and the desk. He cussed as he swept the sticky granules onto the carpet, rubbing them in with his foot.

It was too early to call. He had to sit and wait. Neither of those being his strong points. One cup turned into two. A single cup not being an option. No more sugar. The workout was done. A shower taken. The bed made and the room tidied. The clock was moving, just not fast enough.

. . .

The raid was done just after dawn. Armed response and two detectives. The street had been sealed off at each end and a neighbour who had stepped out had been shouted at to step back inside. DS Sharman was a policeman that had enemies within the force, and even his own department. His arrogance and laziness galled others in the team, and that was without the rumours about him; how he liked to be two sides of the same coin. It wasn't the sound of his alarm that woke DS Sharman, it was the sound of his front door smashing into the wall, causing the framed photo of him as a fresh-faced PC to fall and crack into pieces.

'How the mighty have fallen,' DCI Lacey muttered to himself as he stood over the broken glass and followed his armed response boys upstairs. It didn't take long to find the haul. A half-brick of Charlie, a shed load of bags and a burner phone. Everything needed to be a major mover of narcotics. DS Sharman was still proclaiming his innocence as he was led down the stairs, his hands cuffed tightly behind his back and his head pushed down under the roof into the back seat of a waiting patrol car, which was why, for the third time, he didn't spot someone on a bike lurking in the wings. But it wasn't Harlan this time.

The man on the bike watched as a convoy of cars left the street. It was a big bust. Uniforms, armed response and the serious crime unit. He laughed out loud, loving the fact that a bent cop was getting his comeuppance. He took out his mobile and texted his vice-president. **It's done - he has just been nicked.**

Dolby was in bed when his phone went off. He sat upright and reached across for his phone and his reading glasses. He looked at the screen and read the message. He smiled, took off his glasses, folded them up, put them back on the cabinet, put his phone under the pillow beside him and went back to sleep.

Harlan was already sitting at the table when Lenny walked into the dining room.

'You shit the bed?' Lenny asked.

'Just can't keep away from your Michelin starred cuisine.'

'By that, I take it, you want a fry-up?'

Harlan laughed, he had gotten to like Lenny and his sardonic wit.

The dining room needed a facelift. Two different types of wallpaper with a border running across the middle. All the rage in the 90's. It had started to dog-ear in places. The skirting boards had been over-glossed and fake wooden flooring had started to lift and shift.

Lenny arrived with Harlan's mug of tea. 'Much on today?' he asked.

'Just meeting up with some friends,' Harlan replied. A smirk coming over his face.

Lenny didn't twig the irony and headed back towards the kitchen. Another guest came in, dressed in manual labour clothing and sat down. He had cropped hair, shaved and faded up high and one of his ears had a small stud. He sat off to Harlan's right and had taken the newspaper from the stand, starting off on the back page. A football fan.

Lenny arrived with Harlan's fry-up. There was fried bread, toast and bread and butter. The bacon was pink and with the fat removed. Three sausages and two fried eggs. A hearty meal, slightly let down by the fact it was bad for his heart. Harlan was chewing on a mouthful of sausage and egg when he saw a message appear on his screen: It was from Dolby, just one word: **Done.** Harlan smiled to himself and then carried on chewing.

.   .   .

264

She would be awake by now. Harlan pictured Carla reading a story with her son, snuggled up next to her in her bed, hanging on every word. They would have breakfast together, or rather he would have some cereal, maybe with some fruit added in. Strawberries. Or bananas. Carla would be having a coffee. Harlan wasn't sure what type. Coffee didn't interest him, neither did its extortionate price. He went into his call history, having not stored her name. They weren't ever to become lovers. When this was over, they wouldn't even be friends. Carla was now, soon it would be tomorrow. Harlan didn't like looking back. As a biker, you only ever faced forward.

Carla answered, sounding sleepy.

'Hey, you. Good morning.'

'Morning. All good with you.'

'Yes, fine – thank you. Just got my little man here beside me.' Harlan had been right and he could hear Connor in the background making car noises. Innocent imagination.

'You know that thing we spoke about the other day, I need you to do it this morning.'

'OK – but are you sure you want to do this?'

'Sure? I'm looking forward to it.'

Carla could hear in his voice that he wasn't lying.

'What time?'

'Make the call at 10:30am. Text me when done.'

'10:30. Okay, that's fine. I'll set a reminder.'

'I appreciate it.'

Harlan was about to end the call but sensed she had more to say. 'What's wrong?'

'Nothing... really. I'm just... I'm just worried for you.'

'There is no need to worry. I need you to realise I'm not a nice man. As, they too, will find out.'

'What do you mean, not nice? You seem nice to me. A gentleman, in fact.'

'I am neither. I hurt people for a living. I'm not someone you want your son to know.'

The line went quiet. He knew she was thinking. Wondering who actually it was that she had slept with the other night. Harlan waited for her to speak. Finally, she did. With conviction.

'I disagree, you're that young girl's hero. I know that you care, even if you think you don't.'

Harlan didn't reply. Just held the phone to his ear. A million memories in his mind. 'You still there?' she asked.

'Still here.'

'I'll call them at 10:30. Be safe, please.'

'Always.'

His plate was empty and the mug of tea beside it had just a small mouthful left. As always. Harlan never finished his drinks. It was a weird quirk of his, one of many. Or maybe a subconscious ritual? He didn't know. Nor was he inclined to find out. Lenny came and took his plate, looking flustered. He had a busy dining room and the stress and the sweat was plain to see. Harlan wanted to help but he needed to get over to the wine bar. He had chosen the time for a reason. Carla would call at ten-thirty, and he allowed himself thirty minutes for them to get in their gangster gear and drive over.

There would be fifteen minutes of posturing with kick-off at quarter past. From there it would be over quickly. A little longer than normal as there were two of them, but no more than five minutes. Then the cavalry would arrive. It should be all done and dusted before Guy got there. It was time to leave. He put his knife and fork together, like he was brought up to do, and left the room. The man with the hearing aid was attempting the crossword and as Harlan walked past him and looked over his shoulder, it was evident he was shit at them.

Harlan parked up around the back. There was no need to make a spectacle, he wasn't selling ringside seats. This needed to be as close to behind doors as possible. He had a set of keys from Guy. Harlan always asked for a set of keys to whatever pub or club he was working at, it was part of his T's and C's. He opened the back door and stepped inside. The alarm started to beep. Little small blips of sound, the calm before the deafening storm. He paced over to the control panel, entering the four-digit code from memory and the annoying beeps ceased. It always amazed him with pubs and clubs the contrast between night and day, or rather, open and shut. When closed, they all looked so peaceful, no matter where they were, from a champagne bar in Chelsea to a shit hole in Soho. It all changed when the doors opened. That's when the fun and games started.

Harlan entered the office. The hub of Guy's business. Manilla folders and box files. A calendar on the wall and free samples on the floor. There were a few invoices on the desk to pay but nobody appeared to be screaming. Harlan was in the office for a reason. The security system. He entered the password, went straight into the set-up, found the settings and pressed what he needed to press to stop it from recording. The screens were still showing all four corners of the building but the cloud wasn't getting the intel. Just the way he liked it.

Carla was busy wiping down the shower screen when her phone started to chime. It wasn't until she saw Connor at the top of the stairs that it clicked. It was her reminder. It was 10.30.

She gave him a kiss, thanking him for bringing mummy

her phone and asked to go back downstairs, watching him as he went. Carla waited at the top, her head hanging over the banister, just to be sure he was out of sight and earshot. Carla stepped back into her bedroom and shut the door. She took a deep breath. And then another.

It felt like hours between each dialling ring, and she felt her stomach starting to turn.

'Thought you had died?' Buzzcut said. It was meant to be as menacing as it sounded.

'I'm sorry about that, I... I just had a lot. A lot going on.'

'I don't care. The deal is simple. We call, you answer. That's how this works. You'll do well to remember that. You'll also to do well in remembering who we are.'

Scare tactics. Designed to intimidate. Designed to put her in her place.

'I'm sorry. It's just that last week. I got... I felt...I was frightened.'

Carla was playing her part well. Clambering for forgiveness, wanting them to know she had done wrong. Letting them know she was a subordinate. So far, so good.

'You better be ready for tonight. And any more silent treatment and you're gone.'

This was Carla's way in. The reason for the call. Another deep breath.

'That's why I've rung. I was just at the wine bar dropping off some stuff for later. Glitter, tan, stuff like that, and I saw him.'

'Saw who?'

'The man with the beard. The man who took the newbie. It was him.'

'Yeah, we know. It's his place now.'

Shit – their comment had thrown her a curveball, she needed to adapt quickly, before she came unstuck, or worse, found out. Another quick intake of breath.

'He said that I wasn't welcome there. That there were no more strip nights happening.'

'Did he now?'

Carla could hear in his voice that he was taking the bait. She pressed on.

'He said he wasn't afraid of you. That he had spoken to one of you that night and you were both pussies. He didn't seem fazed by you at all and just told me to do one.'

'Who was with him?'

'No-one. He was on his own.'

'Just be there tonight. And you have some making up to do.'

The call ended. He had hung up. Harlan's plan had worked. She sent him a message:

I think they are coming. Please be safe. C xx

She had done it. It would all be over soon. She looked down and noticed her hand was shaking.

Harlan had made himself a tea and was sitting in the office, his feet were up on the desk. He was watching the monitor. The screen split into sections. Out the front looked busy. Cars were coming into view. Parking up or leaving. He could see people's feet on the screen, not their faces. The cameras inside were showing empty tables and a desolate bar. It was missing punters; it was missing its heartbeat. The camera showing the loading bay around the back had nothing to report, not even a stray cat to look at. But his focus was the camera at the front, looking at the cars coming into the courtyard, driving across the cobbles. He was looking for a particular car. A Mercedes. And in it would be his guests. He was getting bored, his eyes starting to strain from staring at the black and white screen and it was then that his phone buzzed. A text. It was on the desk. He dropped his feet down and leaned forward to grab his phone. It was from Carla: **I think they might be on their way. Please be safe. C xx**

It had worked. It would soon be showtime.

They arrived on schedule. Thirty minutes from Carla's call. He watched them pull into the courtyard car park. He watched as they got out, looking around, pulling down on their lapels straightening their jackets. Harlan walked through the bar and over to the glass entrance door, propping himself up against it, his arms folded. A stance of strength. They walked over with the same arrogance as before and the taller one spat on the floor. He hated everything about them. Including, now, their disgusting habits. They got within ten feet of him, and stood side-by-side. Their chests puffed out. Harlan gave a wry smile, their attempt to look tough tickled him.

'Well, well, what do we have here?' said Harlan, his arms still folded.

'Someone deluded, by the look of it,' replied the one with the buzzcut.

'Is that right? Care to shine me a light?'

'We've been told that you aren't having our nights here anymore. The deluded part is you think you have a choice.' The taller one laughed at his partner's put-down.

'Think? Didn't we talk about this before? That I think... and you can't.'

Buzzcut eyes narrowed. His face started to grimace. Harlan was still smiling.

'You think,' then realised what he had just said and corrected himself before starting again, 'You believe, you are the shit don't you? Dressed there in your shitty clothes and big bushy beard.'

'Yes, I do – but if you don't, why don't we step out the back and discuss it a little further.'

The suits looked at each other and nodded. It sounded fun, and it was good odds. Harlan turned his back and walked back into the dimly lit bar. He had turned the lights off when he arrived, there was no need to waste money lighting up an empty room.

'Well come on, chop chop,' Harlan said, not even bothering to turn around. The suits followed in single file. Harlan led the way, walking past the empty tables and desolate bar and through the STAFF ONLY doors, past Guy's office and through the back into the wine bar's rear access. The suits stepped out behind him. Harlan closed the door. It was them and him in a makeshift concrete ring. He had already taken out one nobody here, two more wouldn't be a problem.

The suits started to roll their shoulders and twist their necks side to side, loosening up for the battle ahead. This was the part of the posturing time that Harlan had accounted for. Fifteen minutes of them stood there, dick measuring and pontificating. He knew they would be savouring the moment, building up the suspense. What they didn't know yet, but what they soon would, would be the pain they would be feeling very soon. He actually felt sorry for their suits, blood was such a bitch to get out. 'You may want to take those pretty little jackets off.'

Buzzcut stepped forward and undone his buttons on his jacket, not realising he was already doing as he was told. 'How we doing this?' Harlan asked, the smile still on his face.

The taller one stepped up next to his pal, a show of solidarity. 'Painfully,' he sneered.

'You got that right; you may not be as stupid as you both look.'

Harlan saw the taller one's top lip start to curl.

'Well, what are we waiting for, do we need to touch gloves first?' Harlan said, mocking them.

That was enough. It was time to start talking. Buzzcut went to go but the taller one put his hand across his partner's chest, indicating he wanted to dance first. The sparkle in Harlan's eyes stopped shining, the fire was out. Replaced with nothingness. A dark, empty tunnel, filled only with hate and no light at the end. Harlan's opponent shimmied, feigning a punch before switching his feet and changing angles. A middleweight boxer's move. Harlan just watched, his guard not yet up. Just standing there, looking, a predator analysing his prey. The taller one threw his first punch, a jab. Harlan parried it, he was impressed with its speed, but not that impressed. The second punch was a wide right, a schoolboy swing, wild and reckless but Harlan sensed it and stepped back as it whizzed past his face. He raised his guard, his fists closed but not clenched. The next shot from the suit was a jab, same as the first, and this is where it all went wrong for the taller one of the two. Harlan blocked it with his left and came back with a straight right that stopped dead-centre in his opponent's nose. The explosion was instant. The taller one reeled back, clutching his face, his eyes already watering, his nose already bleeding. Harlan caught sight of Buzzcut coming in fast from his left and just as he was in punching distance, Harlan kicked his leg down hard into his knee, and heard bone break.

The shriek from Buzzcut was loud, he needed the noise taken out of him, the stamp into his ribs achieved that, the shriek replaced with a whoosh of air leaving his body. It was back to face the one with the broken nose. Harlan decided to play him at his own game and throw two quick half-jabs, landing due to their speed but he deliberately held back on the ferocity. Harlan was just playing with him. He knew his opponent couldn't see, his eyes already starting to swell, it wouldn't be fair to carry on, but who said Harlan was fair? The taller one threw a punch, it was missing any form of direction, designed only to keep his opponent at arm's length, but it was a mistake. The last one he would make. Harlan parried the punch, and swept away his leg by the ankle sending him falling to his side, hitting the floor hard. He looked up, dazed, blood streaming from his nostrils and tried to get up and that's when the kick came crashing into his head, sending him to sleep.

Harlan turned to face Buzzcut, still reeling around on the floor clutching his broken ribs. Harlan walked over and put his foot on his throat. Hard enough to choke him, but not hard enough to kill him. Yet.

The van pulled into the rear car park pretty much to the second. The driver parked as close as he could, shielding the show from any unwanted attention. The side door swung open and three members of Dolby's MC jumped out. They had on their cuts and were tooled up.

Harlan looked down at Buzzcut, a broken bully struggling for breath. Harlan was right. They were plastic gangsters. Pathetic.

'This is where I give you a pass. If you give me what I want. I want the address of the lawyer. You give it to me; this transit becomes your taxi and you get dropped off at the hospital to get fixed up. But if you don't, the inside of that transit will be the last thing you ever see. Your choice. If you want my advice, choose wisely.'

Harlan eased the pressure on Buzzcut's throat just enough so he could speak.

The answer came as a whisper but it was the answer he was looking for.

Harlan nodded for Dolby's boys to come over. The suits were scooped up, broken, battered, bloody and bruised, and manhandled into the back of the van. Harlan watched as the sliding door slammed shut and the driver lifted his hand off the wheel to signal their goodbye. He saw the van reverse back far enough before turning the steering wheel into a full lock ready to manoeuvre it out of the tight spot it had found itself in before straightening up and flooring itself out of the small car park and out of sight. Harlan looked at his knuckles. They were red but the skin hadn't split. Which was good as there was still another head he needed to bust. That of a lawyer, a certain Edward Broadbent, QC. Harlan took some ice from the freezer and placed it over his knuckles. There were no signs they were starting to swell but it didn't hurt to cool them off.

He went into the office and was surprised to see Guy standing there, staring up at the security monitor, his jaw wide open. 'What the actual f –'

Harlan stood there. Not speaking. Waiting for Guy to process what he had just watched.

'I mean. Like, what was that?'

'I was getting rid of your little pest problem. Like you asked me to.'

Guy found himself falling down into the chair, his legs giving way underneath him. He felt a pain shoot across his chest. 'Does that mean? I mean, is it … is it really over. For good?'

Harlan looked at him. Sitting in the chair was a decent man. Somebody with a good heart. He lacked a backbone, that much was true, but he was somebody who just wanted to grow himself a little business and didn't want to hurt anyone in the process. Harlan liked him.

'Yes. It's over.'

Months of stress and worry left Guy's body. His head

dropped into his hands and he sobbed. It was over. It was really over. Harlan struggled with displays of human emotion in men. It was something he wasn't wired to deal with. His dad had been a man's man. A sailor. He would come into his own when Harlan became a man himself. Buying him his first pint. Rolling him his first fag. But that never happened. Divorce had put a stop to that before cancer had ended it for good.

Guy's head was still in his hands. Months of pent-up adrenaline leaving his body all at once. Harlan put his hand on his shoulder and gave it a light squeeze and Guy put his hand over the top. It was the closet Guy was going to get to an embrace. But it was enough. He wiped his tears, rubbed his hand into his thighs, pulled himself together and then stood up. He was a little shaky on his feet at first. The office was small, not enough room for two fully grown men to be standing facing each other but Guy was glad it was happening here, that he had cried in here. That it had ended, here.

Guy looked down at his watch. They had a deal. He set the clasp free, and slid it down over his wrist. He held it in his open palm, looking at it. He had made a promise to himself that when he could afford it, he would treat himself to a Rolex. And then he had made a promise to Harlan. It was a promise he was going to keep. He pushed his arm forward, his palm still open. The watch was no longer his. It now belonged to the man that had saved his business. And him. Harlan waited for a few seconds before taking it, waiting to be sure Guy wanted to give it. He had given him a choice, the Rolex or the readies. His choice. It needed to be his choice.

Guy nodded his head. It was time to hand it over. Time to pay the man.

Harlan took the watch and put it straight in his pocket.

He didn't want to make it awkward, just in case there was sentiment to the watch. Harlan didn't do sentiment but appreciated that others did. Guy's eyes didn't flicker. Taking the watch was fine. He had now been paid.

'I take it your work here is done?' asked Guy.

'It is,' Harlan replied.

'I guess you'll be leaving?'

'You guessed right.'

'Can I keep in touch?'

Harlan looked at him. His face became expressionless. His tone became flat. 'No.'

And with that, Harlan left the office, the building and Guy's life.

Guy watched the Harley Davidson leave the car park, its tyres bouncing over the cobbled stones. He felt a strange sense of loss. He had hired Harlan to help him, but he now considered him a friend. And now his friend was leaving. Guy started to feel his eyes glass over, he felt stupid, 'Get a grip of yourself,' he told himself, the voice inside his head subconsciously mimicking that of the bearded biker.

25

Harlan knew he was against the clock. Two points of the triangle had been successfully removed. Neutralised. One more to go. He had dealt with the bent and the brawn, that left the brains.

He pictured the suits in the back of the van, surrounded by members of the local MC, each with a tool; a hammer, a baseball bat, an iron bar. The suits would be nervous, not knowing if Harlan would keep to his word and have them dropped at the hospital or taken somewhere, bound and gagged, beaten and tortured and left for dead. The suits had read the books and seen the films; outlaw bikers were bad news. Stone-cold killers. Harlan knew it would feel real to them all of a sudden. Their desire to be seen as hard men, to be feared, had backfired. It's a fact of life that there is always somebody stronger, tougher and meaner than you. Harlan himself hadn't come across this person yet, but they had, they had definitely come across him. The beating wasn't bad; it could have been worse; he had needed one of them to still be able to speak, to grass on his boss. And he had.

Hard men, my ass, Harlan thought as he sped across the city and out into the country.

'Zeus, in. NOW!'

Edward had the rear-passenger door open on the 4X4, and was beckoning his guard dog to jump in. The dog wasn't haven't any of it, he hadn't been in a car before. It was something new to him and dogs don't like the unfamiliar. Creatures of habit, and habitat. 'Zeus. Up. NOW!'

Zeus was unsure. His master sounded different. His calm but assertive manner had been replaced with a sense of urgency. The command sounded more like a plea. His master sounded stressed. And desperate. The dog was right, Edward was in a hurry. Mark had called him, as his one personal call, to tell him that he had been detained, as was his legal right. DS Sharman knew the process. The call was quick, one sentence: 'I've been arrested. Close it down.'

Everything that needed to be said in six words.

Edward wasn't a man to panic in a crisis. He was a confident man. Regal. He had a strong belief in himself and his importance. A man of the justice system. That had changed. The robe and woven wig wouldn't help him. He knew Mark would crumble, that his back bone wasn't straight. The police would turn the screw, his only hope to get a half-decent prison sentence would be to do a deal. To throw Edward to the lions so to save his own, sorry, sleazy skin. Edward wasn't going to be around for that. He hadn't achieved the magical number he wanted, but the crypto account was high enough. And what was to say he couldn't start up this venture in a different country? Corruption and greed were global commodities, and Edward Broadbent excelled in both.

He went back into the house, coming out with a handful

of treats. Little bones. Gravy coloured. He threw them over his dog's head, and they landed on the back seat. It worked, Zeus jumped up onto the leather, his nose instantly snuffling around, starting to salivate. Edward closed the door hard behind him. The boot was already full. A life's work and a tailored wardrobe inside two suitcases.

The door to the house was still open. Edward went back in to get his laptop and to download his bitcoin wallet onto his memory stick then he would be gone. A private plane would be chartered at Luton, arriving in the south of France. From there, he would decide on Monaco or the Caribbean. Edward strode across the driveway, the shingle splintering under his shiny penny loafers.

He took the empty brown leather holdall from the cupboard under the stairs and went to his office. The tips of his manicured fingers pressed into the soft digits on the safe and the door clunked, ready to be opened. He reached his hand in and pulled out the four stacks. 500 notes in each one, each bound by two elastic bands. £40k. Plus a few more loose ones, the start of the next stack. His passport was there, too. He took it out and opened it up, looking at himself, his mugshot, and wondered if he'd appear on a wanted poster. They wouldn't find him. Hard cash and a wallet full of cryptocurrency would keep him safe, and in secrecy. The safe was empty. His holdall now bearing its contents. He went over to the mahogany desk and started to tap his details into the trading account. It was the greed that prevented him from hearing a bearded biker walk across his shingled driveway and enter the house. And it was the sense of urgency that prevented him from seeing the shadow appearing behind him. 'Going somewhere?' Harlan asked, looking over Edward's shoulder. Harlan walked around the desk and stood in front of Edward, his arms folded.

The lawyer's face said it all, a rabbit caught in head-lights. A rabbit that, if not careful, was about to become roadkill. 'You seem to be in a rush?'

Edward didn't speak, instead scanning around his office looking for a weapon. He spotted the silver letter opener on the desk and grabbed it, retreating a few steps before thrusting the knife forward. 'Back off... and get out.' Edward tried to find some words to make himself sound violent.

Harlan had faced blades before, and broken bottles, from men who were prepared to actually use them, and those who would be prepared to do the time that come from using them. He knew Edward was a coward. It was written all over his bony little face, the very same face he wanted to drive down into the wooden desk the lawyer was leaning against. If he got the opportunity, which he would, that's exactly what he was going to do.

'I mean it... back off.' repeated Edward, still holding the letter opener firmly in his grip.

'We both know that isn't going into me. What we don't know is how far it's going into you.'

The comment was designed to make the lawyer stop and think, to turn him against himself. *Did I really want this? Is what I have worth dying for?* But Harlan also knew some people would do crazy shit to protect what they have. Harlan took a step forward. Then another. And another. Ten feet from the tip of the blade. Edward's arm was shaking. He was trying to hide it, but failing. Harlan always looked for tells, or signs his opponent was struggling to contain his own fear, his own adrenaline. The lawyer was in a world he didn't want to be in. To escape he needed to get past the man standing in front of him and get into his car. Edward wished now that his dog had refused the treats, and was still outside waiting on a command from his master. Another step. Nine feet. Another. Eight. And that was when Edward swung his arm, a large arcing swoop, slicing through the wall of air that was between them. Harlan was right, this was a man prepared to do some crazy shit to protect what he had.

Edward brought the knife back to the centre, his arm outstretched, the slash had been a warning. Harlan's senses were ignited. Endorphins travelling through his body like rapids. The tip of the knife was still oscillating, Edward was struggling. This wasn't who he was. He was a public schoolboy turned scholar. This felt foreign to him.

'The next time you swipe at me will be the last time you can walk without a stick.'

Harlan had raised the game. Edward had stepped into his backyard. It was time to dance.

Harlan paused, light on his feet, his body appearing fluid, and then BANG, Harlan rushed forward, his arms folded across his chest, protecting his lungs and heart, using them as both a battering ram and a shield. The force sent Edward backwards, the edge of the desk crashing into his kidneys, the pain and shock sending the knife flying onto the floor. The lawyer was now disarmed and at his attacker's mercy. Edward tried to lift himself up from the desk but a shuddering right cross sent him to sleep. Harlan watched as his eyes rolled and then his neck went limp. The lawyer was unconscious. The threat to his own life, disarmed.

It was a good five minutes before Edward came to. His eyes started to register the daylight and his hand went up to his shattered jaw. His head was spinning. He felt like he had been hit by a train. Harlan was standing looking out of the window when the lawyer came around, turning to face him. 'Morning, sleepy head.' The mockery in his voice was plain to hear.

Edward was still holding his jaw. He didn't know whether to reply, or even if he could.

'Let's have a chat. You and I. Take a seat,' said Harlan, his open arm gesturing towards the leather chair at the other side of desk. He watched as the lawyer walked groggily around to the chair, before slumping down. The pain in the lawyer's face was evident.

Harlan walked around and stood behind him. Edward went to swivel in his chair to face him. 'Don't,' Harlan barked.

Edward stopped and went back to facing forward with the bearded biker behind him. He felt nervous. And afraid. This wasn't how this was supposed to go. It wasn't how it was supposed to end. Harlan spoke. The words coming from behind were said without any sense of expression or feeling. Just cold, hard words.

'I'm not going to lie. What you had going on was good. But it's over. I've stopped it.'

Harlan waited for a reply. None was forthcoming. Harlan pressed on.

'Greed wasn't your downfall, grooming was. You don't get girls to dance because of the fear of doing bird. That was where it went from being clever to being sleazy. But you have talent. You're a lawyer, and judging by the size of this gaff, a good one. So, I have a proposal for you. Want to hear it?'

Edward wanted to turn around but had been told he wasn't allowed. And right now, doing what he was told was keeping him alive. Edward nodded his head.

'Your little leather bag of cash is now mine. Call it the fruits of my labour. I have bills to pay. However, I've seen your little stash of Bitcoin, it's impressive. And I take it you don't want to lose it. So, here's the offer. First option, I beat you some more, just for my own fun. And after, I get some pals of mine to come by, scoop you up and drop you to the feds. You'll get sent down, a proper shitty little prison and if you think I'm nuts, wait until you see my friends inside. Also, whilst you're locked up and Big Baz from B wing takes a fancy to you, this tidy little pad of yours will be used to have some crazy ass parties. You do have contents' insurance, right? Or...there is an alternative, one I think you should take. Are you sitting comfortably? Good, I'll continue. The second one is this little crypto account of yours - which is now mine, well, not mine exactly, but I will be its custodian. I've changed the password and the contents of your wallet are on this memory stick.'

Harlan watched as the lawyer started to tense. His bitcoin was his baby and now somebody was holding it to ransom.

'Simmer down, and listen. If you want it back, all of it, every last penny, then you'll work for us. Satan's Security. You'll be our lawyer, you'll be on call seven days a week, everything from traffic violations to assault charges. Call it pro-bono, if you will. But I'll be fair to you. When we think the value of your service to us has matched the contents of this crypto wallet, you'll get it back. All of it. I'll give you ten seconds to consider your options.'

Harlan counted out loud. Playing with him. 1...2...3...4...

Edward spoke, no mean feat with a broken jaw. 'Option 2.'

'Option 2, what?'

'Please. Option 2, please.'

'Good choice. You know what's kind of funny, though? The more badly behaved we are, the quicker you'll get your readies back. You need to hope we don't become choir boys, hey?'

Edward couldn't share the joke; his jaw wouldn't let him.

Harlan picked up the bag and made for the door, turning just before he left.

'Oh, one more thing. Be nice to that dog.'

Harlan walked down the driveway, his heavy boots crushing the shingle along the way.

The triangle no longer existed.

The clubhouse looked busy judging by the amount of Harleys parked outside. It was the most he had seen, their full charter, or pretty damn close. The drunk was there, singing a Rod Stewart song, but this time he had a friend. Equally drunk and equally out of tune.

Harlan walked over to them and, at first, they didn't see him, and then they saw two of him, their eyes blurry and bloodshot. Harlan unzipped the leather holdall, took out a handful of loose notes and passed them to the drunks. They took the notes, their eyes taking a couple of seconds to process before smiling, with not a full set of teeth between them.

Harlan crossed the street, back to the clubhouse and rang the buzzer. He waited for a reply but it didn't come. The music was blaring from inside, the sound of the buzzer upstairs falling into insignificance. Harlan buzzed again, this time keeping his index finger on the button. A voice crackled through, hardly audible over the music. Harlan looked up at the camera. No need to turn. He was now considered a friend of the club, and it was the same for him. Without their help, he knew it would have been harder, and taken longer, to crush the OG. Harlan waited for the door to open, but he knew he wouldn't be able to hear the sounds of steps. The booming bassline had put paid to that. The door opened and Harlan stepped inside. A member he hadn't seen before was standing there, a big, thick ginger beard covering over half of his face. He stepped forward and gave Harlan a hug, his hand patting him high on his back – a standard welcome for a brother. Harlan followed him up the stairs to the second floor. The room was full of smoke. Some legal. Some not. The music was loud, too loud if you wanted to chat but there were other floors for that. Dolby was at the far end, nuzzling on his Old Lady's neck, one hand on her ass, the other holding a cigarette.

The Sgt at Arms he had met down by the metal merchants went around the back of the bar, came back holding a beer and handed it to Harlan. There were some girls milling around, on the way to being drunk, or being laid. Probably both. A few members came over, trying to start a conversation but it was futile, the Kings of Leon were in full swing and the speakers were close to blowing. Dolby came over and introduced Harlan to his Old Lady. She had a svelte figure; she looked a decade younger than she was but the age spots on her hands gave it away. There were crow's feet around her eyes and her face was heavily made up but she was attractive, he couldn't deny that. The small talk was over. Dolby's missus left to pour some shots for whoever wanted them. Harlan tilted his head over towards the door, gesturing to Dolby that they needed to go somewhere quiet. Dolby took the hint and they made their way out of the second floor and up to the third. There was a member on his phone when they got there, it was to his missus, telling her he would be home soon, all three of them knowing he was lying. They waited for him to finish his call and the member said his hellos to Harlan and went back down stairs to join the party.

'Get it all done?' asked Dolby.

'Yeah. It's done.'

'Any problem with the lawyer?'

'Let's just say that he has gone from *being* the devil, to working for it.'

Dolby laughed at the reference to the Satan's Security patch. Two bouncers stood outside the gates of hell.

'What about your passengers, they get dropped off?'

Harlan was referring to the suits. He had promised them free passage to the hospital if they gave up their boss.

'Yeah. I mean the lads had a bit of fun with them first, but yeah, they were dropped off at the hospital.'

'Define fun?' A smile coming over Harlan's face for what he was about to be told.

'I think it's fair to say their ribs made a good xylophone.'

They both laughed and Dolby took his cigarettes from the top pocket of his shirt, opening up the packet for Harlan. Harlan took one. Dolby flipped the lid of the Zippo and struck his thumb down on the wheel, a flame appeared for them to share. They stood in silence for a few seconds, savouring the taste of the tobacco.

Dolby had seen the holdall but hadn't mentioned it. Wasn't his place to ask. If it was for him then his brother would tell him but he didn't have to wait long before Harlan got down to business. He watched as Harlan knelt down and unzipped the bag before standing back up with a large stack of cash in each hand, the cigarette hanging from his mouth.

'That from the lawyer?' Dolby asked.

'Yep.'

'Well, ain't that a first, normally it's the criminal that pays his lawyer.'

The quick quip made them both laugh. Harlan could feel his shoulders start to relax.

He handed each stack to Dolby. 'There is twenty grand

here. Fifteen of that for the debt. And five for your club. Can you get it to him?'

'Of course, brother but you sure about the other five?'

'I couldn't have done it without you. Put it behind the bar, tell them the drinks are on me. Or use it on a run, whatever, you decide, but just have some fun with it.'

'Fun paid for courtesy of a lawyer, that will be a first.'

Both men laughed. It was at someone else's expense. But that's what made it funny.

Dolby turned and put the two stacks of cash on the metal shelving behind him. The shelving had old bike parts on it; brake levers, a broken headlight, a rusty exhaust, and now, twenty grand in cash.

'How much did it cost you the other night?' Harlan was referring to the set-up to snare the cop. Dolby had outsourced the task – his Old Lady's cousin playing the pimp in the baseball cap. The Russians were real, but they were friends of the club, often invited to strip, or suck.

Dolby shook his head. It was a gift, one brother helping out another. Harlan wouldn't let it lie, all favours that cost, needed to be repaid. It was one of the rules of the code he lived by. Outlaws may be seen as scum by many, but Harlan knew the world would be a better place if the rest of the human race shared their values. 'Come on, man, how much did it cost to sort?'

'Not much. Two ton. Loose change.'

Harlan went back into the holdall and collected all the loose notes, digging into the corners of the bag making sure there weren't any left behind. He handed all of it over to Dolby, the vice president of the Pirates, and now, his friend.

'Probably a grand there, give or take. Take your Old Lady away somewhere nice. On me.'

Dolby took the cash and squashed it down into his jeans pocket. Harlan held out his hand but Dolby declined and stepped forward and gave him a hug. Respect given; respect earned.

'Staying for the party?'

'Nah, man, I'm gonna split. Thanks, though.'

Harlan turned to leave before Dolby stopped him. 'Take care, brother.'

'Later,' replied Harlan, and he walked down the stairs and out of the clubhouse.

The kettle was boiling. There was a teabag in the mug, waiting. Lenny had been in and refilled the sugar. Harlan had stripped down to just his jeans. It had been a long day and his bed was calling. He looked in the mirror, turning his face from right to left. He was toying with the idea of shaving, a task he hated. The sculpted lines of hair running across his cheek were now starting to look like spiders' legs. He ran his hand down past his chin and through the two inches of hair that carried on after it stopped. He thought about Guy.

Guy would have a good night tonight; he would have a new sense of purpose behind his bar. The light at the end of the tunnel, that he'd so desperately wanted, had come. For Harlan, it was just a job. Guy had hired him to sort out his problem and Harlan had delivered.

He thought about Rihanna, too. There was no denying she had been stupid, she didn't need to sell drugs, she had a good job and a nice family and he hoped she had reflected on what her greed had cost her. He hoped she wouldn't make the same mistake twice.

Then there was Carla, a strong independent woman, except she wasn't, not really. She, like nearly everybody else, wanted to be loved. That warm feeling of waking up or coming home to someone. She would find love, he knew that, just as he knew that he wouldn't. Not again, not like he had. The second phone told him that, by its silence. The two people he cared about most in the world were no longer in his life. They had left a void. One he wouldn't replace, the other, he couldn't. Harlan had dealt in pain and punishment his whole adult life; it was what had forged him into who he was. But physical pain, it heals. It may scar, but the pain goes away. The same couldn't be said for his heart, that was still broken. And what made it worse, he knew it always would be.

The sound of the kettle coming to its end stopped his reminiscing in its tracks, which was good, he didn't like looking back. Outlaw bikers only face forward, driving towards life full-on and full throttle. The way it should be.

He tore open the sachets, being more careful this time, and gently emptied the packets into the dark, brown water. He was stirring his spoon anticlockwise, still thinking about the silent phone when he heard the other one chime. He picked it up and stared at the screen. There was a message. In code. It said: **I need you.**

The End.

EPILOGUE

It was one of the many drags to the job that Lenny despised. The early starts. Really early starts. He would love to only have to get up at the crack of dawn but it was always earlier than that. He put his feet out from under the warmth of his duvet and onto the carpet, fumbling around for his slippers that were nearby. Cursing because one of the tartan patterned slippers had gone rogue, ending up out of reach of his foot, resulting in him having to get down on the floor and rummage around under the bed to find it. The room came with its own bathroom, so the next few seconds were spent wearily walking over to the toilet, and sink, in that order. After gargling on the disgusting mouthwash, he spat out a mouthful of pure purple and as he watched it disappear down the plughole, he pulled down on his eyelids checking for any sign of life; there wasn't much. He declined the shower. His guests were greasy food connoisseurs who didn't need a finely dressed Maitre'd' to serve it to them. Lenny pulled yesterday's jeans up over yesterday's pants that he was still wearing, and stood up, trying to find today's t-shirt. Last to go on was a pair of clean socks, annoyed as he always was that he couldn't wear his sliders; his mum had told him open-toed footwear contravened a host of council regulations. Plus, she thought his feet were ugly.

Lenny pulled the door to, then gave it a slight push just to be sure it had locked. There wasn't much of any value in his room, but what was there was his, and he intended it to stay that way. He walked down the stairs and over to the reception desk, checking, as always, for any flashing lights on the answer machine. The first job of the day was to prep the fry-ups, the next was to stand there and cook them for a couple of hours. Hardly the career of dreams, but he was helping his parents cut costs so there was that. Lenny didn't see it at first glance, but then he did, from the corner of his eye. The key fob for room 3. The biker had checked out. Would have been nice if he'd at least said 'Bye', Lenny said to himself, and louder than intended. He walked back upstairs to check the room. It was something his dad had told him to do, 'Always check the room after they've gone – the bastards will steal anything.' He got to the room and pressed the key into the lock and stepped inside. The curtains were open and the bed was made. If he hadn't gone towards the desk, to retrieve the wicker basket bin that was under it, he wouldn't have seen the carrier bag that was on the desk, next to the kettle. The handles of the plain white carrier bag had been tied together. Sitting on top was a note. Two words had been written on it: **To help.**

Lenny wasn't sure what to do, was it really meant for him? To help with what? He stood over it, looking down, but the knot was too tight to peer inside. He clasped his hands on the opposite sides of the tightly compressed bag, still not knowing what was inside. He gingerly untied the knot and then felt his jaw drop. Inside the bag were two neatly stacked piles of notes, side by side and looking proudly up at their new owner. Lenny smiled, and then wiped the wetness from his eyes.

He picked up the bag and as he did so, he imagined the weight lifting off his parents' shoulders. He bent down to grab the waste bin. There was nothing in it apart from three empty sugar sachets. Lenny smiled again.

The wine bar had a light to it, but not one that was created by the sun or strobe lights. It was simply that the dark clouds had lifted. The bar felt lighter. Guy walked around his wine bar; *his* wine bar; the back wall behind the bar displayed the finest wines and champagnes he had to offer. Chosen on their merit, not their profit; Guy's customers came first. Always did. Always would. He looked down at his wrist, a white line of flesh cutting through the fake tan. It was a small price to pay for his sanity, and that's what Harlan had returned to him. Sleep. Appetite. Smiles. That's what the thugs in the suits had really stolen from him. The money, truth be told, was irrelevant. Money comes and goes but someone's self-belief, that's personal. No-one has the right to take that from you. Harlan had been his saviour. Guy took the cap off a bottle of red, poured himself a large glass, and toasted the bearded biker, knowing he would never see him again. The first mouthful of Merlot tasted like sweet success.

Guy took his glass and walked around the bar, looking at his business like it was the first time. He had made mistakes, every new entrepreneur does, but he didn't deserve to be bullied. And he had done many things right; the location, the décor, the service. He had built himself a good little business, and now, thanks to Harlan, he had an even better one. Harlan had taught him how to maximise his margins, how to use his supplier's money before his own, and when to open up during the day. Harlan had become his very own business angel. Another mouthful. Another toast. Guy knew he wasn't the only one who had been affected by the thugs. He was one of many. His phone was on charge, next to one of the tap-screen tills. He pulled the cable free and with the glass of wine still in his left hand, thumbed his way into the phone and used his thumbnail to scroll through his list of contacts. The person he was looking for was the third name down on the list. Alan. Amy. Andy. He pressed down on his friend's name...

Andy was in the gym when his phone rang. He had his headphones in his ears and accepted the call from the lead dangling down in front of him. The workout had been tough, his PT taking no prisoners and Andy was by the water cooler grabbing a plastic cup of water, before the cardio part of the session kicked in, when he took the call.

'Alright mate, you good?' said Andy, out of breath and panting hard.

'Christ, you sound like you're about to keel over, are you OK?' replied Guy, concerned.

'Ha, yes. I'm just at the gym. What can I do for you?'

'It's the opposite. It's what I can do for you.'

'Really? Go on...'

'It's over. Done.'

'What's over? What's done?' asked Andy, unsure what his friend was referring to.

'You won't be hosting any more strip nights. They are finished.'

'Really, like... really? How? Who, like what? Really?'

'I'm telling you; it's done. It's a long story but I promise you that it's over. You have your business back.'

Andy didn't speak for nearly a minute. It was over. Really over. 'Thank you.'

Guy could hear the lump in Andy's throat. He hung up and left him to his smile.

The sun was shining outside, not quite a bright, summer's day but like in the wine bar itself, there were no dark clouds. Guy took another wine glass from under the counter, half-filled it with Merlot and went off in search of the lady from the coffee shop next door.

Rihanna was exhausted. It had been a hard class. She was wearing a black leotard with a t-shirt two sizes too big over the top. Her hair was scrunched into a ponytail. The room was big with a wooden floor. Two walls had graffiti artwork on them, the other two, opposite each other, were mirrored. Full length and width. She was watching herself, trying her best to emulate the woman stood facing them. Rihanna had signed up two weeks earlier.

Until then, she had been hiding from the world, her confidence at an all-time low. She had been wallowing in the sea of shame, caught inside its swirling waves. Slowly drowning, her lungs filling with water. It was her dad who had saved her.

It was late and he had locked up the house for the night. He had walked up the stairs and past her bedroom door, but then he'd stopped and taken a few steps backwards until he was parallel to the handle. He had gripped it, started to turn it but stopped. Unsure what to say if he stepped inside, but she was his daughter. Daddy's little princess. And she needed him.

He had knocked first, listening in case she was asleep but she wasn't. She couldn't sleep. Her mind wouldn't let her. Whenever her eyes closed the copper was standing there inside of them. She was seeing him in her sleep. His seedy smile and his sneering face. He repulsed her. She heard the knock, 'Come in', she said. It would be her mum.

But it wasn't. It was the man she loved most in the world. It was her dad. Her hero.

'Ri, can we talk?'

His voice was soft. Warm. He was hurting, too.

'Of course.'

He walked over and sat down next to her. He didn't know where to put his hands and settled on placing them on his lap, one hand on each leg. Rihanna placed hers on top of them. She needed to feel him. She needed his warmth in her soul. She wouldn't ever tell anyone about the conversation; that was between them. All she would say was that her dad had come to her rescue.

She had stood there that awful night, frozen. Her confidence ripped far away from her. Men had leered at her body. The goosebumps of terror had paralysed her. Her dad had helped her come back from that, which was why she was there tonight, dressed in a leotard with a t-shirt that was two sizes too big, and her hair in a ponytail, learning how to street dance. She felt alive. Fearless. And free.

It was the following weekend that Carla decided it was time. She had kissed her son goodnight after the caterpillar had come for tea. She had left his door ajar and the hallway light on. The babysitter was downstairs and Carla had ordered her a pizza.

Carla was in her bedroom going through her wardrobe, looking for tonight's outfit. It would be another bust-enhancing bra. The only real difference would be the colour or style. Sequinned or lace. Push-up or peek-a-boo. It didn't matter. Not really. It would be coming off and so would her panties. She was paid to dress nicely but leave naked. She had fooled herself that her body was hers, but it wasn't, it was anything but. Harlan had told her to make it hers, not theirs, and that statement had stayed with her. And it was that statement along with her son, who was asleep in his room, safe and sound, that told her that this was it. It was time. It was over. She closed the wardrobe door and went downstairs, wearing her comfy pyjamas, sat down with the babysitter, and shared some pizza.

Carol, meanwhile, was busy sweeping outside her front door. Harlan still hadn't called.

ACKNOWLEDGMENTS

I would like to thank Wendie Michie. Without her tireless dedication to Harlan and expertise in multi-media marketing, this novel would be a much poorer project. Bringing a story to life requires so much more than a narrator, it needs both business acumen and the skill to deliver what a reader wants and this book wouldn't have been born without her insightful input and often thankless tenacity.

Thanks also to Timofey Lazarchuk and Patrik Dahlborg-Lau for helping bring the MC to life with the book, logo and character art.

To my dogs – thanks for letting me sit on the sofa and write whilst you often missed your evening walks but never complained.

To all the MCs out there – keep facing forward, brothers.

AUTHOR Q&A

What was the inspiration behind Harlan?

I felt there was a place for him in commercial fiction. Someone who lives outside the law but who has a strong moral code. Even if those morals aren't aligned with what the majority of us would call socially acceptable. That is what led me to delve deeper. Just because we are seen as 'one' thing, doesn't mean we don't have the same emotions and trials and tribulations as anybody else. A nightclub bouncer doesn't spend all day, every day, courting violence. They do tuck their children in at night and read them a story, they do visit their grandparents. We are quick to judge others when sometimes we should shine the spotlight on ourselves. Harlan is a bad man, with a good heart, and like everybody else, he is three-dimensional and people would be foolish to judge him at face value.

Tell me more about the MC, Satan's Security.

Motorcycle clubs still have a mystique to them, although they are not seen in quite the same way as unicorns are. I have always been drawn to their camaraderie. Public perception is that the outlaw way of life defies social norms but actually, I disagree. I think an MC is more in-keeping in who we used to be, hunters roaming in packs. The 1%ers may live the outlaw life but they look after, and are loyal to, their own. I think MCs get a bad rap because little is really known about their inner-workings. What we don't know we tend to surmise, often with heavy media influence. I think the 70's movies about outlaw bikers made a lasting impression and created their cult status, often with criminal connotations attached, but like I said earlier, everybody comes in a three-dimensional shape and just because something has been said about a particular group, it doesn't make it true.

Why the name, Satan's Security?

Because Harlan is a bouncer – that's his job. He is there to provide security to a venue and keep people safe. The Satan part came with the 'image' we still have of outlaw bikers, as in they are the devils of the motorcycle world. It is an image they play upon themselves with their own insignias, and I thought it would be perfect to combine the two elements: The gates of hell being protected by their very own security team.

Will there be more adventures about Harlan?

Yes. I set out to create a character that couldn't be encapsulated in a single novel. He has too many facets to him and to cover them in just one story would do him, and the reader, an injustice. On top of that are his many encounters. He is a travelling doorman, self-employed and hard to get hold off. Harlan is the man you turn to when no-one else can, or will, do. If you need him, you must send a solitary text, three words long: **I need you.** But even then, you aren't guaranteed his help. You contact him, he chooses you.

What were some of the hardest scenes to write?

I would say the passive scenes, e.g. Harlan sat musing on his bike or in his room. Or the tender moments, only because you need to stand outside of the genre for a second. But I did love writing those moments because it gave not just Harlan, but pretty much all the characters, more depth. Some soul behind their eyes.

What did you enjoy most about writing the story?

I loved writing the dialogue. For me, writing is when I am trying to put the words in the characters' mouths. To *be* them, flipping between each as they speak. Harlan is a character who deals with the seedier end of society, and the prose and turn of phrase must reflect that to make it authentic. Plus, I like humour, quick quips and put-downs so writing those was fun. Sometimes an action thriller can be very full on, scenes at break-neck speed and with very direct dialogue so I wanted to try and give the reader a few laugh-out-loud moments.

Are there any secrets in the book that you purposely let the reader find.

There are some easter eggs planted, yes. More so for the reader to want to know the answers to a recurring reference. All good fictional characters must arrive into the reader's life in the 'now', but make the reader want to know about the 'then'. I hope I have done that with Harlan. One of the highlights for me will come if and when readers want to read the next novel because they find him as intriguing as I do.

Was there someone in mind when you wrote the physical characteristics of Harlan?

Yes, actually there was. I used to work in a fish factory and one of the supervisors was a tall, broad, straggly haired, bearded biker. Someone who was just naturally strong and had a strong, physical presence. He wasn't 6'4 and 220 pounds of perfect muscle, he was more of a farmer's build but he fitted the mould of Harlan perfectly. I hope he reads the book!

Did you find the writing process hard at times?

I don't think you can call it *hard*; it's not like we are carrying bricks for a living. It's not a physical process but it can be draining due to the need for the words to fall, and in order. On top of that - it is a marathon, not a sprint. Each genre has a preferred word count, a remit, and you must get in the ball park, one word at a time. Plus, your mind decides when it wants to be creative, not you. It can't, or won't, be rushed. You can be sat there for an hour and you'll end up with five or six mediocre sentences. Then a few hours later you sit down in front of the screen and you can't type quick enough, ideas coming so fast you're afraid of losing them.

Can anyone write a novel?

I wholeheartedly believe anyone can write a book, yes. I feel we are all brow-beaten into thinking that writing must be taught, learned from a textbook or explained by a professor but creativity doesn't need that, in fact, I think it's the opposite. I wrote Harlan my way. You could give the characters and the plot to someone else, and they would write it differently, and what makes it so beautiful is that each way would be right. Why? Because everybody writes 'their' book. It's a process determined only by thought, nothing else. The way art should be. It is true there are some rules to adhere to, the classic beginning, middle and end, but how you get there is up to you. It's your story, so tell it.

THE NEXT HARLAN ADVENTURE

CHILD'S PLAY

COMING SUMMER 2023

EBOOK AND PAPERBACK

Register for an advance copy at:

www.harlan.store

EXTRACT FROM CHILD'S PLAY

CHAPTER ONE

Harlan ordered from the menu. It was nice enough, not trying to be anything that it wasn't. There were no frills on the menu, pub grub at restaurant prices. Low level lights in crimson-coloured shades over each table. Cheap sauces in ceramic pots. Silver cutlery that had started to stain. He asked for a burger with fries, no pickles and definitely no garnish. And a Coke. He wanted a ribeye but didn't trust the chef to cook it how he liked, whereas anyone with a half-ounce of tobacco between their ears could cook a damn burger. The minutes slowly passed and some of it was spent removing a piece of beef from his tooth with a pick. He wondered what he would be facing this time. Not that it mattered. Not really. Different pub, different part of the country. The same damn problem. A pub that was in trouble; an owner not knowing how to stop it.

They would have turned a blind eye at first, hoping that whatever the trouble was, it would soon go away. Harlan knew that was seldom the case. They would have tried the police, they all do, but that wouldn't have worked. They would be at their wits' end. Not knowing who to turn to. But then someone, some-how, would have handed over a number on a scrap piece of paper. They would have been told 'This is who you need, and this is how you get hold of him.' They would have sat on it for a day, maybe two, not wanting the war to escalate. But they were in a war, and they were losing. Losing their business, their livelihood. Losing sleep and losing money. A downward spiral. Then whatever it was that was causing the sleepless nights and the anxiety attacks would happen again. And then they would go back to that piece of paper. They would unfurl it, smoothing it flat, trying to make it decipherable. They would type in each digit, slowly, checking it through, twice. Then they would add the three words. They would wait a second before sending. Breathing hard and heavy. Their stomach starting to knot. Then the confidence would come and they would press send. It would be done quickly, like ripping off a plaster. There, it was gone. Those three words had been sent: **I need you.**

Michael wasn't sure. Ryan showed him the money in his fake Gucci wallet, a wallet Ryan assured him would be the real deal soon. The wallet contained a stack of twenties. Ten of them. Two hundred pounds. A lot of money for a four-teen-year-old.

'It's so easy, Mikey. You will be minted, mate, proper minted,' said Ryan. Michael, *Mikey* to his friends, knew all about peer pressure. That's what got him into bunking off school. Then smoking. Then smoking weed. But this, this was next level. He couldn't deny that the stack of cash was tempting. Very tempting.

Ryan was the same age as Mikey but more streetwise. It helped, of course, having an older brother who had a rep for being a brawler; that earned him some kudos and some protection. But this didn't involve his brother, this was his own gig, and now he wanted to earn more by doing less. He knew how it worked; it had been explained to him. The more people you have underneath you, the closer you are to the top. He knew he wouldn't ever reach the top, but if he had Mikey working for him, he wouldn't be at the bottom, either.

They were standing in an old shed on an all-but abandoned allotment. They didn't know whose shed it was, they didn't care. It gave them a roof and a closed door. The humble beginnings of a HQ. The shed was old. It had the smell of mould and the shelves contained pots with dead flowers in them and various boxes of stuff that would help make whatever was supposed to be growing, grow. The shed had two deckchairs. The type you find at the beach. A flimsy wooden frame with a piece of sagging cotton to sit on. It was perfect as long as whoever owned it didn't come in, but that hadn't happened in all the times they had been in there, so no reason to suspect that it would now.

'What do you say?' asked Ryan.

'I'm not sure.'

'Look, I can go into town tomorrow and get me what the hell I want. I don't even need to nick it, I can just walk up to the counter and put down dollar. Self-made, that's me.'

There was an air of swagger in his friend's voice. Michael envied that. He was tempted. They left the shed. The padlock was placed through the clasp but not pushed fully home. They found it like this when they first started dossing in there, and saw no reason to change it. They fist bumped and got on their bikes.

Michael had a mountain bike; a Christmas present from his parents. It had been wrapped and put under the tree and Michael couldn't tear the wrapping off quick enough to reveal its beauty. It had twenty-two gears. Soft grip handlebars and his dad had fitted the drinks bottle holder onto the frame. It was so cool. He no longer believed in Santa but he did believe right there and then that he was lucky.

Ryan's bike was different. It was an old-school BMX and it hadn't been wrapped up in Christmas paper and been propped up against the radiator, next to the tree. It was second-hand and had been stolen for him by his brother. He may have had a second-hand stolen bike, but his threads were new, and expensive. He was wearing a North Face tracksuit and Jordan trainers. Typical clothing for a street-wise teenager, and he had a leather man-bag strapped over his chest. Inside was a half-smoked packet of cigarettes, some weed, some Rizla papers, his fake Gucci wallet and 2 phones. One contract, the other a burner. The burner started to ring.

Ryan stopped pedalling and sat stationary, pulling the phone from his bag, he knew exactly who it was. Only one person had that number. He answered and listened carefully. He didn't speak. He was told never to speak. He knew to put his hand over his ear to drown out the noise, he knew never to ask twice for a set of instructions.

'217A, Carlton Road. Pick up. 7pm. At 7.15 I'll call with where to deliver.' The line went dead. He didn't mind the work. £200 just for delivering packages across town. What could possibly go wrong?

FOLLOW HARLAN

Website: www.harlan.store

Facebook: Meet Harlan

Instagram: meet_harlan

Twitter: meet_harlan

JOIN THE CLUB

To join Satan's Security MC, or to purchase
official Satan's Security© merchandise, please go to:

www.harlan.store

Printed in Great Britain
by Amazon

21881364R00182